D1244106

Berkley Sensation Books by Pamela Montgomerie

AMETHYST DESTINY
SAPPHIRE DREAM

AMETHYST DESTINY

Pamela Montgomerie

BERKLEY SENSATION, NEW YORK

THE BERKLEY PUBLISHING GROUP
Published by the Penguin Group
Penguin Group (USA) Inc.
375 Hudson Street, New York, New York 10014, USA

Penguin Group (Canada), 90 Eglinton Avenue East, Suite 700, Toronto, Ontario M4P 2Y3, Canada
(a division of Pearson Penguin Canada Inc.)
Penguin Books Ltd., 80 Strand, London WC2R 0RL, England
Penguin Group Ireland, 25 St. Stephen's Green, Dublin 2, Ireland (a division of Penguin Books Ltd.)
Penguin Group (Australia), 250 Camberwell Road, Camberwell, Victoria 3124, Australia
(a division of Pearson Australia Group Pty. Ltd.)
Penguin Books India Pvt. Ltd., 11 Community Centre, Panchsheel Park, New Delhi—110 017, India
Penguin Group (NZ), 67 Apollo Drive, Rosedale, North Shore 0632, New Zealand
(a division of Pearson New Zealand Ltd.)
Penguin Books (South Africa) (Pty.) Ltd., 24 Sturdee Avenue, Rosebank, Johannesburg 2196,
South Africa

Penguin Books Ltd., Registered Offices: 80 Strand, London WC2R 0RL, England

AMETHYST DESTINY

A Berkley Sensation Book / published by arrangement with the author

PRINTING HISTORY
Berkley Sensation mass-market edition / May 2010

Copyright © 2010 by Pamela Palmer Poulsen
Cover design by George Long
Cover art by Jim Griffin
Handlettering by Ron Zinn
Interior text design by Kristin del Rosario

ISBN: 978-0-425-23470-9

BERKLEY® SENSATION
Berkley Sensation Books are published by The Berkley Publishing Group,
a division of Penguin Group (USA) Inc.,
375 Hudson Street, New York, New York 10014.
BERKLEY® SENSATION is a registered trademark of Penguin Group (USA) Inc.
The "B" design is a trademark of Penguin Group (USA) Inc.

PRINTED IN THE UNITED STATES OF AMERICA

10 9 8 7 6 5 4 3 2

To Anne Shaw Moran

ACKNOWLEDGMENTS

Huge thanks to Laurin Wittig and Anne Shaw Moran for your wisdom, humor, and wonderful friendship. I'd be lost without you two.

Thanks also to my editors, Allison Brandau and Kate Seaver. And to Robin Rue, Kim Castillo, Emily Cotler, and Misono Allen for all your effort on my behalf.

As always, thanks and love to my family for your endless support.

PROLOGUE

SCOTLAND 1668

Talon MacClure spat upon the brown heather, blood and dirt ribboning his spittle as he stumbled away from his home, holding his arm against his aching ribs. The cold winter wind swirled around him, whipping beneath his mud-caked plaid and shirt to chill the bruised flesh of his bare legs. At fifteen, he was barely the size of his mum, his arms and chest no more muscled than a lass's.

A worthless piece of shite.

Snowflakes swirled in the frigid air as he trekked over the heath and prayed he'd caught a rabbit or two in his traps. If he had, they'd eat tonight. If not . . . he'd be hurting more than he was already. The thought of rabbit stew did little to stir his appetite, but no longer was he able to shoot his bow to bring down anything bigger. Not for nearly a year now. Not since his arm healed so poorly from the break last spring. Twice since then, a shank of venison had arrived at their door, a gift from one of his mother's kinsmen. But the gifts only infuriated his da, and at his mum's pleading, they'd stopped coming.

Talon knelt in the snow beside a thick bush and pushed aside a snowy branch. There, in his trap, was a fine rabbit. He removed the wee beast and went to check the others he'd left last eve. Two were empty, but the fourth held another rabbit, scrawny, but large enough to please him.

Satisfied and relieved, he bent to gather his treasure. Tonight they would eat. But as he reached into the trap, his crippled arm twisted the wrong way, sending pain shooting up into his shoulder. Talon cried out, then clamped down on the sound even as hot tears gathered in his eyes and spilled. He tried to wipe his damp cheek on the plaid draped over his good shoulder, but only managed to get an eyeful of mud.

Blinking furiously, he finally gave up the fight and let the tears roll freely as he knelt on the soft ground, spitting the blood and grit from his mouth as pain ran up his arm and into his shoulder on wave after wave of fire. Misery pressed down upon him, the weight of it feeling like it would shatter his scrawny shoulders. If only he'd grow as big as his cousins. As big as his da.

Big enough to protect his mother and himself.

Talon slowly fought back the shameful tears, found an unsoiled bit of plaid to wipe the dirt and moisture from his face, then rose, rabbits in hand. He turned to head for home.

And froze.

Standing on the rock above him, watching him, was the strangest creature he'd ever seen. A little man who, were he to stand at Talon's side, would not even reach Talon's shoulder, he was certain. Though small, he was no child. His stocky build was that of a man grown. His face had lost its youth. But perhaps the most intriguing thing about him was his hair. The riotous mass of orange stuck out from his head as if he'd stepped into a whirl-wind.

The sight almost made Talon feel like smiling. Until he saw the sympathy in the wee man's eyes.

Talon scowled. "I dinna need yer pity, sir." He turned toward the path and home.

"Who hit ye?"

Talon brushed self-consciously at the mud on his cheek with his free hand, wincing as his arm pained him yet again.

"Come here, laddie. Let me see that arm of yours."

Talon ignored him, moving slowly, painfully away. But the man wasn't deterred. Despite short legs, he caught up to Talon easily and fell into step beside him.

"Got you in the ribs, too, did he?"

"I dinna wish to speak of it."

"I've a healing way, lad. It'll only take a minute and I can help you."

Talon glanced down at him. "My arm has healed. 'Twill not be improving." He let his curiosity get the better of him. "Who are ye? I've ne'er seen ye before."

A cheeky grin split the man's face, mischief dancing in his eyes. "The name's Hegarty."

Part of him wanted to turn away, but there was a kind-ness in those eyes he'd seen little of in his life and he was pulled against his will. "Are ye an elf, then?"

"Nay. A dwarf. Of sorts."

Talon nodded, accepting the explanation.

Hegarty motioned to a large rock. "Sit ye down, laddie."

Talon hesitated, gripping his rabbits tighter.

"I've no need for yer food, lad. Now sit."

Talon hesitated, then did as bade, lowering himself to the rock. Hegarty reached for him. Talon tensed, but did not jerk away as one small, thick hand curved around his elbow.

From so close, Talon could see the faint lines around Hegarty's eyes and no sign of stubble on his face, as if he had no facial hair.

Hegarty closed his eyes. Odd words came from his mouth in a rush of sound.

Almost at once, Talon's arm began to tingle and seep with warmth. "What are ye doing?" he asked, amazed and a little frightened.

"Hush, laddie." Hegarty resumed his odd chanting.

The warmth sank into his flesh, traveling up into his shoulder and down through his body as if a soft, warm wind blew inside him. The aching in his ribs ceased. Even his eye began to lose its swelling.

As quickly as he began, Hegarty stepped back and nodded as if satisfied. "Would that I could rid ye of the mud as easily."

Talon blinked, his vision once more clear. "What have you done?" he asked breathlessly.

"Straighten that arm o' yours, lad."

"I canna . . ." But he raised his poor right arm and reached it out straight as an arrow. With nary a hint of pain. Talon's eyes widened, a grin slowly lifting the corners of his mouth. "Yer an angel."

Hegarty cackled. "An angel. That I am not. Just gifted with a wee bit o' magic."

Talon didn't question the claim. He knew all too well he'd been given a miracle. "My thanks, sir."

"What's your name, lad?"

"Talon. Talon MacClure."

"Ha!" A youthful voice shouted from the rocks above. "Talon *Manure*, ye mean."

With a sinking gut, Talon looked up at the three large youths staring down at him from above. His cousins.

The largest, Dougal, leaped down from the rock to land

at his side, towering over him. In a flurry of whipping plaid, the twins joined him. Though only a couple of years older than Talon, all had gotten their growth four or five summers before and were strong, braw lads.

With a quick move he should have seen coming, Dougal snatched the two rabbits from Talon's hand and tossed them to one of the twins.

"Looks like we found dinner."

Talon stared at the rabbits, his stomach cramping from the hunger pains as much as the thought of the beating that would come.

Dougal grinned at Hegarty, a cruel look in his eyes Talon recognized all too well.

"What is he?" one of the twins asked, disgust dripping from his words.

"A rodent, by the looks of him." Dougal grunted, an ugly look entering his eyes. "I say we drown him."

"Nay!" Talon feared his cousins would do just that. He shoved himself in front of Hegarty. "Leave him be."

"Talon *Manure*," Dougal said with mock dismay. "Have ye not learned yer place, laddie? 'Tis beneath my boot." His meaty hand slammed into Talon's chest and sent him flying past Hegarty, into the snow and mud. Then he grabbed for the dwarf.

Nay. In a fit of desperate fury, Talon launched himself off the ground and leaped at the far bigger lad. His useless fists managed only to clip Dougal on the chin before a hammer of a hand smashed into his middle, stealing the air from his lungs, knocking him to his knees.

"*Leave him be*," Talon gasped. Hegarty had helped him. Healed him. He would not let them hurt him!

But as he struggled to his feet, he watched with disbelief as the three bigger boys sank to their knees in pain, clutching their stomachs as if they, too, had been slugged in the belly.

Hegarty stood over them, his arms crossed, his toe tapping. "Ye'll be apologizin' to Talon, lads."

Dougal spat on the ground. "That be my apology to Manure."

He cried out and doubled over, his long dark hair swinging down to obscure his face.

"And ye'll be givin' me yer waistcoat, laddie. I've an eye for sheepskin."

"Go to the . . . *devil*," Dougal gasped.

Again he cried out, moaning in obvious agony.

Talon stared at his hated kinsman. "What are ye doin' to him, Hegarty? Are ye killin' him?"

"Nay, laddie. Just teaching him his place."

One by one, the twins rose and lurched away, running as fast as the pain allowed them.

Dougal tried to rise, but collapsed again with a piteous moan. "Make it stop," he wailed. "I'll give ye the damned waistcoat."

"Apologize to Talon, lad."

"My . . . apologies, Talon Manure."

"*Lad* . . ."

"Talon . . . MacClure. MacClure!"

Dougal's tense body relaxed with a suddenness that took Talon by surprise. Would that his own pain would disappear as easily.

Gasping for air, Dougal rose slowly to his feet. But as he stared at Hegarty, his face turned into a mask of fury and his hand balled into a fist.

Hegarty faced him calmly. "Yer waistcoat."

Dougal lunged, but before he could swing, fell once more to his knees with a cry of pain.

Hegarty winked at Talon. "He doesna learn quickly, does he?"

Talon laughed for the first time in as long as he could remember.

Dougal shrugged off his plaid and struggled out of his waistcoat, tossing it onto the ground. "Let me go, ye devil."

"Go, then."

Dougal stared at the small man, his eyes spitting hatred even as they glistened with fear. Slowly, warily, he struggled to his feet, his face lined with pain. He stared at the two of them a moment more, his breathing hard and uncertain, then turned and stumbled away.

Hegarty picked up the waistcoat and put it on, the garment falling nearly to his knees. He adjusted the shearling, plucking at his own shirt beneath, preening a bit before he turned to Talon and held out his hand.

Talon wasn't certain what the dwarf wanted, but placed his hand in Hegarty's without hesitation. Almost at once, the pain in his middle washed away.

"I wish I could do that," Talon murmured.

Hegarty's lips compressed thoughtfully. "Mayhap ye can."

"I can?"

Hegarty released him and pulled something off his finger and handed it to him.

Talon opened his hand and Hegarty dropped a thick silver ring with a square-cut stone the color of blooming heather into his palm.

"'Tis an amethyst," Hegarty said. "The ring is magic, laddie. Put it on yer finger and wear it always. When ye be needin' something, anythin', rub the stone and make the wish, either out loud or silently. The ring will hear either way."

Talon made no move to put it on. "I canna keep it."

Hegarty continued as if he hadn't spoken. "I'll be warning ye, the ring has a mind of its own." He scowled at the thing. "It'll be givin' ye what ye need, lad, but not always in the way ye want, aye?"

Talon thrust his hand at the dwarf. "My da will not allow it. If Dougal sees it, he'll take it from me. I'm not worthy of such a fine gift, Master Hegarty. Ye should ken that."

Hegarty looked at him, his eyes clear and kind. "Ye be worth more than those three wicked lads combined, young Talon. Someday, mayhap, ye'll believe it. But until then, the ring is yours."

Slowly Talon closed his fingers around the gift and drew it close. With slow, deliberate movements, he lifted it from his palm and slid it onto the middle finger of his right hand.

It fit him perfectly. And disappeared.

He gaped at his hand. "'Tis gone!"

Hegarty cackled. "Nay, 'tis not. Feel it."

He could indeed feel the weight of the ring still on his finger. "You hid it?"

"The ring hides itself. None will take it from ye, wee Talon, for none will know 'tis there but you and me. Ye cannot have it forever. When yer grown, I'll return for it." Hegarty nodded to the east. "Now be off with ye before this snow settles in. Godspeed to ye, laddie."

Talon looked down at his bare hand, marveling at the invisible ring, then up again.

Hegarty was gone.

"Godspeed to ye, Hegarty." Talon picked up the two rabbits the twins had left behind in their hurry to escape. His step was light, his body strong and without pain, and he ran nearly the entire way home. But as he neared his small, sorry cottage, he heard the thuds of his father's fists and his mother's pained cries.

The old, familiar helplessness tore at his innards, clawing at him with hatred and anger. He made a sound like an animal deep in his throat, part plea, part growl. "I wish he would leave us *and never return*."

He swallowed hard, shaking inside, hating that he

couldn't help his mother. Knowing that if he went in there now, if he tried, the bones that had been miraculously healed would only be broken again.

As he stood in the yard, the snow swirling around him, the bitter cold piercing his skin, he felt it. That same odd, warm tingle that had danced upon his skin as Hegarty healed him. Was the healing not done, then?

An eerie silence washed over the glen. The sounds of the beating had ceased. Then a heavy thud sounded in the silence and terror pierced his breast.

He'd killed her!

But the cry, when it came, was his mum's.

Talon ran for the house and pushed through the door. As his eyes adjusted to the dim light, he realized it was his father lying on the floor, his mother kneeling at his side, her mouth bloodied, her eyes wild.

"He's dead."

Talon's eyes widened. Relief washed through him like a fine summer rain. Was this not what he'd wished for?

His breath caught. His heart stuttered. *The ring.* He'd wished for his father to leave and never return.

He'd done this.

With a rush of horror, he grabbed the ring and yanked it off his finger. His heart began to pound. He'd done this. He'd killed his own father.

His mother began to cry in great sobbing gulps.

Talon stared at his dead sire without grief. Without triumph. He felt nothing. As if his soul had fled.

But he'd not regret his wish.

Understanding washed slowly over him. With the amethyst, he was no longer weak. No longer powerless.

No longer Talon Manure.

His jaw hardened. Slowly, he pushed the ring back onto his finger and curled his hand into a fist around the stone.

ONE

Julia Brodie gripped the handle of her suitcase, the muscles of her arm and back straining as she lugged the heavy piece of luggage down the ancient stairs of the inn deep in the Highlands of Scotland.

"Can I help ye with that, lass?"

Julia grimaced. The question was almost certainly directed at her, since the voice came from directly behind her, but she ignored the question as she ignored the man, whoever he was. At five foot two and a hundred and five pounds, she might look as fragile as a butterfly, but she wasn't. She could lug her own damned suitcase.

"Aye, lassie," came a second voice. "Let us be helpin' you with that. 'Tis too heavy for you."

Julia growled under her breath and glanced back to find two of the yokels she'd seen at the wedding. "I've got it," she said tersely.

Ignoring her, one of the men closed the space behind her, his hand brushing hers on the handle.

"Let me help ye with that."

Julia clamped her hand tighter around the handle. Did the moron not understand English? "Back off. I don't need your help."

The man made a sound of disapproval deep in his throat, but backed off, as she ordered, muttering about rude Yanks.

As if it were her fault he couldn't take no for an answer.

But as she neared the bottom of the stairs, she looked up to find her cousin Catriona watching her, soft rebuke in her odd, mismatched eyes—one brown, the other pale green. Eyes the exact colors of Julia's own.

"Off so soon?" Cat asked as Julia set the suitcase on the worn carpet and pulled up the handle. "I thought your flight wasn't until tomorrow."

Though they shared the mismatched Brodie eyes, their similarity in appearance ended there. Catriona was tall and curvy, with a shining mass of long, dark curls. Julia was flat-chested and short, with straight blond hair she'd recently cut into a chin-length bob.

"My flight is at seven in the morning. I'm staying at the Glasgow airport tonight so I can roll out of bed and onto the plane." Besides, she'd had all the family she could handle. Especially since her aunts had apparently decided she needed to be the next one married and had been pushing *nice Scottish lads* at her for three days straight. Yokels, every one.

She'd made it more than clear she wasn't interested. Most of them were giving her a wide berth by now. The two on the stairs had been the exception, with *had* being the operative word.

Cat clucked her tongue softly as the men strode off, clearly put out with her. "Ye push them all away, Julia. Someday yer going to have to let one get close."

"Don't count on it. I don't need a man, Cat. I don't need anyone."

Catriona cocked her pretty head. "Even your favorite cousin?"

Julia rolled her eyes. "Who says you're my favorite?"

Cat laughed. "We both know it's true. Just as you're *my* favorite."

Julia looked up at Cat in surprise, but then frowned. "Right."

"'Tis true, Julie. I ken ye, aye? I understand you better than you think. Better than you do yourself, I'm thinking."

"Oh, I know myself just fine. I'm a bitch." Julia grinned. "A happily single bitch."

But Catriona didn't smile in return. "Nay, lass. Underneath it all, you're fine, Julia. Fine and bright and good. But ye hide it from everyone. Mayhap even yourself."

Julia's smile died. "Favorite cousin or not, you're overstepping yourself, Cat."

"Aye." Catriona reached for her hand and squeezed it. "But ye'll remember what I said, Julie. Just remember."

"Sure, whatever. I'm fine. I always knew that."

"'Tis not the *fine* I mean." Cat turned as if to give her a hug and Julia stiffened and pulled back.

She didn't need this shit. Catriona might be her favorite cousin, but she didn't need hugs or cousinly advice.

Why had she come to Scotland at all? She'd asked herself that question at least a dozen times since she got here three days ago.

"I have to go, Cat. Good luck with your marriage and all that stuff."

Catriona's expression turned serious, her eyes going razor sharp. "Wait, Julia. I need you to do something for me. I need you to take something back to America with you. It's . . . a gift."

"You don't have to give me anything, Cat."

"No, I do. I truly do. Come with me, please? 'Twill not take five minutes."

Julia stifled her impatience and nodded. Another five minutes with family wouldn't kill her. After all, she'd flown all the way from New York to attend Cat's wedding, acting on some odd and errant need for a dose of family. And since her dad's Scottish relatives were the only ones she had, family meant Scotland.

If he hadn't died last fall, she'd probably have sent her regrets in response to Catriona's wedding invitation. But there was something about knowing that she didn't have anyone else that had spurred her to accept the invitation and book the flight.

She doubted she'd come back again. It had been ten years since she'd seen any of them, not since her sophomore year at Princeton, and she hadn't enjoyed the visit. They all knew one another as if they'd lived together all their lives. Which they practically had.

And she barely knew them at all. Or they her, despite what Cat claimed.

Cat was right, though. The two of them had hit it off that first summer Cat joined the family, the summer Julia was ten and Cat was thirteen. At least they'd hit it off as well as Julia ever hit it off with anyone. Probably because for a short while they'd both been outsiders.

No one knew who Cat was or where she'd come from. Not even Catriona herself. She'd appeared at the gates of the family home one spring, twenty years ago, dirty-faced and lost, remembering little but her name. Her parents had never been located, but there'd been no denying she was a Loch Laggan Brodie with those mismatched eyes, and she'd been swept beneath the collective family wing.

Looking a world away from that lost kid, Catriona led

her to the back of the inn where the stylish bride and her new husband had spent their wedding night. The couple would be leaving soon to head north to spend a few days honeymooning on the isle of Orkney in the Hebrides. Julia had heard at least a dozen people wonder why they didn't fly south to Spain or southern France for a spot of sunshine and warmth. But September would still be hot in the south and Catriona had admitted once that she wanted to see every inch of Scotland someday.

There was something about Cat's love of her homeland that Julia understood, despite having turned into a jaded city girl. There was something about the wild, rugged land that pulled at her, as if her Scottish blood recognized the place. And maybe even longed for it.

Which was too damn bad. Julia hadn't always been a New Yorker, but she was a New Yorker now, and no way in hell was she ever moving again.

Cat led her into the room as her husband, Archie, zipped up the suitcase on the bed.

"Have ye the stone?" she asked him.

"Aye." He looked at Julia with speculation, then reached into the outside pocket of a duffel bag and pulled out a small fabric pouch pulled closed by an attached silk cord. He didn't hand it to Cat, but instead placed it on the bed beside her.

Catriona glanced at the pouch, then at Julia, but made no move to reach for it. "I want you to have this, cousin. Put it in your purse and don't touch it until you get home."

Julia raised a skeptical brow. "What is it?"

"A necklace. It was mine, but I want you to have it, now. Don't ever bring it back here."

Cryptic words. "Do you mind explaining why not?"

"I do mind, aye. Why isn't important. Just do as I say, Julia, please?"

Julia nodded slowly, deciding she was probably taking some unwanted jewelry off their hands. A gift from an old boyfriend or something.

"Okay." Julia picked up the small pouch and slipped it into her purse. "Thank you."

Catriona's gaze met Archie's and something passed between them, a look of profound . . . relief?

Odd.

But when Catriona turned back, the smile that slid across her pretty face was so pure, Julia found her own mouth tilting up into a wry smile.

"Someday you're going to have to tell me the whole story, Cat. You know that."

"Aye." Catriona smiled broader. "Someday when we're old ladies, I'll tell ye everything."

Julia pursed her lips and nodded. "Deal."

This time when Catriona opened her arms, Julia allowed herself to be swallowed in the hug. With a wave, she said good-bye to Cat and her new husband, one of the decidedly non-yokels, then retrieved her luggage from the foyer and headed for her rental car.

Hours later, as she sat in stalled traffic, waiting to get around an accident on the A9 on her way to Glasgow, she rued not spending the extra money for a flight out of Inverness. Looking for a diversion, she reached for the small pouch Catriona had given her, curious about this necklace that her cousin no longer had any use for. She opened the pouch and dumped the small pendant into her palm. The stone was small, oval, and purple, about the size of her fingernail, in a fine silver filigreed setting. The stone reminded her of a purple garnet she'd once drooled over at the jewelry store. A pretty little necklace, if badly in need of some silver polish.

Julia rubbed her thumb across the face of the stone,

watching the sunlight catch in the facets. Very pretty. The delicate chain didn't have a clasp, but looked to be long enough to fit over her head.

She stared at it for two seconds as she remembered her promise to Catriona to wait until she got home to put it on. As if anyone would know.

With a grunt, she pulled it on over her head, letting it settle between her breasts. It was a little long, but looked good against the moss green turtleneck sweater she'd donned that morning.

Finally, the traffic started moving again. It was dark by the time she pulled into the car rental lot at the Glasgow airport. She turned off the engine and was about to reach for her coat and purse when she realized there was still a light on in the car.

With confusion, she looked down, seeking the source . . . and stared. What the hell?

The purple stone was glowing.

"Great. Just great." The thing was probably radioactive. Either that or Catriona had turned into a practical joker. Either way, she wasn't wearing a glowing necklace in public like some ten-year-old kid.

Not only was it glowing, but it was starting to heat. She could feel the warmth through her sweater. Yeah, this thing definitely had to go.

But as she reached for it, she was hit by a violent wave of dizziness that made her stomach roll. Around her, the car began to spin. She grabbed for the steering wheel, desperately needing to ground herself. If this didn't stop soon, she was going to be sick all over the rental car. Which was bound to cost money.

The warmth seeping through her sweater began to turn hot. If she didn't get the thing off soon, it was going to burn right through the fabric. But she couldn't bring herself to let go of the steering wheel. An illogical fear gripped her that it was the only thing holding her tethered. If she let go, she'd go spinning off into God-knew-where.

Catriona's words rang in her ears. *Don't touch it until you get home.*

How was the necklace doing this?

Come on. That's ridiculous. The dizziness doesn't have anything to do with the necklace.

But a strange, crawling sensation began to blossom all over her skin. A buzzing sounded in her ears. Ridiculous or not, her instincts told her the dizziness and the stone were related.

Putting on Catriona's necklace had been a terrible mistake.

Talon strode purposefully down the passage deep within Castle Rayne, his white chaplain's robes brushing his legs, hiding the knives he had strapped around either calf. In one hand he held a lantern against the darkness. In his other, a carafe of holy water. For a bloody fortnight he'd walked these passages, visiting every room, pretending to bless the castle and cast out the evil spirits residing here.

In truth, he searched for the treasure he'd been sent to find.

Or at least some small clue to its whereabouts.

"Ye worthless piece of metal and rock," he muttered under his breath to the amethyst ring that had clung to his finger for the last score of years. He pushed open the door of yet another bedchamber that would remain empty until the lord and his retinue returned. "Ye tell me to come to Castle Rayne and here I am. Here I linger. Have ye deserted me, now?"

The sounds of drunken laughter lifted from the Great Hall below and he thought of the dram of whiskey he'd begged from the ring earlier that very eve and moments later found dripping through the floorboards at his feet.

Nay, the ring had not deserted him. The irksome thing toyed with him, as it had always done.

The lost whiskey had been his own fault. He'd long ago learned not to ask the ring for anything directly. Hegarty had warned him as much when he gave him the ring years ago. *It'll be givin' ye what ye need, lad, but not always in the way ye want, aye?*

Never in the way he wanted, was more the truth, though he'd learned to get his way more often than not. If he needed silver, he couldn't ask for silver. Or money. He had to ask the ring to fill his belly. Nine times out of ten, he found silver in his purse afterward. On occasion, the spiteful stone would send him food. Real food, and he'd feel his sporran fill with oats, or leak with soup.

But if he was hungry and in need of food, he only got sustenance if he complained to the ring he was growing weak and demanded the ring strengthen him.

Setting the lantern on the washstand, he searched for the Fire Chalice of Veskin, or anything that might tell him where to find the treasure that was his latest mission. The bloody amethyst had sent him to Castle Rayne for a reason.

None knew he had the ring, for none could see it but him. His fist closed tight. The ring might be a pain in his arse, but he'd not give it up, even if Hegarty returned for it as he'd promised he would. The ring was his life now. Everything had changed for him that dark day all those years ago.

The Wizard had been born.

He'd learned to manipulate the magic, soon realizing no task was beyond him. At seventeen, having gotten his growth at last, he'd left home and sold himself and his talents to the highest bidder.

None but him knew he actually possessed magic. They

simply believed him a man who could do anything. For the right price.

Over the years he had indeed accomplished an abundance of impossible tasks. He'd delivered a brigand to his hanging, a lost child to her mum, a cache of gold to one who sought to steal his enemy's treasure. Talon cared not who hired him or why.

The Wizard never failed.

He grimaced. Until now.

A fortnight he'd tarried in this castle to no avail. Now only two weeks remained of the month he'd been given to find the chalice and deliver it as promised. But the damnable ring refused to cooperate. Every day, ten times a day, in every way he could think of, he asked the ring to show him how to find the chalice. So far, all it had done was tell him to come to Castle Rayne.

Finding nothing, he reclaimed the light, left the chamber, and started up the narrow, twisting tower stairs. The light flickered along the whitewashed stone as he rose.

"All right, ye worthless piece of rock. How can I put this that ye'll understand? How about this . . . help me find what my client, Niall Brodie, seeks?" His words held a hard, frustrated edge, for he was fast running out of patience. The Wizard never failed. *Never.*

Yet he was utterly dependent on the ring, for without it, he had no chance of finding the chalice. The Brodie chieftain knew only that it had been stolen sometime within the past twenty years. He knew neither when, nor why, nor by whom. The chalice could be anywhere. But he was willing to pay a king's ransom in silver to get it back.

And the Wizard had promised to do just that.

Bloody, traitorous ring.

Talon continued up the tight, turnstile stair, then stopped suddenly as the familiar prickle of magic rushed over his skin. With a leap of his heart, he stilled, waiting for the slight change in the air that presaged the ring's magic. But the air dropped to frigid, charging as if he'd stepped into the heart of a thunderstorm.

The hair rose at his nape and his pulse began to pound. He was well used to the feel of magic by now, but this was different. Like a winter gale instead of the usual spring breeze.

From far below, he heard shouts of fear and knew he wasn't the only one feeling it. Excitement and anticipation raced through his blood.

"Chaplain!" The voice echoed from far below, seeking his chaplain's cross, no doubt, to ward off what they would believe was evil.

He made no move to answer, but held his lantern high as he stood poised on the stairs.

Waiting.

The firelight flickered. The magic burned through him in a quick, tingling rush. And suddenly he was not alone.

His pulse raced as he stared at the woman. She appeared into empty air a half-dozen steps above, bent as if sitting, then sat hard on the step behind her with a yelp. Her head jerked up, her gaze wide as the moon as she stared at him with the strangest eyes he'd ever seen—one brown, the other pale green. Though clearly a woman grown, she was a wee bit of a thing with shorn golden hair that just brushed her jaw, and odd, male clothing that molded to her slender form.

She scrambled to her feet, facing him with a wild confusion of fury and terror. Never had he seen a more bonny lass.

Slowly, he raised the ring to his lips and kissed the stone. "I take back every bad thing I've said about ye."

God in heaven, the ring had sent him an angel.

"Chaplain!" The steward's voice rang over the stone, nearer now. By the sounds of it, he was climbing the stairs a couple of floors below.

Bollocks.

Talon pursed his lips. He needed to hide the lass and he didn't have much time. Her appearance would raise too many questions, questions he was neither inclined nor able to answer. Who she was. *What* she was. How she'd gotten here.

"I have to hide ye," he told her, wondering if she spoke Scots or English.

"Where am I?" she asked in English, a strangely accented English. Her voice at once demanded and trembled. Her already pale face was losing color by the moment.

"Come." He raced up the few stairs and grabbed her arm, then pushed past her and pulled her with him.

"No," she gasped, but stumbled after him.

He pulled her into the passage then opened the door of the nearest chamber and ushered her inside. The space was small and dusty—the chamber of one of the lady's maids. It would have to do.

The lass stumbled and he grabbed her to keep her from falling.

"I'm going to pass out," she gasped.

"Aye. 'Tis for the best."

"No!" She fought the weakness, struggling to free herself from his hold.

From below, he heard the steward calling for him again.

"I must leave ye, lass." She needed to be out and he feared she'd not go willingly. With a sigh, he set down the lantern and clipped her under the chin with his fist, hitting her just hard enough to knock her unconscious.

He caught her as she went down and lifted her into his arms, marveling at the lightness of her. "My apologies, lass."

With quick steps, he strode into the window alcove and deposited her on the cushioned bench, deep in the shadows where none would find her unless they searched. "I'll be back for ye."

At last, the ring had sent him the tool he needed to find the chalice and complete his mission. But . . . *a woman*? From whence had the amethyst pulled her? Questions knotted in his head. Was she even human? Foreboding wound through his gut.

His jaw clenched tight, he grabbed his lantern and hurried back down the stairs, reaching the chapel just as the steward stormed out.

A man of medium height, little hair, and sharp, suspicious eyes, the steward scowled at him. "I felt magic, Chaplain. Black magic."

Talon gathered the cloak of the chaplain's serenity about him and smiled calmly. "Nay, my good man. Not magic at all, but the gates of hell opening to accept the evil souls fleeing this place. 'Tis as I told ye, aye? Bad spirits haunt Castle Rayne. What we felt was the first lot of them leaving. My work hasna been for naught."

As always, the ring had provided him an alias when he arrived at his destination. A role. But, although the steward had accepted him and allowed him entrance, he'd never entirely trusted him.

A smarter man than most, unfortunately.

A bead of sweat rolled between his shoulder blades. Finally, *finally*, the ring had answered his plea. He needed the steward to believe in him just a bit longer.

"I'll persist with my work until the evil spirits are all returned to the hell where they belong."

The steward eyed him sternly. "One more day, Chaplain, then ye'll leave us. The lord is due back at any time."

Talon held tight to his serene expression. "Aye. 'Twill be enough." Now that he'd been sent the lass, he believed it might be so. Perhaps, finally, the ring would reveal his purpose for being here. He would know he'd found that purpose when the chaplain's robes and the full beard on his face disappeared with the role, as all ring-given tools vanished once he'd used them to the amethyst's satisfaction.

The moment the steward was out of sight, Talon retraced his steps to the room where he'd left the lass. He pushed through the door and strode to the tiny window enclosure where she now lay in a pool of moonlight, sleeping her unnatural sleep. Jesu, but she was a strange and bonny thing. He reached for her, lifting a silken lock of soft, golden hair. Aye, an angel. An angel with missing wings, shorn hair, and lad's clothing.

Was she human? His skin prickled at the thought she might be other.

That was the problem, he supposed. Though he'd used the ring's magic for more than twenty years, he'd never understood its source. Just as he'd never been certain who or what Hegarty was. Until now, he'd given the question only passing thought, for what did it matter so long as the ring's magic was his to control?

But now he found himself fiercely curious and more than a little wary as he stared at the woman. A lass, he was most certain, who was not of this world.

TWO

Julia woke slowly, her head aching, her body uncomfortable as sin on the lumpy mattress. Her cold nose twitched against the musty smell of old wool, though the rest of her felt warm beneath the blankets.

Nothing resonated as familiar to her sleep-dazed mind and she forced her eyes open, trying to remember where she was. She started, staring at the man sitting not three feet away. Confusion fogged her mind. She tried to lever herself up, but pain ripped across the base of her skull and she stopped abruptly.

"Easy, lass."

A Scotsman. She was still in Scotland. Memories flooded back. Catriona's wedding. The drive to Glasgow.

Had she been in an accident?

And just where was she? Because this sure as heck wasn't a hospital. The room was tiny and Spartan in appearance. Big enough only for the small bed she found herself on—if the lumpy thing could be called a bed—a tiny wardrobe, a washstand, and the spindly chair upon which the man sat. The only normal-sized thing in the room was the fireplace. It was tucked into the wall beside a deep window alcove where sunlight trickled in through ancient-looking glazed panes.

And it sure as heck didn't smell like a hospital. Her nose twitched at the strong smell of oil. Lamp oil? And urine. She must have ended up in some country yokel's hovel. Great. Just great. She'd almost certainly missed her flight.

The man leaned forward, his forearms on his knees. He clasped his big hands together. "I didna hit ye hard. Ye should be fine in a thrice."

Julia nodded, her jaw smarting. So there had been an accident. Carefully, she sat up, turning her head until she could face him fully.

The guy wasn't bad looking for a yokel with a full beard wearing a choir robe. He was big, but from what she'd seen, the Scots tended to grow them that way. His beard probably hid a weak chin and jaw. Who else would wear a beard like that these days? At least his cheekbones were high and well-defined. His nose was slightly crooked, though a nice size and shape, and his eyes were a pretty shade of Carolina blue. If she had to guess, she'd put him in his mid-to-late thirties.

"How damaged is my car?"

"Your *car*?" His brows drew together in confusion.

She stared at him. "I wasn't in my car when you hit me?" God, why couldn't she remember? "Did you hit me with a car?"

That look of confusion in his eyes turned wary. "I dinna ken yer car, lass. I hit ye with my fist."

Julia gaped. Slowly, the memory returned—a hazy memory of him dragging her up an ancient, twisty stair-well and into a dark room, then turning to her. Or on her.

"*Why?*" Outrage began to burn through the pain.

"I'm sorry I hit ye, but I couldna have ye wandering the castle."

"The castle?"

"Castle Rayne. I'm the acting chaplain. Talon, I'm called."

"Talon." She frowned, trying to move backward from that moment she'd first seen him on the stairs. The last thing she remembered before that was . . .

The necklace. She'd been ready to get out of the car in the rental lot when the necklace Cat gave her had started to act funny.

Her breath caught as she remembered how everything had begun to spin. And then the car seat had fallen away behind her and she'd landed on a stone stair. *In a twisting stairwell.*

Impossible. Clearly, she was missing a chunk of memory.

She met the man's gaze, her own hard and demanding. "How did I get here?"

His brows drew down. "How is it ye have two different eyes?"

Julia groaned. If one more person mentioned her weird eyes . . . "It's called heterochromia, it's perfectly natural, if unusual, and it runs in my family. My cousin's eyes look just like mine. As did my aunt's and my grandmother's."

He smiled at her, taking her by surprise. It was a smile meant to wheedle or charm, but it was breathtaking. To her annoyance, her body reacted like some inexperienced teenager's, her pulse absolutely fluttering. Fluttering!

"I meant no offense," he murmured. "I'm thinking I rather like yer eyes, lass. Having two the same color is muckle plain."

Julia groaned at the blatant flirtation even as she fought her body's ridiculous pleasure in his words.

"I'll ask you again, Braveheart. How did I get here?"

The man cocked his head, a small smile playing at that well-sculpted mouth. "Braveheart, eh? Well now, how do you think you got here?"

She made a sound deep in her throat, a mix of pain and frustration. "I'm not up for games. If I was in an accident, I don't remember it." She frowned "Did you kidnap me?"

"Did I steal ye? Aye, 'twould seem so."

"*Why?*"

He studied her. "I need your help."

Julia frowned, trying to make sense of his answer. Trying to make sense of any of this. From what she remembered, she'd been alone in her car when everything had started to spin. She must have been drugged. But when? *How?* She'd been alone the entire day except for the quick stop for petrol and soda outside of Glasgow. The soda bottle hadn't been opened, so it couldn't have been tampered with.

He was playing games with her. She was sure of it. And yet . . . "If you needed my help, why didn't you simply ask for it?"

His mouth turned up, forming that devastating smile. "I did, in a manner of speaking."

Oh man, he was too cute. Even with the beard. But she wasn't some kid, susceptible to a handsome face. And, dammit, this wasn't funny.

"You're making jokes. I want answers."

"As do I."

She scowled. "*You* want answers? You're the one calling all the shots here, dude."

He looked at her quizzically. "I wish to know who ye are."

Blinking, Julia stared at him. "You don't know? You just grabbed me at random?"

"I doubt there was anything random about it. But, nay, I dinna know ye."

She made a sound of disgust. "I can't believe I have to introduce myself to my kidnapper. I'm Julia Brodie."

He frowned. "A Brodie."

"Is there a problem? Other than the fact that you *kidnapped me*?" She turned slowly, pressing her back to the wall. "Why did you bring me here? *How* did you bring me here?"

Talon cleared his throat, his expression turning boyishly engaging. "I have a talent, ye might say. When I need help with something, I ask for it. And God provides."

Julia lifted one hard brow. "God?"

The man nodded earnestly. "God."

"You expect me to believe God snatched me out of my rental car at the Glasgow airport and handed me to you?"

Once again, his expression took on that look of confusion, as if she were speaking another language. She knew the Brits had different words for things, but come on. Was he being intentionally obtuse?

Julia scowled. "Try again."

"'Tis the truth."

"I don't think so. I'm willing to believe God works in mysterious ways, but this is a little too blatant, even for Him."

"'Tis a miracle, aye?" Dimples appeared in his cheeks just above his beard. *Dimples*.

The butterflies moved into her chest. She bit down on her rising frustration. "This is not a joke!"

He was trying to tease her, cajole her. What was really scaring her was the fact that he wasn't trying to tell her she'd fallen asleep. Or been knocked out. Or something minimally logical. He was acting as if she had indeed poofed from her car into this castle. Just as she remembered.

He lifted a single brow, keen intelligence lighting his eyes. "Do ye have a better explanation?" Only a hint of his smile remained, but the look he gave challenged her.

"No." Her voice began to rise. "But people do not simply disappear into thin—"

He moved so fast, she barely saw him coming. One moment he was on the chair, the next he was on the bed, one hand clamping over her mouth as he grabbed her. He pulled her back against his chest, the solid band of his arm across her middle pinning her tight.

"Wheesht!" His voice was low in her ear, but no less sharp. "Dinna shout like that, lass. No one kens yer here and I would keep it that way."

Her heart began to race. Acting purely on instinct, she struggled to free herself from his iron hold, shaking her head to dislodge his smoky-smelling hand from her mouth.

Pain bolted through her jaw and she quieted, groaning.

Never in her life had she been physically overpowered like this, despite her small stature. This man overwhelmed her in every way. Yes, he was bigger and stronger than she, but who wasn't? Much more frightening was the certainty that he was a man who would do whatever he damn well pleased. She could feel it in the way he pressed her against him, in the sure, unflinching way in which he'd grabbed her and controlled her. Hadn't he already hit her once, hard enough to knock her out?

Fear began to cloud her mind. He could do anything to her, anything, and she couldn't stop him. She was completely and utterly at his mercy. If he decided to rape her, he'd rape her. And if he wanted to kill her, she wouldn't be able to do a thing to stop him.

The iron band across her chest loosened, though he didn't let her go. "Easy, lass. I've said I'll not hurt you."

His hand moved away from her mouth.

"You already did hurt me."

"I've already apologized for that." He released her slowly, then moved away from her and returned to his chair. She opened her eyes to find his smile gone, as if it had never been. He watched her without softness. "Are ye human?"

"What do I look like, a donkey?"

A glimmer of humor lit his eyes, but did nothing to soften the hard line of his mouth. "Nay, not a donkey. Yer human, then. That's good."

This had to be the most bizarre conversation she'd ever had in her life. "What would I be if I wasn't human?"

"I dinna ken. Ye'll tell me from whence ye came."

Did that mean he wasn't the one who'd kidnapped her? God, she didn't remember being kidnapped. "I'm from New York. But the last thing I remember was sitting in my rental car in the Hertz lot at the Glasgow airport."

His eyes narrowed. "Ye speak strangely lass, and of things I dinna ken. But I know Glasgow."

"Am I in Glasgow?"

"Nay."

"Still in Scotland, at least?"

"Aye, ye are that."

She sighed. They'd probably shoved her in the trunk of a car or the back of a van. "How far are we from Glasgow?"

"A week's ride, mayhap."

She frowned. Scotland wasn't that big a country. She was pretty sure she could get from one corner to the other in a day. Two at the most. "On what? A bicycle?"

His brows drew together again.

"Oh, quit it," she snapped. "You know what a damned bicycle is."

But his eyes continued to hold that wary, uncomprehending look. "I was speaking of a horse."

She stared at him, then laughed, a harsh exhalation of air. "Who in their right mind would try to ride a horse across *this* country?"

"'Tis either ride or walk."

"Chaplain!" a male voice called from just outside the door.

Again Talon leaned forward and covered her mouth with that less-than-clean hand. "I'll be there forthwith!" He caught her eye, his expression hard once more. "I must leave. Do you wish me to hit you again and make you sleep, or tie and gag you?"

Great set of choices. Being kidnapped sucked.

Her eyes shot daggers at him, but when he lifted his hand, she hissed, "Don't hit me."

"Then ye'll cooperate and be silent." He grabbed a rag and twisted it, shoving it between her teeth and knotting it behind her head, just like in the movies. The linen texture felt gross against her tongue, and tasted worse, but she reminded herself the alternative was probably another fist to the jaw. No thank you.

As he tied her hands behind her back and looped the rope around the bed frame, she belatedly wondered if she'd missed her opportunity to get some help. She probably should have started screaming when she first heard the other man. But the truth was Talon scared her. One moment he was flashing that killer smile, the next he was looking like he'd happily kill her for real.

Definitely a man to tiptoe around until she figured out where she was. Then she'd formulate a plan for escape.

Before he reached for the door, he sent her a sharp, warning look. "Silent."

She glared at him, but didn't make a sound. Julia Brodie was no coward, but neither was she a fool. And right now, staying quiet . . . and alive . . . seemed like the wisest thing to do.

Talon left the room and closed the door behind him. A moment later she heard voices through the wall.

"My wife, Mary." The voice was the same deep tone as

the one who'd called through the door. ". . . babe due in June. Same as the queen's."

Julia's brows pulled down. Queen Elizabeth was a little old to be having kids, wasn't she? Unless Prince William had gotten married and been made king when Julia wasn't looking. Despite being half-Scottish, she was all American and had never paid much attention to the British royals.

". . . praying the queen gives birth to a girl. We dinna need another papist on the throne. King James is naught but a pope lover."

King James? Clearly they weren't talking about the English monarchy. Had Scotland finally declared independence after all these centuries? Or was her head injury more serious than she thought?

The conversation ceased, replaced by a low murmur she thought was Talon's. A murmur that reminded her of a minister's mutterings. As if he were a chaplain for real.

Ha. No way. If that guy was a man of God, she was a sumo wrestler.

A few minutes later the other man thanked him. A woman did the same. Then the door opened and Talon slipped back into the room. He closed the door and stood there, watching her with a contemplative look she wasn't sure she liked.

Fear had taken the place of the butterflies, but she glowered at him, refusing to be cowed.

"We need to talk, lass." Talon crossed his arms over his chest, his eyes hard. "If you try to scream, I'll knock you out again. Do you ken?"

If her hands were free, she'd have been tempted to flip him off. Instead, she gave him a single hard nod, then winced at the ache in her jaw, losing her glower.

As her vision cleared, Talon sat beside her and removed her gag.

She raked her tongue across the roof of her mouth, trying to get rid of the nasty taste of linen. "Why do they think you're a chaplain?"

"Because that's what I am."

"Right. And I'm the King of Siam."

His mouth quirked up on one side, a dimple flashing as a gleam of humor, and maybe respect, lit his eyes. "The King of Siam, eh? And why do ye not believe me?"

He turned her to face away from him, his hands surprisingly gentle, then began digging at the knots at her wrists.

She glanced over her shoulder at him. He had to be kidding. "Do you want the entire list, or just the highlights?"

That gleam in his eyes deepened, encouraging her.

"Try kidnapping and assault, not to mention the fact you're skulking around, hiding me. Not very chaplain-like, in my experience."

"And what do you think I am?"

She turned back, glancing at the intricately carved cross hanging on the wall. "If I had to guess, I'd say a con artist. But more than that. You're into dangerous stuff. Maybe spying. Maybe drugs." And she should probably shut up now before he decided she knew too much and needed to die. *Smooth move, Julia.*

He was silent for more than a minute as he dug at the ropes. Finally, he sighed. "Ye ken the truth, Julia Brodie. I am not who I claim. There is something I seek and ye will be helping me find it."

As the ropes went slack at her wrists and disappeared, Talon rose and returned to the chair. Julia turned to face him, rubbing her wrists where the ropes had chafed.

She hadn't realized that she'd begun to calm while her back was to him. But the moment she faced him again, the moment she met that sharp, intense gaze, her pulse began to speed and her body began to flush.

The man disturbed her on a fundamental level. He scared her, and yet, her reaction to him wasn't nearly that simple. She couldn't breathe with him so close, with him watching her like a tiger getting ready to spring.

Without consciously deciding to move, she found herself scooting toward the end of the bed, away from him.

Talon rose, towering over her, crossing his arms over his chest like a Roman jailor. "Ye'll not try to leave."

She stared up at him, hating the physical inequality between them. "I wasn't leaving. I just . . . need a little breathing room. You have a bad habit of pushing me around and I'm getting tired of it, dude."

Talon again watched her as if she'd started speaking Farsi, then shook his head and went to lean back against the door, blocking any chance of escape. "Stand where you wish."

She didn't have to be told twice. She scrambled off the bed and strode as far away from him as she could in the matchbox-sized room, straight into the shallow window alcove. Sunlight streamed in through the ancient window and she went toward it, drawn by the warmth as much as by curiosity. If she ever got the chance to escape, she needed to know if the window was an option.

But her hopes were dashed as she saw they were at least four stories up, high above the castle courtyard. With disbelief, she took in the scene below, a scene from another time. This was clearly no modern castle, but one designed to run like a fortress from centuries past. The busy, bustling courtyard was filled with people dressed in period costume, carrying baskets and tools as if they'd stepped out of some late-medieval play. Was this the Scottish version of an Amish village, then? Filled with people who shunned modern ways?

Or maybe she was being held in some kind of tourist trap, filled with reenactors. She scanned the crowd, searching for modern people with cameras or event brochures, and finding not a one.

A girl caught her eye, a young teen in a simple gown and bare feet who reminded her markedly of the way Catriona had looked the first time she'd seen her. Cat could have come from this place.

Julia blinked.

To her knowledge, no one had ever figured out where Cat *had* come from. What if she'd escaped this place and run, winding up at Loch Laggan?

Her thoughts began to spin, her mind leaping, making connections. It was Cat's necklace that had started acting so strangely right before the car started spinning. Right before she'd landed on Talon's stairs.

Which was interesting, certainly. But what could a piece of jewelry have to do with anything?

It was that same necklace that Cat had told her to take far, far from Scotland and not touch. Did it have some kind of locator in it?

For heaven's sake, it was a gemstone. Not a teleporter.

There had to be a perfectly logical explanation for all of this. She'd been in an accident and probably suffered a head injury. She'd lost a chunk of time. As for Talon . . . she clearly couldn't believe a word he said.

As she watched out the window, a man stopped along a corner, whipped out his penis, and began to urinate. *You've got to be kidding.* No one seemed to notice. Or if they did, they didn't seem to care. Good grief. This place was way too real. If she didn't know better, she might think she'd been plucked out of the twenty-first century and dropped into the past.

Which was utterly ridiculous.

Her scalp began to tingle.

Snatches of overheard phrases popped into her mind like comic book thought balloons. . . . *babe due in June. Same as the queen's. King James is naught but a pope lover.* Talon's assurance she could ride to Glasgow in a week's time. *On a horse.* Cat's admission that she hadn't known how to read or write when she'd first come to them. As if she'd grown up in a world of horses and bare feet. And King James.

Julia grabbed for the windowsill, her fingers clutching at the wood.

No. She was being ridiculous even *thinking* of such a thing. Magic wasn't real. Time travel was not real.

Cat's voice rang in her head. *Don't touch it until you get home. Don't ever bring it back here.*

As if she'd known something would happen.

As if she'd known *this* would happen.

Cold sweat dampened her body. Talon claimed God had delivered her to him, like he knew she'd been plucked out of thin air and handed to him. For God's sake, he'd asked if she was *human.*

Her hand gripped the window frame so hard that the muscles in her arm began to quiver. There was a logical explanation. There had to be.

But the question that pressed at her mind wouldn't be quieted. What if the stone did possess some kind of . . . magic? What if it had somehow snatched Catriona from *here* all those years ago and delivered her to the Brodies?

And had now snatched Julia from there and dropped her here.

Where exactly was *here*?

She stared out the window, her gaze riveted to the sight as her mind supplied the answer, then violently rebelled.

She was *not* in the past.

Swallowing hard, she turned around and met the gaze of the man watching her with a pair of intense blue eyes.

She looked at him, really looked at him, searching for some telltale sign that her imagination was running wild. But his robe, his boots, all screamed *the past*.

Her gaze scanned the room. No electrical outlets. No cables. No light switch on the wall.

It didn't matter. Her imagination was running away with her, probably a result of a head injury.

She forced herself to meet his gaze. "What's the date, Talon?" Her voice sounded calm and even, but the moment the words were out, her heart began to pound in her chest. Because she knew. Deep down, *she knew*. Everything fit. As insane and improbable as the answer was, it fit.

"Seventh of April."

"The rest. The year."

He looked at her quizzically. "The year of our lord 1688."

She nodded. 1688. *Sixteen* . . .

Her stomach lurched. The air turned the consistency of molasses, refusing to enter her lungs.

Talon rose with a worried expression. "What is amiss, lass?"

The blood drained from her face. She was going down.

Talon grabbed the lass and sat her on the edge of the bed, shoving her head between her knees.

"Breathe, lassie. Easy, now." His fingers slid into her soft hair as he gripped her small skull. "Breathe."

Her hands came up, her fingers pressing against her temples. "I'm okay. I don't faint." But her voice sounded as pale as her skin looked.

"Aye. Ye fight it most thoroughly."

Had he hit her too hard? Had the magic harmed her mind? He'd felt the blast of it. The whole castle had felt it.

Talon released his hold on her and squatted on the floor

before her, his hands resting on her knees. "Tell me what ails ye."

She looked up and met his gaze, her face as white as milk, shock in her eyes.

Shock. She'd asked the date and he'd told her. It was then she'd nearly swooned. Why?

A chill raced along his spine.

He'd asked her from where the magic had pulled her. Perhaps that had been the wrong question.

He studied her—her oddly short hair that appeared not hacked, but carefully shaped. Her clothing, like nothing he'd ever seen, the fabric and knit of remarkable fineness.

He thought of her speech—English, but accented as he'd never heard it. Her strange, strange words—and her disbelief that he hadn't understood them.

"Julia?" he asked softly. "Ye'll tell me, lass. Ye were not expecting the year I gave you, were you? Did the magic pull ye through time as well as space? When were ye in Glasgow, Julia? A different year, aye?"

Her gaze clung to his, a lost look in those intriguingly mismatched eyes that pulled at the strings of his heart.

"The future." The words came out as little more than a whisper from between tense lips.

Gooseflesh raised on his arms. *The future*. A future when lasses dressed as lads and intentionally hacked off their own hair.

"How far into the future, Julia? From when have ye come?" He held her gaze as he gripped her knees, uncertain whether he supported her or held on for himself.

Her bonny mouth opened, then closed as she visibly swallowed, then opened again. "2010."

Talon's eyes widened, the hair rising at his nape as he rose and stepped back. He'd thought forty or fifty years, mayhap. Not . . . *Jesu*. "*Three hundred twenty-two years*."

He glanced at his ring with new respect. The rock had

power greater than even he had suspected. It was little wonder the blast of magic had been felt throughout the castle.

Excitement began to pulse beneath his ribs.

Mismatched eyes implored him. "Send me back."

"I cannot."

Twin fires ignited deep in those eyes, anger fanned by desperation. "You have to send me back." Once more, her voice began to rise. "You said you were the one who brought me here!"

"Wheesht!"

She flinched, her face paling even more, a thing he'd have not thought possible, as she lifted her hands as if to ward off a blow.

Or him.

He glanced at the door, but made no move toward her. "Ye must settle, Julia, or you'll bring the whole castle down upon us." He fought to keep his voice low and calm, sensing she was near hysterics. "I'll not hurt you again."

She watched him with eyes too big for her face, breathing too fast. "You have to send me back."

"You've a job to do, aye? And once you do it, you'll return to your place and time."

A flare of temper tightened her expression. "If you can send me home *then*, you can send me home *now*."

"Nay, I cannot. I did not bring you here apurpose. I canna control it."

"Then how did I get here?" The color was slowly returning to her cheeks. "And don't give me that crap about God's will. God didn't do this and we both know it."

With a mix of admiration and frustration Talon accepted that this lass was too canny to believe anything less than the truth. But would she *believe* the truth? Even if he were willing to share it?

Nay, he'd not share his secrets. He'd never told anyone about his ring and was not about to do so now.

Claiming magic of any kind was a dangerous game. Though the witch hunts had died down, there were still those all too willing to believe. And to destroy those they feared.

But the lass deserved an explanation. Indeed, by the look on her face, she demanded one.

And what would he possibly tell her, if not the truth?

A partial truth, perhaps.

"'Twas magic that brought you to me, lass. I asked for help in finding the item I seek, and you appeared. You must ken something from the future that will help me."

She stared at him with a look of growing frustration. "I don't know anything." Her voice quavered.

He rose and poured a dram of whiskey from the carafe the ring had gifted him with late last night and handed it to her. "Drink it slow, aye?"

She took the glass, the liquid sloshing against the side, her hands visibly shaking. Slowly, she raised it to her mouth and took a sip, her tongue darting out to lick the moisture from a pair of lush, feminine lips.

With a sweep of lashes, she caught him in the agitated chaos of her gaze. "How could I possibly help you? I'm not even from Scotland. I'm a New Yorker. An investment analyst. I don't *know* anything about this time, or this place." Lightning tore through her eyes, a keen desperation. "Tell me what I have to do to get home."

Talon sat on the chair and leaned forward, his arms on his knees. "Help me find that which I seek, Julia Brodie."

Impatience tightened her pale features. "Which is?"

Talon felt his lips twitch, admiration sparking inside him at the grit with which she faced this most untenable situation.

He shrugged. "I dinna ken." His pulse lifted in anticipation. "Have you heard of the Fire Chalice of Veskin?"

"No."

Ah, well. He had hoped . . . "'Tis said to be made of gold with fine etchings around the rim. But 'tis likely what I seek in Castle Rayne is not the chalice at all, but something quite different. Something that will help me find it."

Julia lifted a fine brow, a sharp look of disbelief in her eyes. "How can you not know what you're looking for?"

Her shrewish tone chafed at his pride and he shrugged. "The magic can be fickle."

She raked her golden hair back from her face. "You're losing me here. How will you find it if you don't know what *it* is?"

"Ye dinna understand."

"Clearly. Maybe if you explained this magic of yours a little better, I might. Who did you ask for help? A crystal ball or magic mirror? God, I can't believe I'm even saying this. Do you have some kind of magic lamp that grants you three wishes? Or a genie in your pocket?"

He scowled. "Nay."

"That's it? Just *nay*?"

"Ye dinna need to know."

"Right." She buried her face against her knees, her hands over her head. "I wish I didn't know any of this. I would give anything right now to make it *all* go away. I don't believe in magic," she whispered, a soft lament.

A minute passed. And another. Slowly she lifted up, straightening again, her eyes tormented. She took a deep, shuddering breath. "Your magic brought me here to do something for you. How am I supposed to help you if you keep your secrets from me?"

He'd never told anyone about his ring and he wasn't starting now.

"You have to give me something here, dude. Is the magic yours personally? Again, I can't believe this stuff is coming out of my mouth. Are you a witch or something? Or . . . what would a male be called? A warlock? A wizard?"

"I am not."

"Then you get your magic through an object or spell book or something."

His jaw clenched.

"I'm right, aren't I? I can see it in your face. Jeez, Talon, do we really have time for a game of Twenty Questions? I'm going to figure it out eventually. Can't you just tell me and save us both the annoyance?"

Bollocks. He supposed it made little sense to keep the truth from her when she'd already witnessed the results. "My magic comes from a ring."

Her gaze fell to his hands. "Do you wear this ring?"

"Aye."

"I don't see it."

"None can see it but me."

A small smile breached her defenses, but the smile turned sour and she made a sound that was part grunt, part laughter. "That is the most ridiculous thing I've ever heard."

Anger sparked inside him, then flickered out as he watched her mask slip, and he glimpsed the anxiety she was trying to hide.

She tossed back the rest of the whiskey with a single swallow, shuddering violently. A shudder, he suspected that had little to do with the spirits.

She met his gaze, a pained understanding in her eyes. "Almost as ridiculous as time travel."

He studied her face and her eyes. "Ye believe me."

Their gazes met, then locked, as if two halves of a whole had clicked into place. It was a strange feeling. A feeling he wasn't sure he liked. Yet he couldn't look away from her.

Through her gaze, he felt her reach for him, cling to him as if he alone could give her the answers and strength she needed. As if he alone could see her through.

A strange and unwanted feeling of protectiveness rose inside him.

With a quick lick of her lips, she broke the connection and looked away, her gaze scanning the small room.

"I'm withholding judgment on whether I believe you until I've seen a little more than a bedroom and the courtyard. But if I've really traveled back in time, then not believing in your magic ring seems kind of ridiculous."

She turned to him again, the strength back in her eyes.

The calm logic of her mind pleased him.

"I think we'd best find ye some garments that better suit this time, aye? I'm not for certain what we'll do about your hair. Mayhap we can say you took a knife to it in grief."

"Excuse me," she said with asperity. "This is a hundred-dollar haircut. Does it *look* like I hacked it with a knife?"

His jaw dropped. "A hundred dollars?"

"American dollars. With over three centuries of inflation. Expensive, but not what you're thinking, so close your mouth."

He did, and found a smile breaking over it.

"What?" she asked warily. "Why are you smiling?"

"You please me, lass. You've every reason for hysteria and swooning, yet you fight it every step of the way."

"Thanks. I think." She slapped her thighs lightly. "Okay, let's get me some clothes and find your chalice so I can get home. I've got an important meeting next week that I can't afford to miss." Her mouth twisted thoughtfully. "I wonder if time moves the same in both places. Or if I'll wind up right back in the car as if I'd never left."

Talon shrugged and rose. "I dinna ken. All right, then." He rubbed his ring with his thumb. "The lass's clothing will give her away as not of this time, putting her in danger. Keep her safe."

Her mouth twitched. "You're asking your magic ring?"

His ire tried to rise at the faintly teasing tone, and failed. He might have a magic ring, but she'd traveled from the future. They were more than even, to his mind.

"Aye." The look he gave her was stern, but not entirely serious.

"Why not just ask it for clothes?"

"The ring's a wee bit fickle, aye? It does as it pleases." He shrugged. "Ye may get new clothes soon or not at all. And if . . ."

He felt the tingle of magic over his skin, then stared as the lass's outlander clothing disappeared to be replaced by a simple, threadbare shift. The yellowed linen clung to her form, the neck wide, revealing creamy skin, the sleeves extending to just below her elbows. The fabric itself was so worn, he could see straight through it.

Jesu, but the sight of her dusky nipples and the thatch of hair between her thighs moved him. His blood rushed, heating his skin. Hardening him.

Julia looked down at herself and gasped, covering those finely curved breasts with her arms. The only things she wore that she'd come with were her boots and the necklace around her neck.

Her head jerked up. "You did this on purpose."

Talon's mouth kicked up in a sideways grin, his body growing harder still. "Nay." Though he couldn't say he wasn't enjoying the moment.

"Quit looking at me like that and get me some clothes!"

With a low chuckle, Talon rubbed the ring again. "The lass is in danger of catching a chill, ring."

A servant's bonnet blossomed on her head.

Julia scowled.

Talon began to laugh. The ring had a mind of its own,

to be sure. And for once he was enjoying the rock's impudence.

"This isn't funny." Though her voice was waspish, her eyes began to glitter with unshed tears.

His heart went out to her. She'd been through shock after shock, finding the strength to withstand each. But now her clothing had been stolen from her and she stood undressed and vulnerable before him. Taken from all she knew.

He sobered. "You're right," he said softly. Lifting the blanket from the bed, he wrapped it tight around her as she stood still as stone. Feeling the need to offer a bit of comfort, he cupped her shoulder and squeezed lightly. "I'll find ye a gown. Without the ring's dubious help."

As he reached for the door, he turned to her, to where she stood looking small and lost and vulnerable. "You'll go nowhere?"

Her eyes widened and she shot him a disbelieving look as sharp as daggers. He ducked out of the room, grinning. Slowly, he leaned back against the wall, fighting for control over his humor even as he willed his body to quiet from the need throbbing low.

"You're playing with the two of us now, are ye?" he asked the ring as he tipped his head back against the wall and looked up at the ceiling. "You couldna bring me a plain lass, could you? Or dressed her in sackcloth?" Nay, the bloody ring had to send him one who made his loins ache and his admiration rise. A bonny lass with fire in her eyes and steel in her spine.

A lass who might pose a threat to his very life. She knew more about him than anyone ever had. The secret behind the Wizard's success.

Magic.

THREE

Julia stared at the closed door, pulling the blanket tighter around her as the last of her control shattered. The tears that had threatened with the loss of her clothes spilled over, running down her cheeks as great, wracking sobs tore through her shivering body.

"*I want to go home,*" she whispered into the empty room. Crying, she crawled onto the sorry excuse for a mattress and huddled beneath the blanket, wrapped in misery.

She hated to cry, but the storm was upon her and she knew it wouldn't end anytime soon. She'd handled being flung through time and being hit by a barbarian with killer blue eyes. Even the news that she wasn't going home until she performed some mysterious and unknown task hadn't laid her low.

But losing her clothes was the last straw. She loved that

sweater. And, dammit, that had been her best bra. It was too much!

Too much to accept. Too much to process.

How could she possibly be in the past? Yet if she'd harbored any doubt that she was dealing with magic, it had disappeared along with her clothes.

Magic.

The tears only ran faster. By the time they'd finally run their course, her skin was chilled and clammy, her headache had worsened, and her eyes had grown heavy and swollen. She felt awful. And scared. And horribly, horribly alone.

As badly as she wanted to blame everything on Talon—after all, he certainly seemed to believe he was the one who'd called her—she couldn't forget the way the garnet had turned hot and begun to glow just before the car started spinning. The necklace had played some part in her time shift, she was sure of it.

Cat's words rang in her head. *Don't touch it until you get home.* But she'd put it on anyway.

She had only herself to blame.

Reaching inside the blanket, she felt for the stone and found it still lying cool against her chest. She fingered the purple garnet with a mix of relief and wariness. There was no doubt the thing was dangerous. Putting on the necklace had been a mistake of monumental proportions. But if the rock had been her ticket to the past, it might also be her way home.

"Send me back," she murmured to the stone, much as Talon had spoken to his ring. "Dammit, *send me home.*"

Lifting the thing where she could see it, she held her breath, watching for the telltale glow, willing the stone to begin to heat in her hand.

But nothing happened.

With a huff, she dropped the necklace to settle between

her breasts and pulled the blanket tighter around her, the musty smell of wool enveloping her. One thing was certain. She didn't dare tell Talon her suspicions that her jewelry was at least partly to blame for the magic. He'd probably take it from her.

Despite the fact the man knew who she was and where she'd come from, she didn't trust him. She'd never met anyone wrapped in so much subterfuge. He was a thief and a con man. Yet, there was something magnetic about him, too. Something that attracted her on the most basic level. An appeal deeper than his killer smile or those blue eyes that danced with intelligence and mischief, charming even as they manipulated.

There was something not quite civilized about him. The way he'd grabbed her without hesitation. The way he'd knocked her out, then offered her a smile that had stolen her breath.

Talon wasn't like any man she'd known in her own time. He was far more physical. More confident, but in an entirely different way than the well-dressed Wall Street types. This man could take care of himself and he knew it. What's more, she suspected anyone entering his orbit sensed that strength on the most primitive level. That danger.

It wasn't that he was all fists and manhandling. He'd been gentle enough with her some of the time, even giving her shoulder a light squeeze as he left the room. Not that she needed gentleness. She didn't need anything from anyone. But she'd found that small offer of comfort a reassuring trait in a dangerous man.

And he was definitely a dangerous man.

God, she had to get out of here. She had to get home. If time passed equally in both places, her plane would have left this morning. Tomorrow, she was due back at work and four days from now she was scheduled to give the presentation that just might land her the promotion she'd been working toward for three years. She *had* to be in New York by then.

Feeling a surge of stress-induced adrenaline, Julia scooted to the edge of the bed, then rose and went to the window, keeping the musty wool blanket tight around her. Chills sent goose bumps popping up on her arms as she stared again at a world so distant from the one she'd left.

If only she knew why she'd been yanked back here.

Her gaze followed a young boy chasing a chicken across the courtyard, lunging and failing to catch it again and again, yet the kid never gave up. And neither could she. What she *could* do was keep her eyes and ears open, believe nothing without proof, including the time traveling.

And trust no one but herself.

The same as always.

Julia heard the click of the door and turned, holding the ends of the blanket tight in her fists as Talon walked in. He closed the door, then grinned at her, flashing a pair of killer dimples as he held up a skirt and a little jacket thingie. Seventeenth-century clothes, apparently. The skirt, navy blue and probably made of wool, looked as if it had been mended a million times. The jacket, or maybe it was just a heavy shirt, was dark red with a vivid grease stain on one side. Lovely. Clearly these were loaners.

"Where's the rest of it?"

"'Tis all ye need, lass. Ye have the shift and the boots, aye?"

"What about underwear?"

He turned his head as if uncertain he'd heard her right. *"Underwear?"*

Julia groaned. "What do women wear under their clothes in this time? Pantaloons? Corsets?"

Talon made a tsking sound. "Lasses who are not fine

ladies wear a shift. Which you have. You've no need for anything else."

She liked her situation less and less with every passing minute. "Easy for you to say. I thought this thing was a nightgown."

"'Tis both."

"Of course it is." No need for luggage if you carried your nightgown around on your back everywhere you went.

Talon laid the skirt and top on the bed, then motioned her closer with his hand. "I'll be your lady's maid."

"Yeah, right. I can dress myself. You can turn around."

A smile played at his mouth, but he did as she asked.

Julia tossed the blanket onto the bed and picked up the skirt. No nice, neat little zipper, just a lot of strings and ties. She dropped it to the bed and picked up the jacket instead. Even more ties . . . or laces . . . all the way down the front.

Talon turned around, shaking his head at her. She crossed her arms over her breasts, but needn't have bothered as he focused his attention on the skirt, opening it wide.

"Hands over your head, lass."

"You don't follow directions well, Braveheart."

His eyes laughed at her. "I dinna have all day and ye do not seem to be making much progress."

If she'd been twenty years younger, she'd have stuck out her tongue at him. With an ill-humored growl, she lifted her arms and let him lower the skirt over her head, then crossed her arms again.

Stepping closer, Talon bent to settle the skirt on her waist. His light brown hair fell forward, nearly brushing her cheek, his face so close she could see the faint scars at the corner of one eye and along the side of a nose that looked like it had been broken more than once.

His scent wafted over her, an infuriatingly intriguing smell of wood smoke, wool, and rough, attractive male. Why didn't he stink of body odor or something?

He fiddled with the skirt, placing it just so. His broad hands cupped her hipbones then slid to her waist, where he slowly, carefully, adjusted the fabric. Wrapping the strings from back to front, he stepped even closer to tie them.

Her pulse began to accelerate. Her body temperature began to rise. His nearness overwhelmed her and it was all she could do not to step back. The moment he released her skirt, she snatched the little jacket off the bed and stepped away.

"I can do it myself," she said a little too sharply, and turned her back on him.

The jacket's laces kept the front panels together, so getting into it was no easy feat, especially with the shift underneath, but she was determined to dress herself without his help. She managed to get the jacket over her head and her arms through the sleeves without pulling the laces entirely loose. But her shift bunched awkwardly beneath it, pulling too tight in some places and hanging out in others.

"What I wouldn't give for a simple bra," she muttered. She fought with the outfit, reaching beneath the skirt to try to pull the fabric down, shoving and yanking at the bodice, trying to hide her sole undergarment, but there was no way the shift was disappearing. Was it *supposed* to show? She could seriously use a fashion magazine about now.

She felt his fingers in her hair. Strong, male fingers lifted the locks as his knuckles trailed sensuously down the side of her neck, sending a shiver through her startled body.

Julia jerked away from his touch and whirled to face him. He was too close, towering over her with that damnably engaging smile, half-boyish, half-sexy-as-hell. She had to steel herself against the urge to step back, to retreat to safety.

Instead, she glared at him. "I'm going to tell you this once, caveman, and you're going to listen to me. Don't *ever* touch me without my consent. Not for any reason and not with any part of your anatomy, do you understand?"

His half-smile turned chilly and the look in his eyes hardened. Something about that look made her think of a cat toying with the mouse he was getting ready to make his dinner.

"Aye," he said softly, sharp-edged amusement sparkling in his eyes. "I'll have your consent, then, for you look as if you were dressed by a blind lady's maid."

Julia stared at him, her frustration rising even as her anger drained away. She sighed loudly, unhappily, and gave him a rueful twist of her mouth. "You're obnoxious, do you know that?" With a quick grin that reached his eyes, he grabbed the ties of her skirt and hauled her closer, then set about loosening the ties of her jacket.

"If we were in my time, Braveheart, I'd haul you up on sexual harassment charges so fast your head would spin."

His hands stilled.

She hazarded a glance up, afraid she'd really offended him this time. But the look in his eyes was an ocean away from offense. Heat flickered within the Carolina blue.

"'Tis not sexual harassing I wish with ye, lass." His voice was low and husky. "But sexual pleasuring."

Liquid warmth gathered low in her body. "Back off, Scotty." But her own voice sounded breathless and almost as husky as his.

With that infernal little smile of his, he jerked her closer, brushed his lips against her temple in a quick, surprisingly sweet touch, then went to work straightening her dress with sure, skilled hands. Though, if she'd thought he'd spent an inordinate amount of time on the skirt, it was nothing compared to the top. His knuckles brushed her upper chest over and over as he tugged and straightened. His palms slid beneath the jacket, cupping her shoulders, smoothing the shift, then reached beneath it in back, smoothing and adjusting.

Finally, he turned her to face him and pulled the edges of the jacket together, right over her breasts, lingering too long.

"Keep moving."

His mouth kicked up at one corner. "Yer as skittish as a new filly."

"There's nothing new about me."

His expression and voice softened. "'Tis no shame being unused to a man's touch, lass."

Unused . . . ? "I'm not a virgin, if that's what you're getting at."

"No?"

"Not at all."

"Have ye a husband, then?"

"No. And I never will."

"Never? Do ye prefer the lasses, then?"

Julia rolled her eyes. "I am *not* having this discussion with you. No, I don't prefer women. But that doesn't mean I want or need a husband. Or you."

He pulled and tugged at the lacings, working them tight down the front of the jacket. "But ye do want me."

"In your dreams." Her body might be hot and bothered by his overwhelming presence, but that was a natural reaction to being too close to a far too masculine man. Something she generally avoided.

"You respond to me, Julia," he said softly. "Your body warms to me. Dinna think I cannot tell."

That sexy know-it-all smile was really getting on her nerves. She grabbed his hands. "Let go. I can finish."

He ignored her, watching her with a gentle intensity. "The lad who took your virginity. Did he hurt ye?"

"No. And it's none of your damn business anyway."

"You've a mouth on ye, lass."

"Go to hell."

"Did ye find it . . . pleasing?" His hands had stilled on the laces. He continued to watch her with that probing gaze.

She looked away. "Sure. Of course."

God, what a liar. It had been awful. The worst two weeks of her life. She was mortified to feel the heat rising up her neck and into her face.

"'Tis rarely pleasant for a lass the first time," Talon said quietly.

"Yeah, well, there was a second time, and a third." With a defiant lift of her chin, she met his gaze. "I've had four lovers, Braveheart. Enough experience to know you're not my type. I'm through talking about my love life, so finish dressing me and *back off*."

With her words, his eyes had narrowed, the smile dying from his mouth. She saw the disapproval plain as day, and it hurt.

"Don't you dare judge me, Talon," she said heatedly. "Things are different in my world. Sleeping with lots of men is normal."

If only she could believe it herself. And maybe she would if they'd been relationships strung out over years. But they hadn't been. And she judged herself bitterly.

Talon's jaw hardened as he turned his attention to her laces. Finishing quickly, he turned away.

"Ye'll stay here." The flirt was gone. All humor and softness had fled.

A fist tightened in her chest.

He strode to the door, his back to her. "As the chaplain, I have responsibilities I must fulfill. I'll return when I can."

Without a backward glance, he left, shutting the door behind him.

Julia stared at the door as the flush of embarrassment receded, stealing the blood from her face. She sank onto the bed, cradling her head in her hands, feeling emotionally battered. She knew enough history to know that in this time there was only one word for an unmarried woman who'd known four men. *Whore.*

Not that she cared what he thought.

She dug her fingers into her hair, tears starting to burn her eyes. Okay, maybe she did care, but she had no one to blame but herself. There was no reason in the world he'd needed to know her sexual history, but he'd been acting too sure of himself and she'd been feeling a little too unsettled by him.

Stupid, Julia.

But, honestly, did it matter? Her only goal was to figure out what she had to do to get out of here. Once she did, she'd never see him again.

And that couldn't happen soon enough.

FOUR

Talon muttered under his breath as he sprinkled water along the inner walls of the Great Hall, pretending to be blessing the room with holy water, as he had the others. After last night's blast of magic, the castle's scarce inhabitants were skittish and fearful, looking to him to protect them from the evil spirits.

But if any got too close to hear his mutterings, they'd hear not prayer but railings at a woman. A woman who'd known four men, yet turned her nose up at the suggestion she lift her skirts for him.

Judge her for taking men to bed when she was unmarried? Aye, it was hard not to even though he himself had bedded . . . *Jesu*, he didn't know how many lasses. Scores. Maybe hundreds. Any likely lass who held out her hand to him and lifted her skirts.

In the two weeks he'd been at Castle Rayne, he'd

tupped four lasses. No, five. Ah, he'd forgotten the one in the root cellar. Make that six. And two of them twice.

He had no right to judge. But a lass who'd taken four lads to bed could be persuaded to take a fifth. Aye, she could. And this lass was not unaware of him, no matter what she pretended.

A small, determined smile lifted his lips.

Before she completed her task and returned to her time, he would seduce her.

The Wizard never failed.

Several hours later, Talon returned to his chambers, a supper tray in his hands. He held the tray with one hand as he opened the door, praying the lass had remained in the room as he'd bade her. He didn't think she would leave on her own, now that she knew she wasn't in her own time. But he'd not put it past the fickle ring to snatch her away just when he'd set his sights on her.

Grabbing the lantern he'd set down, he lifted it high as he pushed into the dark room.

Julia whirled to face him, fury in her unusual eyes, her hands clenched into fists at her sides. "The sun's already gone down. You left me in here *all day*. Without food. Without drink. *Without light*. With nothing but a stinking chamber pot. I had *nothing* to do and no way to know if you'd driven off . . . *walked* off and left me."

Talon listened to her tirade, delivered, at least, in a voice little more than a whisper. He set the tray on the bed and stepped back.

"Your supper."

She grabbed the ale and took a long swallow, but she wasn't through. "I didn't know if you'd been caught and thrown in the dungeon, or if you'd just conveniently forgotten I was here. Twice . . . *twice* . . . someone knocked on the door looking for you. I had to shove myself under this damned bed. If anyone had come in and sat on it, they'd have flattened me. This has been the longest, most frustrating day of my life!"

Talon watched her grab up a slice of meat and tear into it, his mood swinging between amusement and annoyance. She was a high-strung lass, true enough. Mayhap even a bit of a shrew, though he supposed she had a right to her high dudgeon. He hadn't intended to leave her for so long.

With a small grimace, he conceded maybe he had meant to, mistakenly believing she'd be so glad to see him when he finally returned that she'd throw herself into his arms in relief.

He'd misjudged her reaction badly. And he'd given no thought to how long she'd been without food before the ring called her.

She dug into the meat as if she'd not eaten in days. In between bites, she glared at him. "When I'm through eating, you will get me out of this room or I'm going to start screaming and never stop."

He raised a harsh brow, his amusement fleeing. "You make any noise approaching a scream and I'll either gag you or knock you out again."

She stared at him as she chewed, then scowled. "I didn't mean that literally. I'm claustrophobic, Braveheart. I wasn't before today, but after at least a dozen freaking hours in a ten-by-six room, I am now, thanks to you."

"You're claus . . . ?" He didn't know what she was trying to tell him.

"Claustrophobic. Afraid of closed spaces. Going stark-raving mad. Insane. Loony. Nutso. Are you catching my meaning *at all*?"

"Aye." And, yes, definitely a shrew. Though in her ire she was, if possible, even more bonny. Her color was high, her eyes flashing. He rather enjoyed her fury.

"When you've finished your supper, I'll take you into

the tower for a wee spell. Mayhap we can figure out why you're here."

She stared at him as she tore off another chunk of lamb with her teeth, then nodded, the stiffness draining from her body as if the mere promise of escape was enough to keep the desperation at bay. She sank onto the bed and pulled the tray onto her lap, careful not to spill a drop. Her fury seemed to dissipate as she devoured the meal.

Not until the food was more than half gone did she look up at him again, pleasure warm in her eyes. "This lamb is amazing. The best I've had."

The praise for the food pleased him almost as much as that glimpse of warmth. "The cook is surprisingly fine to have been left behind when the marquess is not in residence."

"Do you know the marquess?" She took another bite.

"Nay. I've not been to Castle Rayne before a fortnight ago. I'd not be here now if not for the ring." He eyed the bed beside her and took a step toward her, intending to sit at her side and test the attraction he knew existed between them. But as she realized his intent, she stiffened, her hand stilling, her supper forgotten. So he changed his path and leaned against the wall, instead.

Julia watched him warily as she finished taking the bite. He would test that attraction later, when it wouldn't interfere with her meal.

"Why are you looking for the chalice?" she asked.

"I've been paid to do so."

"Someone hired you to find it?"

"Aye."

"They know about your magic ring?"

"Nay. None know of it. None know I have magic at all. But for you."

She eyed him, a lovely brown eye pinning him. "1688. Isn't this prime witch-burning time?"

"'Tis why I tell no one."

"They just think you're really good at finding things?"

"Aye. *The Wizard* they call me."

To his surprise, a flash of humor gleamed in her eyes. "Cute. And ironic."

Many of her words made little sense to him, but he gathered their meaning through context well enough. *Cute* meant nothing to him, but *ironic* he understood. And he'd, too, oft thought it ironic he was known as the Wizard.

Her expression sobered as she chewed another bite. His gaze lingered on her mouth and he watched the movement of those supple lips, wondering if she would taste as good as she smelled. He was certain she would. A small, secret smile lifted his spirits. He'd find out for himself soon enough.

"You're really taking a risk trusting me with the truth, aren't you?" A glimmer of wariness entered her eyes.

"Aye. But not so much, I'm thinkin'. You're an outlander, lass. Your speech and hair give ye away as not Scottish, though most will have trouble placing your origins. Nay, I dinna think most will listen to you if you accuse me of magic. And if they believe magic's been done, they'll almost certainly point the finger at you."

Julia watched him thoughtfully. "You're probably right." She finished her meal, leaving not a morsel uneaten, then set the tray aside and rose from the bed. At the washstand, she rinsed her fingers with a bit of water from the washbasin and dried them on her skirts.

He watched her, intrigued by the grace with which she moved. When she turned, fervent desire lit her eyes and sent his pulse soaring. The blood pounded through his veins, gathering between his legs. He was about to close the distance between them when she spoke.

"To the tower?" she asked hopefully.

Belatedly, he realized the desire in her eyes had naught

to do with him and everything to do with freedom from her day's confinement. He stood rooted, struggling to gain control.

Jesu. A simple look and she had him nearly on his knees with wanting her. He whirled away from her, picked up the lantern, and opened the door. Neither seeing nor hearing anyone, he held out his hand to her, not terribly surprised when she ignored it.

Her fury might have dissipated, but she was far from smitten with him. A temptation and a challenge she would be, of a certainty. He enjoyed a challenge as well as the next man, but rarely had his body risen as quickly and as thoroughly as it did with this lass.

The thought of her ultimate surrender brought a smile to his lips. For the first time in as long as he could remember he was tempted to put off seeking whatever the ring had sent him for, at least for a few days. Because once he found it, he feared the lass would be gone. And he was loath to see that happen yet. Not only did he fully intend to bed her, but she intrigued him mightily.

She followed behind him as he lifted the lantern and lit their way up the tower stairs, the very ones on which she'd first appeared a night ago. As they passed the spot where he'd first seen her, he reached back and took her hand, half-afraid he might lead her through a hole from which she'd return to her own time unless he held her tethered.

To his surprise, her cool hand closed tight around his.

"I hate these stairs," she murmured, as if feeling the need to explain her sudden willingness to accept his touch.

He didn't care why she didn't pull away, only that she didn't. Her hand in his felt small and delicate, yet surprisingly strong. Surprisingly right.

They climbed the stairs without incident and he led her into the passage at the next level. As soon as they were off the stair, she tugged her hand from his and he released her. He hung the lantern from a wall post and led her into the large lady's chamber beside the one where he'd hidden her last eve.

"You don't want to bring the light?" Julia asked.

"'Twouldn't do for the guards upon the wall walks to see it. This tower is supposed to be closed until the marquess returns. The moon is already risen and nearly full and will provide adequate light."

"This room is huge," she breathed.

Though he'd been in this guest chamber several times already, on the pretense of blessing it, he looked around, trying to see the space through her eyes. Though it was now draped in colorless shadows, he knew it to be adorned with wealth and beauty, expensive red and green papers covering the walls, the high, curtained bed draped in the finest red satin.

How he would love to lay Julia Brodie on that bed and lift her skirts to her waist, parting her thighs . . .

Heat rushed through his body as the thought took on a life of its own inside his head. He could almost feel the silken skin of her inner thighs against his fingertips. Could almost hear the racing of her heart. Heaven knew he could feel the pounding of his own.

"This isn't the room where you took me last night," Julia murmured.

"No. You'll forgive me for hitting ye, lass. I couldna let you draw attention to yerself until I had a chance to figure out who and what you were. And explain to you why you were here."

She turned to him sharply. "You could have broken my jaw."

"Perhaps. But you were far from the first I've sent into an unnatural sleep. I knew where to hit you and how hard. You were in little danger."

Silhouetted as she was in moonlight, he watched her lift her hand to her jaw. "Easy for you to say."

Talon tried to close the distance between them, but she backed up a step.

"Let me feel it, Julia. I would know how badly I injured you." He would take any excuse he could find to touch her.

As if she understood that all too well, she replied, "I'm fine." But she didn't fight him when he slid his fingers along the line of her face, cupping her soft skin.

"Does it pain you, still?"

"No, not really. Only when I touch it."

"Or I touch it."

She shrugged and stepped away from him again, then turned to roam the room.

"Dinna step into the moonlight, lass. The guards may see ye."

Her low, determined voice floated back to him. "I need to figure out why I'm here. There has to be something I know, or something I can do, that would help you. Can you read?"

"Aye. Well enough."

"So you don't need me for that. What languages do you speak?"

"English, Gaelic, and French."

"More than me. I have some French, but I'm not fluent. And I know almost nothing about Scottish history." She turned back to him, cocking her head. "I thought Scotsmen wore kilts or plaids or something, yet watching the courtyard all day, I never saw a one."

"Highlanders wear the plaid."

"And we're not in the Highlands?"

"Nay. Castle Rayne is north of Edinburgh, but not in the Highlands."

"Have you ever been to the Highlands?"

"I was born there. Only a Highlander would speak the Gaelic, eh?"

"Then why aren't you wearing plaid?"

"I wear the robe of a chaplain. The ring dressed me much as it dressed you."

"Seriously? Would plaid have given you away as an imposter?"

"I could have sought work in the clothes in which I travel, which is generally not the plaid. But that is not the way of the amethyst. I requested a reason to be in this castle, which the ring had already directed me to through a dream. The stone responded to my request by providing me with the robe and trappings of a visiting chaplain. I'll know when I've completed my task here, for the robes will disappear and I'll once more be standing in my travel clothes."

"More than just a nightgown and boots?" she asked dryly.

Talon grinned. "Aye." But his body heated, remembering all too well the way her slender body had teased him through the thin shift, a shift that even now caressed those womanly curves. Curves his hands itched to trace.

The longer he watched her pace the room, the more he thought about taking her into his arms, the more he longed to taste her.

And the more certain he became that he was going to have to employ a bit of trickery if he hoped to make that happen. He feared wooing this lass would take far more time than the ring would give.

Julia paced the room, glad to be able to walk more than three steps before she hit a wall, as had been the case all day. She hadn't been kidding when she'd told him this had been the longest day of her life. Every minute she'd wondered if she should try to leave the room and escape the castle. Doubts had preyed on her mind that she was really in the past.

They still did. How did she know she wasn't merely locked up in some mock-up of a castle designed to reflect a seventeenth-century way of life?

She didn't. Not for sure. Maybe Catriona had come from here, but that didn't mean she'd been a time traveler.

Then again, such a scenario neatly overlooked the fact that her clothes had disappeared. No, as much as she'd like to pretend otherwise, there was no denying magic was involved.

Which was why every time she'd thought about leaving the room, she'd lost her nerve. Deep down, she was all too afraid everything Talon had told her was true. And while he was willing to accept her strangeness, that didn't mean anyone else would.

Minute after minute, hour after hour, she'd waited, wondering where he was, wondering if he was in trouble, if he'd ever come back. They were going to have to have a serious talk. If she was going to help him, he was going to have to show her a little more consideration. At the very least, leave her with food and something decent to drink. And some small sense of how long he might be gone.

She reached the far end of the room and turned back, only to stop as Talon rushed toward her through the shadows, his body radiating a sudden tension.

"Someone comes," he whispered urgently.

Julia's pulse leaped.

Talon grabbed her arm. "We must hide." He pulled her into the corner and into the tight space between a large, carved armoire and the wall. The space was barely wide enough for both of them, forcing them to squeeze together, chest to chest. The scent of his wool cloak teased her nose.

His hands slid over her shoulders, one slipping behind

her and tugging her closer as if he were trying to pull her into his arms.

She stiffened, intensely uncomfortable with the closeness even as she strained to hear the sounds of footsteps over the pounding of her heart.

"Calm, lass," Talon said softly. "Your heart is about to race from your chest." His hands slid back and forth over her shoulders, a light touch that was probably meant to calm her, but was having the opposite effect.

He was too close, everything about him too much. Too virile, too physical, too charming. Her pulse sped instead of calming, her body warmed, flushing with heat. Sexually experienced or not, she'd never been comfortable around men and this man less than most.

His warm, male scent filled her senses and all she wanted to do was put some distance between them, yet she didn't dare move. Not when someone could walk into the room at any moment.

Talon's fingers slid beneath her hair. His thumbs began to trace light, gentle strokes up and down the sides of her neck, sending her breathing into an awkward unevenness.

Deep and low inside, her body began to ache.

"Calm, lass," he whispered leaning down until his mouth was against her temple, his warm breath stirring her hair and smelling faintly of beer. He smelled . . . so good.

Other than to bend his head toward her, she'd swear he hadn't moved, yet she suddenly felt as if he were closer, enveloping her in his warmth and scent, in his overpowering maleness.

The fingers at her nape slid down, caressing her upper back, then slowly moved to the base of her neck where her shoulders were bare. Everywhere his fingers touched, her skin flushed and heated.

"Don't." Her voice lacked its usual firmness, sounding soft and breathless to her ears.

His mouth touched the corner of her eye, making her swallow hard against the intimacy. "I only mean to calm ye, lass."

"I don't need calming. Remove your hands."

"I havena anywhere else to put them."

Julia groaned at the oh-so-innocent tone. "Yeah, I think you do." She tried to shift away from him and only managed to brush her hip against his pelvis. The unmistakable feel of a thick erection jolted through her.

He was hard as a rock, pressing against her, touching her, his mouth on her temple, on her eye, as if he were in full seduction mode.

She froze with a shock of realization. He wasn't acting like a man hiding from imminent danger. This was a man playing at danger to worm his way closer to a woman.

"You *jerk*. Let me out of here." She shoved away from him and into the room.

"Julia . . ." he said urgently.

"Can it, you liar. God, what a cheap, sleazy trick. You didn't hear anyone, you just wanted to rub yourself against me. What a pervert!"

He grabbed her and shoved her against the wall, none too gently. Julia's heart leaped into her throat as she stared up at him, her breathing suddenly harsh. Would he hit her? She kept pushing him, kept forgetting he was nothing like the civilized men she knew.

His hands pinned her shoulders to the wall, his face lowering angrily to hers. "Ye'll ne'er call me a pervert again."

She stared up at him, torn between trying to placate him, which went utterly against her nature, and retaliating with a swift, hard lift of her knee. But the thought of *his* retaliation had her swallowing her pride. No one else had ever hit her before, but she had little doubt he'd do it again if she provoked him.

"I'm sorry," she said stiffly. "For calling you a pervert.

But you took advantage of the situation. Of me. And I don't appreciate it one bit."

Half his face was lit by moonlight and she watched the anger slowly drain from his features, though the hardness remained. "Ye want me."

"No. I don't. I don't want anything to do with you."

"Do ye not? I feel the heat rising from your skin, lass." His lips grazed her temple, sending shivers through her body. "Now who's the liar?"

Julia struggled to free herself, but to her shock, he grabbed her by the upper arms and lifted her off the floor until her feet dangled, until her face was even with his. Before she could gather her wits, he pressed against her, pinning her to the wall, and covered her mouth with his.

Shock turned to disbelief, her senses swamped by sensation. She couldn't breathe, couldn't think. His lips moved over hers, at once hard and gentle. His tongue swept inside her mouth, stroking her own. Her pride tried to protest his high-handedness, but the heat and pleasure swirling inside her kept her silent, stealing her will.

He tasted wonderful, a hint of beer and clean rain.

Raw desire flowed through her limbs, spiraling low inside her until she was meeting his kiss, meeting his tongue, and moving her lips in time with his.

A sound of primal satisfaction rumbled deep in his throat, his hips pressing against hers, pushing that thick erection—an erection that was not well-controlled behind a firm zipper—into her skirts, pressing between her legs, seeking her heat through all the layers of clothing.

Julia wrenched her head sideways, freeing herself from his mouth. "Let me go!" She tried to kick him, but he had her tight against the wall.

Talon released her, dropping her fast and backing up a step, out of the reach of her boots.

She caught her balance, pressing the back of her hand

to her mouth, shocked by the way she'd responded. And furious at him for forcing himself on her.

But instead of looking apologetic or the slightest bit abashed, she saw him grinning in the moonlight.

"Aye, ye warm to me, lass. Ye'll not deny it again."

"You asshole." Her temper spit and snapped. Leading with her fury, she yanked the unlit candle stub from the small brass candleholder sitting on the table beside her, and threw it at him.

Talon caught it, chuckling, infuriating her more. She grabbed the brass holder and threw it, too, but her aim was off and it clattered to the wood floor, making enough racket to wake the dead. The sound startled her out of her temper.

"Whoops." A bit of retaliation was one thing. Getting them both caught, and God knew what would come after that, wasn't what she'd intended.

Talon stared at her, his body still and tense.

Then she heard it. The sound of shouts outside. The pounding of running feet.

Her heart began to thud in her chest. Surely all the commotion couldn't be over one thrown candlestick.

"Has your temper run its course?" Talon asked evenly.

"Yeah."

"Then let's leave this place at once." He held out his hand to her.

Julia didn't think twice before she placed her hand in his. Together, they ran for the door.

FIVE

Julia held tight to Talon's hand as he grabbed the lantern and started down the stairs. The infuriating man descended the narrow, uneven wedges as nimbly as a mountain goat, moving far faster than she felt comfortable with.

"Talon, slow down."

To her relief, he did, even as he squeezed her hand. "I'll catch you if you fall."

She believed him. But not three steps later, he lurched suddenly, careening into the wall, and she thought they were both going down. The lantern swung wildly, slamming against stone, the glass breaking with an awful crash that made the thud of the candlestick in the bedroom sound like a light tap on the floor in comparison.

The flame sputtered out, casting them into utter darkness.

Julia tightened her grip on Talon's hand. "Are you okay?"

He didn't answer.

"Talon?"

His only response was a groan as he slowly slid into her, pressing her down until she was sitting on the narrow wedge behind her, the back of Talon's head listing onto her breast.

"Talon, what's wrong?" Had he had a heart attack?

Her heart pounded. All day she'd wondered if anything had happened to him. Now something had and she didn't know what to do to help. He was far from her favorite person, but he was the only one she knew in this entire world. And very possibly the only one who could get her home.

Like it or not, she needed this guy. Desperately.

"Are you sick?" She lifted his head from her breast, her fingers sliding through the soft, wavy strands as she stroked the hair back from his face, encountering the cool, clammy skin of his brow.

"Nay." His voice was low, but strong. "The ring sent me a vision. I finally know why it sent me to this castle."

"Why?"

He reached for the hand on his forehead and tugged it to his mouth for a soft kiss. "'Tis a lamp I must find. A golden lamp."

"A golden lamp, a golden chalice. This ring of yours has a thing for gold. Where's the lamp?"

"In the laird's chambers. Hidden in the wall."

"So, what now? You'll just go pluck it from the wall and leave?" *What about me?*

Talon squeezed her hand, then stilled.

The pounding of heavy footsteps sounded below. "You must hide, lass. Back up the stairs you go. Quickly!"

"I can't see a thing!" With a groan, she pulled herself up, lifted her skirts, and felt her way up the dark, uneven steps, praying she didn't miss one and tumble into Talon and the broken glass.

In the total dark, her other senses heightened. And not in a good way. She heard the scratching in the wall of a rodent and smelled the unpleasant, if faint, odors of excrement and mold.

She kept going until she reached the hallway above. If she had to, she could probably find the door to that big bedroom again, but she wasn't sure that was a great idea since she'd made so much noise in there.

From below she heard the sound of voices.

"Lost my footing." Talon's calm voice carried to her clearly. "And hit my head, but 'tis clearing, now."

"I'll help ye back to your chambers," a deep male voice offered.

Julia heard the crunch of broken glass and the sounds of footsteps fading away. She hugged herself, her back to the wall as she stood in complete darkness. A bead of perspiration rolled between her breasts.

A draft breezed over her face, chilling her to the bone. Ghosts were known to haunt castles, weren't they? Would they haunt someone who wasn't even supposed to be here? Someone who wouldn't be born for close to three hundred years?

Her hand clasped around the garnet at her throat. "Start glowing again, please? Send me home. If my being here was your doing, *please* send me home."

But the stone remained dark and cold and the wall at her back refused to spin.

She wasn't sure how long she'd stood there when she heard the crunch of broken glass. Her heart leaped into her throat. Talon? Or someone else? Before she could decide whether or not to start searching for a door, she heard his low voice.

"Julia, lass?"

With an exhalation of relief, she pushed away from the wall.

"Here." She hurried back toward the stair, watching the light of another lamp come into view, followed closely by Talon. His strong face and piercing eyes were an intensely welcome sight.

He held out his hand to her and she went to him without hesitation.

"We have to hurry, Julia Brodie."

"What's going on? Did they hear us up here?"

"Nay. Did ye hear the shouting?"

"Yes, but I couldn't make out what they were saying."

"The marquess has returned. His retinue is less than a mile down the road."

She glanced at him with dismay. "That can't be good."

"Nay, 'tis not. We'll ne'er get into his chambers to get the lamp if we dinna do it quickly."

"You keep saying *we*. Does that mean I'm going with you?"

"The ring sent you to me for a purpose. Now that it's told me where to find the lamp, you'll stay with me until I know what that purpose is."

They reached the bottom of the stairs and he led her down the hallway, the opposite direction from the way they'd come.

"Where are we going? Where's his room?"

"In the south tower. The chambermaids will be opening the towers and readying the chambers."

She wanted to point out that they'd almost certainly get caught if the maids were heading to the same place they were, but that seemed kind of obvious. And maybe it didn't matter anymore. Once the castle was swarming with the people who really belonged here, someone was bound to see her sooner or later.

Two women scurried past, carrying piles of linens in their arms. While one looked to be of legal age, the other couldn't be more than thirteen or fourteen. Were these the maids? Both eyed Talon with blushes. The younger eyed Julia with curiosity, the older one with a sharp look of jealousy, but neither said anything as they passed. And Talon paid them no attention.

The hallway grew lighter and lighter as they moved down the passage. She saw why as they turned the corner and passed a teenaged boy lighting wall sconces with rapt concentration. He didn't seem to notice them at all.

Talon led her up another flight of twisty stairs. Julia grabbed her skirts a second before she tripped over them, and followed him, still clinging to his hand. At least these stairs were well lit, sconces flickering with firelight every full turn. The candlelight gave the space a cool, atmospheric feel, though she'd enjoy it more if it were all part of some tourist attraction instead of the real, honest-to-God thing.

As they climbed, the sound of activity above grew louder and louder. They were definitely going to have company. But Talon's steps weren't slowing.

At the top of the stairs, he led her down a short hallway and into a palatial room, far bigger even than the one they'd briefly hung out in earlier. This one was lit up like a movie set, light flickering from no fewer than a dozen brass sconces. A mammoth unmade bed sat in the middle, framed by red velvet bed curtains. The walls were covered in fancy gold and black wallpaper and the furniture was beautifully carved and must have cost a fortune, even in this time period. Especially in this time period, when all that carving had to have been done by hand.

They paused in the doorway, drawing the attention of the three young maids. Two changed the sheets while a third dusted the furniture with a rag. All three glanced at Talon with pleasure and her with curiosity that turned to pity as they caught sight of her short hair.

She wanted to yell, "It's a hundred-dollar haircut!" but knew she wouldn't impress them. Short hair was clearly out, out, out in this time period.

Talon released her hand then moved away, murmuring and making movements like some kind of priest. Under his breath she thought she heard the word *distraction* and wondered if he was talking to his ring instead of God. Probably. Slowly, he walked around the room, stopping every few steps to make the same kinds of holy motions.

Not a bad plan, really. Maybe no one would notice when he stopped and opened a door in the wall. Maybe. He was seriously going to need that distraction.

The sound of grunting and heavy footsteps preceded the arrival of two well-muscled young men each carrying a large bucket in each hand. As water splashed onto the floor, the girl doing the dusting released a squawk of disgust.

"Lachlan, ye dolt, ye'll be cleaning that up!"

"Aye, Morna," Lachlan replied evenly with a voice that sounded more boy than man. "I always do."

The two youths carried the buckets to the dark hearth. While the other young man knelt before the hearth and started the fire, Lachlan pulled a round brass tub from behind a dressing curtain and rolled it across the room until it, too, sat in front of the hearth.

The pieces clicked into place. The tub. The buckets of water sitting in front of a soon-to-be-roaring fire, warming nicely. Apparently the marquess liked to be greeted with a hot bath. And without a bathroom and running water, this was the way he'd get it.

Lachlan straightened and started back toward the door,

catching sight of her for the first time. "And who will you be, lass?"

Julia stiffened, meeting his curious gaze. She opened her mouth, uncertain what to say, when Talon beat her to it.

"Leave her be, lad. She suffered a blow to the head and hasna been right since. I'll be taking her to the abbey soon enough."

Julia resisted the urge to glare at him.

Lachlan studiously looked away from her as he left the room, as if she were some kind of leper. It pricked at her pride that Talon had led him to believe she was a nutcase, even as she knew it was better this way.

Talon's words seemed to have had the opposite effect on the others. The remaining boy and all three girls stared at her now with open curiosity, as if they no longer believed she'd notice.

She stifled a groan and looked down, plucking at the ties on her top to keep from glaring at them all.

Out of the corner of her eye she saw Talon pull a painting down off the wall. Her pulse sped. Had he found it, finally? As she watched him surreptitiously, he ran his hand over the wall.

She felt the strings loosen beneath her fingers and grimaced, realizing she'd accidentally untied them. A quick glance up told her the girls were laughing at her.

The young man who should have been paying attention to his fire building was instead watching her with anticipation. What did he think she was going to do, undress herself? He looked to be a little older than the girls, but not much. Or maybe he only looked older since his face had obviously seen a dozen too many fistfights.

Talon found the opening. Out of the corner of her eye, she saw a small door swing out and the glitter of gold within.

With a flutter of nervousness, she knew she had to keep the kids' eyes on her, not him. With suddenly shaking fingers, she began to loosen her laces. Just a little. Just enough to keep them watching her.

Huh. Was she the distraction Talon had asked for? She and her hundred-dollar haircut? Seemed like a bit of overkill to haul her all the way from the future just for this, but that ring of Talon's did seem to be as annoying as its owner.

Warming to her role, she began to hum the theme to *Friends* and sway her hips back and forth as she ran the loose ends of the laces between her fingers. With a bit of false awkwardness, she began to retie them. Nothing too overt. She didn't want to do anything so strange they'd look at Talon to see if he'd noticed or was going to do something about her.

The sound of heavy footsteps sounded in the hall. Her breath caught, her skin going cold. Anyone walking into the room would have a direct line of sight to Talon's theft.

"Time to go," she sang to the *Friends* theme.

She saw the hidden door swing closed, but not quickly enough.

Lachlan stood in the doorway, staring at Talon. "Thief!"

Julia's gaze swung to Talon. He whirled around, a small golden lantern in his hand.

"Now," he muttered.

She tensed, confused, as a strange warm tingle raced over her skin. Now?

Lachlan's shout of alarm had all their gazes swinging to the hearth, where the fire had leaped free and spread to a small pile of kindling nearby. Lachlan rushed toward the hearth, splashing water everywhere from the buckets he carried, as the youth who'd been tending the fire leaped to his feet and reached for another bucket.

The girls screamed and fled the room.

Talon raced toward her, the golden lantern in his hand. "Hurry." He took her hand.

She raced out the door after him. "You're not going to help them put out the fire?" The whole castle could go up in flames.

"'Tis the distraction I asked of the ring. They've plenty of water. They'll put it out easily enough."

Probably.

As they reached the stair, she felt that strange tingle a second time. In a flash of magic, Talon's white chaplain's robe disappeared to be replaced by black pants and a white shirt that set off his male body to perfection. His beard, too, evaporated, revealing a strong jaw and a breathtakingly handsome face.

Julia gasped.

Talon grinned at her, a new man. "'Tis certain I have the right lamp," he told her. "My reason for being in this place is done."

"I hope the castle survives your mission."

He threw her a wry look over his shoulder as he started down the stair, holding her hand tight. The twisty stair continued down, and down, and down some more. The damned stairs seemed to go on forever.

"We must be halfway through the center of the earth by now," she muttered.

"Nay. We're nearly to the Great Hall." He said something more, something she didn't catch.

And suddenly, out of nowhere, a blanket fell on top of her.

She squeaked with alarm. Fabric tangled under her feet and she cried out as she pitched forward. Talon whirled and caught her in his arms. Barely pausing, he set her upright, steadying her on her feet, then pushed the blanket off her head.

Julia stared at him. He was wearing a brown hooded robe. A quick glance down confirmed she'd acquired one just like it. Not a blanket at all.

She frowned. "We look like a pair of Jedi knights."

"Jedi . . . ?"

"Your ring's doing?"

"Aye."

"Wish it'd give me a little notice next time." She looked down to find the robe dragging the floor, a good six inches too long. "Order me a size extra-small next time, would you please?"

Talon leaned forward and grabbed up the extra fabric and shoved it into her hands. "We must hurry." He pulled her hood over her hair again and whirled to continue the rest of the way down the stairs, the lantern hidden beneath his robe.

Moments later, they erupted into a large, cavernous room she assumed was the Great Hall, though it didn't much look like she'd imagined. Instead of rows of wooden tables and weapons hanging on the walls, this one actually had upholstered chairs and sofas situated in seating groups around the several hearths, like an oversized living room.

"Fire!" Talon shouted. "Fire in the lord's chambers!"

As the men and women readying the hall for their master's arrival took off running, Talon grabbed Julia's hand, leading her toward an entryway.

He glanced at her. "Can you ride?"

"A *horse*?" She looked at him with horror.

He scowled, then began muttering to his ring again.

The others had left the thick doors wide open. Talon and Julia raced through them and into the courtyard scattered with frantic people. Firelight flickered from torches and lanterns, sending shadows dancing in the dark. Some of the men carried buckets of water into the castle, but most of the people were fleeing. Two young men led horses out of the stables.

With a shout, one of the men lost hold of two of the horses, a pair that appeared saddled and ready for riding. Talon whistled low and the pair swung toward them.

They were going to run them down!

Julia leaped behind Talon, her already speeding pulse beginning to thunder as she imagined being trampled to death.

But the pair stopped abruptly in front of them in a cloud of dust.

Talon pulled her around. "Mount, Julia. Now!"

"I don't know how to ride!"

"Aye, you do."

She stared at him. How in the hell would he know whether or not she could ride?

"The ring, lass. *Mount.*"

The ring? Understanding swept through her frantic mind. She whirled to the horse, grabbed the reins, and swung into the saddle—skirts, oversized Jedi robe, and all—as if she'd been doing it all her life.

Holy shit.

Talon mounted in a single, fluid move and together they took off toward the open gates. She didn't even have to think about it. Her body knew what to do to make the horse obey.

Amazing. A million possibilities for that ring ran through her head. She could learn anything with a single wish. A black belt in karate? Instantly. Nuclear physics? In the blink of an eye.

"Stop them!" The shout echoed into the night behind her. "They've stolen the laird's treasure!"

"*Bollocks.*" Talon's softly uttered curse carried back to her.

Julia's pulse sped as she leaned forward, urging her

mount faster. A single guard raced to stop them, his sword raised. But Talon pulled a sword of his own and swung as they galloped by. With the clank of metal on metal, the guard's sword flew from his hand.

Talon looked at her over his shoulder, met her gaze, then turned forward and urged his horse faster as if he expected pursuit.

As Julia followed, the cool wind in her face, adrenaline pouring through her system, she felt the strange and inappropriate urge to laugh.

She'd never felt so alive! If she were home, she'd be in front of the television or curled up with a book, reading about another woman's adventures. She'd never longed for adventures of her own. She'd thought the stress of her job was all the excitement she'd ever need.

But there was something about running for your life that cleared the senses, wiping them clean of all the minutiae. She couldn't call this fun, exactly. Not when they could well be executed if they were caught. But this little detour on her way back to New York had certainly gotten her blood pumping.

This little detour to the past that should be over.

Julia frowned as the wind whipped her hair back from her face. Talon's robes and beard had disappeared with his retrieval of the lantern. If her purpose had been to act as Talon's distraction, shouldn't she have disappeared, too? Shouldn't she be home by now?

She felt the necklace thudding lightly against her chest, lifting and dropping with the gait of the horse, and was reminded, all too clearly, of her suspicions that it hadn't been his ring that had brought her here at all. It had been Cat's purple garnet.

Which meant she had no idea what to do to get home. A chill settled over her heart. She tried to shake it off. Maybe the ring was still in control. Maybe she simply hadn't performed whatever task it meant for her to do.

She had to believe that was the case. The ring would send her home. Because the alternative was too frightening to contemplate.

If the necklace alone controlled her fate, she might be stuck here for good.

Six

❧

Talon pulled up at last and Julia did the same, bringing her horse to a stop beside him. They must have been riding for hours, though it was still fully night.

She glanced up at the nearly full moon shining across a sky filled with far more stars than she'd ever seen, noting with dismay that the moon hadn't moved far since they set out. They hadn't been riding long at all. It just seemed that way.

Time in this place moved at the speed of Manhattan traffic. A snail's pace.

Her rear was numb, her body sore, and her adrenaline spent. All she wanted was a hot bath and a warm, soft bed.

Which were about as likely as suddenly riding upon a 7-Eleven. She'd finally accepted that she was well and truly in the past.

"We'll hide," Talon said in a low voice, dismounting.

A cool, woodsy-smelling breeze tugged at her Jedi robe.

Night insects clicked and chirped against the tinkling sound of a nearby creek. No sound of horses met her ears.

"Have we lost them?" She pulled up her robe, preparing to attempt a dismount as Talon walked to her.

"'Tis unlikely." Talon reached up and grabbed her around the waist, then swung her down off the horse like some kind of old-fashioned gentleman.

His face was in shadow, but as he lowered her to the ground, she was suddenly all too aware of him. There was something about him, a raw and powerful masculinity that turned her inside out every time he got too near. That made her forget to breathe.

He released her and turned to the horses. As she grabbed at her robe, pulling the extra length out from beneath her feet so she didn't trip, he slapped the horses' rumps. In a spray of grass and pebbles, the pair raced off.

Julia stared after them in surprise. "We don't need them anymore?"

"'Tis my hope they'll lead our pursuers away from us. Like as not, they'll find their way back to Castle Rayne."

"And what are we going to do? Walk?"

He reached for her, his hand closing around hers. "We'll worry about that come morn." With a tug, he led her into the shadowed and spooky woods.

An owl hooted nearby, making her jump.

Talon squeezed her hand gently. "'Tis only an owl."

Of course it was. She knew that, but knowing it didn't do anything to settle her suddenly racing pulse. There was something unnerving about dark woods in the middle of the night. Or maybe she'd just watched too many movies.

Talon led her deeper and deeper into the shadows as her disquiet grew. How well did she know this guy? He could be an ax murderer for all she knew. Though, considering the size of the sword he carried, he probably didn't need the ax.

A twig snapped beneath her foot. Maybe he really was a witch and was leading her into some kind of gingerbread prison.

"Calm yerself, lassie," he said softly beside her. "They'll not find us."

Right. Exactly what she was thinking. Maybe no one would *ever* find her. Yet, perversely, her fear only made her sidle closer to him and cling to his hand harder.

Despite the direction of her thoughts, she really did trust him to keep her safe. Which was a revelation.

The woods grew more dense, their scent rich and loamy, as they continued to walk for several more minutes. Finally, Talon pulled up. "There's a cave ahead, but it's behind a thick stand of brush. Be mindful, lass. I wouldna have the branches scratch your bonny face."

The offhand compliment annoyed her as such compliments from men always had. Yet his words softened the knot in her chest and sent a pleasant, tingling warmth flowing through her blood.

Her own mixed reaction confused and bothered her. She tried to shove it away.

"Are we're going *in*?" she asked when they seemed to have reached a wall of dark.

"Aye."

"I don't suppose you have a flashlight. Or any kind of light, for that matter."

"I cannot tell how close our pursuers are. We canna risk a light."

"Great." How was she supposed to protect her face when one hand was holding up her robe and the other was firmly caught in Talon's?

Talon seemed to realize her problem. He pulled her hood over her head and curled his arm around the back of her neck, pulling her face-first against his chest.

"Stay close," he murmured, then eased her through the bushes. As he'd predicted, the branches pulled and scraped against her robe, but with his help, left her unscathed.

He released her in utter darkness. The air of the cave felt cooler than that of the forest, and more damp. And it smelled faintly of . . . A shiver tore through her. *Wet fur.*

"An animal," she whispered. What if there was a bear sleeping in here? Or a wolf? Or a whole pack of wolves?

She grabbed for Talon, her hand encountering a thick, muscular arm beneath the robe, and she hung on tight.

"Easy, lass. I dinna think there are any beasties in here at present." To her surprise, he pulled her close, almost like he was giving her a hug, before he set her away from him, prying her fingers loose from his arm. "Stay here while I make certain."

Her eyes went wide, her pulse leaping. She could see nothing. *Nothing.* And he was going to blithely walk around and see if he kicked something awake? He was out of his mind.

As his fingers slipped away from hers, the darkness swallowed her. The pounding of her heart stole all sound. Talon could be in a fight to the death with a dragon and she doubted she'd hear it over the thundering in her ears. Her flesh crawled with goose bumps, sweat starting to bead along her hairline.

What was the matter with her? She'd never been afraid of the dark before. Then again, when had she ever really been in true dark? In a place that was anything but safe?

She pulled the robe tight around her, fighting the panic, struggling against the urge to push out of the cave and race into the moonlight.

The seconds turned to minutes. The minutes felt like they were turning into hours, though it was probably just another case of time holding still in this place.

Still . . . what if Talon had been attacked and she hadn't heard him go down? What if he never came back? What if whatever attacked him was, even now, stalking her?

Panic twisted her insides into knots, turning her body into a sweating, shaking mess. *Send me home*, she silently begged the necklace. *Send me home, send me home, send me home.*

"'Tis safe, lass." The sound of Talon's voice nearly had her knees buckling in relief. He took her hand and looped her arm into the crook of his own. "The cave isna large, little wider than the chaplain's chamber in Rayne, but about three times as deep." He took a step and she followed. "We'll sleep in the back."

The thought of sleeping in this utter dark didn't please her at all, but she allowed him to lead her without voicing her dismay. It wasn't like they'd passed any Holiday Inns along the way.

They hadn't gone far when Talon took her hand and tugged her down. She felt around, feeling dirt and stones and . . . *euww*. Something sticky. No way in hell was she going to be able to sleep in here.

She remembered thinking her accommodations were rustic at Cat's wedding when she'd discovered her room didn't have a private bath and the only showerhead in the bathroom was a handheld attached to the tub spigot. Right now, she'd give just about anything for that clean, warm inn with the down duvet and the hot, flowing water.

And light. Lots of light.

"Come, lass," Talon said softly, tugging on her hand.

She let him pull her close, not realizing his intent until he tried to pull her into his arms.

Julia stiffened and jerked away. "What are you doing?"

"I'll keep you warm while you sleep."

She snorted and pulled her hand from his grasp. "I'll bet. Thanks but no thanks, Casanova. I'm fine over here."

The thought of him holding her close, his hands roaming God-knew-where, sent a strange combination of chills and warmth fighting one another for dominance over her body.

Maybe she was too aware of him, but that didn't mean she wanted anything to do with him. Not like that. She knew what he really wanted. Sex.

A cold, hard knot formed in her stomach. She'd been there, done that. And she wasn't doing it again.

"Then lay ye down, lass. You need sleep."

Unfortunately, she couldn't argue that one. With a shudder of revulsion, she slowly lowered herself to the ground, glad for the Jedi robe between her skin and the actual dirt. But as she laid her head on the hard ground, she knew it was a lost cause.

She lay there shivering until the sound of some small creature running nearby had her shooting upright again. A *mouse*? She didn't mind mice, not in theory, but no way was she letting one use her as a jungle gym.

Maybe it wasn't a mouse. Maybe it was a rat. *Or a snake*. No, snakes didn't scurry. Not unless they grew Scottish snakes like they did Scottish men—big, with too many hands.

She pulled up her knees and buried her face against them, once more silently begging the stone to send her home. Either stone—hers or Talon's ring. She wasn't particular. She wanted a pillow. A hot shower. Clean clothes.

She listened for the sound of Talon's breathing and heard nothing. Did he sleep as silently as he walked, or was he still awake, too? The thought was comforting. And yet not comforting at all. Everything about the man disturbed her. The way he manhandled her. The way he kissed her. The way he sent her pulse into overdrive every time he came near.

Her heart began to beat a hard, insistent rhythm in her chest. Why couldn't he make just a little noise so she knew he was still there? What if he'd vanished as surely as his clerical robes and beard?

The pounding in her chest intensified, thudding against her ribs. A cool sweat dampened her scalp. Her fingers itched to reach for him, to be sure he hadn't left her, but the last thing she wanted to do was wake him. Or make him think she needed him. She didn't. Julia Brodie didn't need anybody.

Oh hell, who was she kidding? It was exactly that she needed him. Desperately. What in the world would happen to her in this place if she lost him? Not only might she never get home, but she was unlikely to even survive.

Swallowing her pride, she reached out.

Talon heard her. Jesu, half the forest probably heard her. She had no understanding of silence, this one.

When her fingertips grazed his cheek, he slid his fingers around her hand before she could snatch it back.

She gasped.

"Easy, lass. What ails ye?"

"Nothing."

He tugged lightly on her hand. "Come here."

She jerked her hand away from him. "No. I'm fine."

But she wasn't fine. She was scared. He could feel it in the faint tremble of her hand and hear it in her voice, just as he'd been listening to her uneven breathing. Yet she refused to let him hold her.

Why? Was she, as she'd said, simply not interested in him? No. He'd felt the truth of her attraction when he'd kissed her. Was it *him* she was afraid of? But then why had she reached for him?

He'd never understand the mind of a woman. She sat

there shivering with fright and cold and refused his warm arms. If he wasn't good enough . . .

Julia sneezed.

"Lass . . . come here."

"I'm fine, I just . . . wanted to make sure the ring hadn't poofed you out of here."

He heard the fear she tried to hide and again wondered if she wasn't just a little afraid of him. And why would a lass who'd known many men be afraid of a man's arms around her? She wouldn't. Unless one of them had hurt her.

Whatever her past, it was clear demons haunted her still. Perhaps she tried to shut out all men.

All people?

The thought found purchase deep within him. Aye. He could feel her solitude, feel the walls she'd built around herself. They felt surprisingly like his own.

With a sigh, he sat up. The lass was a mystery he'd not solve in a single night, not when he was dead tired. He needed rest. They both did.

"You're not sleeping, Julia."

"I'm not tired."

"I canna sleep either. As you fear the ring's power, so do I. I keep thinking the ring will steal you away." He resisted reaching for her with effort. "I might be able to sleep if I could touch you, lass. Just to know you're there. Perhaps you'll feel the same."

He heard her soft sound of disbelief, but her waspish tongue remained silent. So he did the reaching this time. "Take my hand, Julia-lass," he said softly.

His fingers encountered her arm then moved slowly toward her hand. When his fingers closed around her chilled ones, he squeezed softly. "Come lie down, Julia. If ye get no sleep, 'twill be a hard day tomorrow."

She didn't pull away this time, but neither did she allow him to tug her forward.

Talon shifted closer until he sat beside her. With his free hand, he touched her silky hair, stroking ever so softly. "Drop yer shields, lass. Just for tonight."

"I don't have any shields."

"Aye, you do. Let me keep you safe, Julia. I'll treat you with honor, lass. No seduction, I vow it."

"I don't want you to hold me."

But he heard the sound of a stubbornness that lacked conviction and took the choice from her hands. She needed to be held. And, though he didn't understand why, he needed to do the holding.

"Come here." He scooped her up and pulled her onto his lap, sensing that trying to lie with her immediately would have her fighting to free herself.

"You just do whatever you want, don't you?" Though her words held a hint of frustration, they contained no real anger and far too much exhaustion.

To his relief, she didn't try to pull away, though she remained stiff and straight. Sensing she'd bolt if he pushed too fast, he held her lightly and stroked her back.

"I do what you are too stubborn and prideful to admit you want, lass."

She tried to pull away.

Talon held her. "Easy, Julia. Forgive me. Dinna go." He ran his hand lightly up and down her back, calming her. Gentling her. When he felt her begin to soften, he shifted her slightly, pulling her shoulder against his chest. If she would just unbend a little more, he could tuck her head beneath his chin. "I know you're tired, lassie. Give in to it."

She ignored him for long moments, then the last of her stiffness melted away and she sank against him with a sigh, her small head fitting perfectly beneath his chin, as he'd known it would.

"Don't take advantage, Talon. Please?" Her words throbbed with exhaustion.

He rubbed his chin lightly against her hair. "I vow it, Julia. I'll hold ye while ye sleep and keep ye safe. Nothing more."

He wondered at himself. He never slept with a lass, never wanted to, except for reasons of the flesh. But this one . . . there was something about her. A feeling, perhaps, that the face she showed the world was just a mask. A mask designed to keep others at bay. Designed to keep others from seeing the real Julia.

He knew what it was to wear such a mask, for he'd done so for years. The mask of the Wizard.

He supposed the why didn't matter. The plain fact was the lass needed comforting. She needed a strong man at her back. Despite her shrewish tongue, she was one of the most vulnerable females he'd come across in a long while.

Almost at once, she slept, her face pressed to his chest. Certain she was well and truly asleep, he pulled her down and wrapped his arms around her, pulling her close. The feel of her soft, warm body against his, and the trust with which she'd gifted him, pulled at something deep inside him.

Protectiveness welled up, strong and fierce. Holding her felt surprisingly, disturbingly, right.

Deep in his chest, something eased.

And warmed.

And grew.

"Are ye awake, then?"

Julia blinked at the sound of Talon's low, cheery voice, and turned her head to find him settling on the ground a few yards away, the golden lantern in front of him. Daylight dimly illuminated the small, close cave, revealing their true surroundings. Spider webs hung on the walls near the uneven ceiling. Stones and twigs scattered the ground. In the corner lay a pile of dead grasses—a nest of some kind.

With a shudder, she sat up and looked away. The morning air felt chilly against her face, but her Jedi robe had kept her surprisingly warm.

Or had Talon done that? She'd woken at one point during the night to the scent of warm, male flesh and found her face tucked against his throat, his strong arms tight around her. Warm and content, she'd fallen quickly back to sleep.

The memory of how he'd held her . . . of how she'd allowed him to hold her . . . made a blush rise to her cheeks.

She hadn't been herself last night—afraid of the dark, clinging to a man. The woman inside her who left male business associates quaking in their Guccis was disgusted. Then again, that woman wasn't here, was she? That independent, supremely confident woman had gotten lost somewhere between the Hertz rental car center and the seventeenth century.

This Julia wasn't entirely sure who she was anymore.

She watched as Talon pulled out the small flask of lamp oil he'd tucked inside the lantern and poured oil into the lamp's reservoir.

He glanced up, meeting her gaze. "How did ye sleep?" His question was simple, the look in his eyes warm and kind.

That warmth seeped inside her, filling her chest with a deep, pleasurable pressure. She remembered little of the night, only the feeling that she'd been utterly safe. True to his word, Talon had taken no advantage of her that she was aware of. And she was pretty sure she'd have known.

"I slept . . . surprisingly well."

A soft smile lifted his mouth. His blue eyes watched her with satisfaction. Her stomach tightened, fluttering until he finally turned that intense gaze back to the lamp and she could breathe again.

Part of her really hated to admit she'd liked sleeping with him. She hated being wrong about anything. Or anyone.

Talon was a flirt and a con man, and way too physical, but he wasn't all bad. He might not be bad at all, though the jury was still out on that one. At the moment, with her, he was playing the part of a good guy. And she couldn't help but respond.

He lit the wick on the lamp. The flame rose.

"Show me the place where the fire chalice rests," Talon murmured.

Julia sat, still as stone, watching Talon, holding her breath. Minute after minute passed until she had to fight not to squirm.

"'Tisna working," Talon muttered at last.

"What's supposed to happen?"

The handsome Highlander took a deep breath and let it out slowly, never taking his gaze from the flame. "The answer should appear to me. I saw it in my vision."

"You saw how it worked in your vision?"

"Aye." Still he didn't move.

"Maybe it needs a different question."

He glanced at her, then nodded as he turned back to the lamp. "Show me the Fire Chalice of Veskin."

But still nothing happened.

Talon pressed the heels of his hands to his eyes with a groan. The flame had to be imprinted on his eyeballs by now.

"Is it possible we grabbed the wrong lamp?" Julia asked carefully. If anyone had gotten the wrong lamp, it was him. And he might not appreciate the reminder.

But he didn't seem to mind her question. "I've been wondering the same thing, but there were no other lamps in that nook. And this is identical to the one shown to me in my vision. This has to be the lamp. But I dinna ken why it isna working."

"Can I try?"

Talon lowered his hands, blinking as if trying to clear his gaze. "Aye. Mayhap 'tis the reason you're here."

Julia tried to crawl over to him and nearly landed on her face. Crawling in long skirts was impossible. But as she stood, her bladder complained. If this didn't work soon, she was going to have to find a place to relieve herself. Only the thought that helping him might suddenly send her back to her own time where she might find a public restroom close by, complete with toilet paper, kept her from seeking relief immediately.

She stood and walked the few steps, then sat down opposite him.

Talon met her gaze. "Ask it a question, lass."

Her breath quickened. She broke away from his gaze to stare into the flame. "Why am I here?" She waited, watching the tiny flame dance, but like before, nothing happened. "Show me the chalice Talon seeks."

Still nothing. Finally, she couldn't stand it any longer. She rose. "I need to . . ." What was the proper term? *Go to the bathroom* sounded like she wanted a bath. Which was true, but definitely not her most pressing concern at the moment.

But Talon understood. With a nod, he motioned toward the cave entrance. "There's no one about. Mind your face as ye push through the bushes. I'll not follow."

With a quick nod, she hurried toward the mouth of the cave. Privacy was good. A flush toilet and a roll of toilet paper would have been better.

As she'd tried to squat over a chamber pot yesterday for the first time, she'd finally understood the advantage of not wearing panties. She lifted her hood and pushed past the branches, then walked a short way from the cave, looking around. They were in the woods, though the trees were still winter bare and not nearly as dense as they'd appeared last night. Above the treetops, the sky appeared gray and heavy, and the air felt damp, smelling of rain.

Great.

She found a likely spot and managed to hike her skirts and squat, groaning. She was good about going to the gym three or four days a week at home, but she usually spent her time on the treadmill or weight machines. Not squatting. Definitely not squatting.

Once she was done, she stood with her feet apart, attempting to air dry. God, how much longer was this impromptu medieval camping trip going to last?

With a sinking feeling, she realized she should have been back at work today. Her presentation wasn't until Thursday, but getting back to her own time was only the first step. Would she simply appear somewhere, without purse or passport, looking like a homeless person? How would she ever explain where she'd been or how she'd disappeared?

She didn't want to think about it. Even if she got back to her own time this morning, it might take her days to get back to New York. And she didn't have *days*.

At the thought of returning home, of never seeing Talon again, she felt an odd twinge of regret. She had yet to really figure him out, but there was no doubt he'd been the most dynamic presence in her life in a long, long time.

Birds sang to one another in the trees overhead as she headed back to the cave. Pushing through the bushes, her eyes had to adjust once more to the far dimmer light.

Talon was sitting where she'd left him, legs crossed before the lamp, one arm extended from his side over something flat and dark and round.

Not until her eyes adjusted to the dim light did she realize what she was seeing. Her heart stuttered. The dark round thing was a puddle.

Of blood.

SEVEN

"Talon!" Julia raced into the cave, squatting beside him where the blood dripped from his hand, forming a small puddle in the dirt by his feet. The blood was flowing from a thick, open cut at his wrist. "What happened?" Surely he hadn't slit his own wrist.

He looked stunned. Maybe even in shock. "I demanded the ring tell me how to work the lamp."

"And it attacked you?"

His gaze rose to hers, his eyes a little glassy, yet thoughtful.

"Nay." He turned back to the lamp, his brows drawing together. "I wonder . . ."

With his uninjured hand, he picked up the lamp and blew out the flame, casting them into a dull gray daylight. To her surprise, he tipped the lamp and poured the oil into the dirt.

"What are you doing?" Was he already delirious?

He didn't answer. Instead, he held his bleeding hand straight down over the oil reservoir. Blood dripped onto the lamp, some dropping into the reservoir, some running down the sides.

"Talon, you're beginning to worry me," she admitted softly.

He didn't look up. "The lamp wants my blood."

She cocked her head. "Dude, I hate to tell you this, but blood is not flammable. The lamp can't do anything with your blood but get wet."

His gaze flicked up with a lift of his brow. "'Tis why it is called a magic lamp, aye?"

A magic lamp. Right. "You really think it needs your blood to work?"

"I asked the ring to show me and almost immediately felt the cut on my wrist. Have ye another thought?"

"I suppose not. But you're losing a lot of blood." And he was. He swayed ever so slightly, but she saw it. "You're getting pale. Talon, seriously, screw the lamp. If we don't get a tourniquet around your wrist, you're going to bleed out and die."

His gaze flicked to hers once more, a small charmer's smile playing at his mouth. "And would ye miss me?"

She gave a long-suffering sigh. "Considering you and your ring are my only way home, I'd have to say yes. I'd miss you terribly," she added dryly. But, God help her, she would.

Starting to feel a little frantic, she stared around her, trying to think of what she could possibly use to stop the bleeding. In the movies, the heroine would simply rip off a strip of her shift. Right. This shift was pretty damned thin, so it would probably rip easily enough. But what if it ripped the wrong way . . . right up to her navel? Or was there something about the way the fabric was made . . . the bias or something?

She knew squat about sewing. More about first aid and Talon was seriously bleeding too fast.

"I need a knife, Talon. Now," she snapped.

The look he threw her was tinged with impatience, but he dutifully pulled a knife out of his boot and handed it to her, hilt first. While he bled into the lamp, she lifted her skirt and hacked at her shift until she finally had the bottom strip free. She stared at the frayed remains with dismay. In the movies, the strips always came away neat as a pin.

Dropping the knife on the ground, she grabbed his forearm, above the cut, but when she tried to pull it toward her, he turned a look on her of pure granite.

With a huff, she let go of him. "Talon, it already has enough of your blood. You need the rest."

"If it had enough, I wouldna still be bleeding."

She stared at him as comprehension slowly stole over her.

"Since the ring cut you, it will also mend you when you've bled enough?"

"Aye."

"Great." She sat back on her haunches with a disgusted sigh. "You could have mentioned that *before* I destroyed my nightgown. I hope the ring has the sense to heal you before you die."

He cut his eyes at her, a smile pulling at his mouth, but said nothing more as the steady stream of blood slowed to a drip, then finally ceased altogether.

"Is it over?"

"Aye."

She let out an impatient groan. "At last. Let me see your cut."

To her surprise, he gave her his hand without argument. Instead of using the strip of linen as a tourniquet, she used it to wipe away the blood from around his wound, needing to see for herself he was healing.

Sure enough, the cut had closed as if it had been healing for days. She seriously needed to get one of those rings.

"Healed, is it not?" he asked drowsily.

Her head jerked up and she looked at him. "Your arm's healed, but you're not." He was white as a sheet. "Talon, you need to lie down before you pass out and spill the blood from your lamp." Damn. She dropped his hand onto his thigh and grabbed up the bloody lamp before he did just that. She set the lamp on a rock on the other side of the narrow cave and hurried back to Talon's side before he pitched over. Though how she'd stop him was beyond her. He must outweigh her three to one.

"I'll be fine in a thrice." But his words were soft, his eyes unfocused.

"You're going into shock."

She grabbed his strong jaw, leaving bloody fingerprints on his skin as she tilted his face to where she could get a good look at him. "Don't pass out on me, okay?"

His eyes focused on her, slowly gaining in intensity until the look in them started doing things to her insides. Hot, quivery things.

"A kiss would make me feel better," he mumbled.

Julia rolled her eyes. "A kiss would send all the blood rushing to your groin, which would do nothing to help you stay conscious, Braveheart. No kisses."

Oh, but the thought of feeling the sweep of his tongue in her mouth again sent pleasure rushing through her body. If she didn't turn her thoughts, she was going to be as light-headed as he was.

Without warning, he listed forward, right into her arms.

"Talon." She grabbed him, the solid weight of him almost too much for her. "I'm going to push you back and lay you down, okay? You need to lie down." Thank goodness he was already sitting on the ground. If she had to get him off a stool or a rock, they would really be in trouble.

One hand behind his head to cradle it, she pushed him back. He looped an arm around her waist and took her down with him. He settled back onto the floor of the cave with her locked on top of him, her cheek pressed against his.

"Talon, let me go."

"Wheesht, lass. Quiet now. I'll be right as rain in a few moments, but the feel of you eases me. Let me hold ye, Julia, until the cave stops listing, aye?"

She tried to lever herself up, but dizzy or not, his strength was like steel.

"Shh, lass. Quiet now."

With a sigh of frustration, she gave in, relaxing against him as best she could, but she was too far forward. There was no way to rest her head except to press her cheek to his. Which she finally did. His sleep-warmed scent stole through her senses.

His lips pressed against the lobe of her ear, sending a shiver of pleasure running through her body. She opened her mouth to admonish him, then closed it again knowing it wouldn't do a bit of good. In a few minutes, he'd be recovered. She hoped. Then he'd let her up. Once again, *she hoped*. There was no telling what might happen with this man.

His lips moved, pressing against her neck just below her ear. His warm breath sent excitement churning in her blood.

As his injured hand slid into her hair, the arm that pinned her loosened, his hand sliding down to grab her rear. A dose of cold reality dampened her desire.

"That's it. You're fine." She pushed against his chest. "Let me go."

Amazingly, he did. As she scrambled out of his reach, he sat up and then dipped his head between his knees.

She was kneeling at his side a moment later. "Are you okay?" Without consciously intending to, she pressed her palm against his back in case he passed out.

He lifted his head and met her gaze. "Aye." His face was still too pale, but not the scary white of before.

"You're getting your color back. That's some seriously potent magic, Talon."

He nodded once, an enticing blend of mischief and warmth lighting the blue depths of his eyes, doing funny things to her insides. "I thank ye for seeing to my wound."

"You're welcome." She felt off balance again. How could he knock her feet out from under her with every look, every smile? It was so unfair.

To her dismay, he moved as if he intended to try to stand.

Julia clamped her hand on his shoulder. "What do you need? Let me get it for you."

"The lamp."

"Wait here." She jumped to her feet and retrieved the bloody lamp, then set it in the dirt in front of him.

She settled, cross-legged, on the ground beside him as he tried to light the macabre thing, wanting to be close enough to snatch it away, or grab him, if he started to get faint again.

When the fire flared, nearly bursting from the lamp, she gasped and reared back, staring with disbelief. She'd never really expected him to be able to light the blood.

"It worked," she said with surprise.

"Of course." He tossed her a quick grin. "Like magic."

Julia rolled her eyes.

Talon leaned forward. "Show me where to find the Fire Chalice of Veskin."

Almost at once, something started to happen. The same oddly warm tingling she felt every time Talon called his magic ran over her skin.

A picture formed in the flames, a surprisingly clear picture of a castle—a lovely castle with a pinkish cast to the stone and four large towers, one of which was round.

"Look at it," she breathed.

"I dinna recognize it," Talon muttered. "Show me the nearest town."

The castle disappeared. Moments later, a new picture took its place. A small village, this time, from the vantage point of someone walking right through the middle of it. It reminded her, in a way, of Williamsburg, Virginia, with its row of painted shops squished together. A sign above one of the stores read *Jamie McBean, Merchant*.

"Bollocks," Talon muttered.

"Do you recognize it?"

"Nay, I do not." He took a deep breath and let it out on a frustrated huff. "Show me . . . how to get there from here."

As before, the village disappeared. Moments later, another scene arose. Nothing but trees and bushes, looking just like . . .

"That's the view outside the cave," Julia said.

"Aye," he said with some asperity. "'Tis clearly the direction we must travel, though a bit more help would be appreciated. This lamp is almost as troublesome as the ring," he grumbled.

Julia looked up at him. "Can I try one?"

Talon met her gaze and nodded. "Aye."

She leaned forward, belatedly realizing she'd gripped his thigh at some point, and snatched her hand back. Chewing on her bottom lip, she debated how to ask the question she had to know. Her pulse began to thrum. Finally, she simply blurted the words.

"Show me what I have to do to get home."

But the scene of the woods outside the cave remained. Nothing changed. Nothing happened. Time stood still as she held her breath, waiting.

The lamp wasn't giving her an answer. Either that or it didn't have an answer to give.

A cold, damp sweat crawled across her scalp.

Please, God. Please don't tell me I can't go home.

Talon's gaze swung to Julia as she stared at the flame. He was still feeling a bit light-headed from the loss of blood, but far less so than moments ago. When the ring's magic injured him, it healed him just as quickly. Now it was Julia whose cheeks had paled. And not from lack of blood.

No. The flame was refusing to answer her query, and she was reading much into that. Her fearful thoughts were clear in her eyes.

He squeezed her shoulder lightly, feeling the need to reassure. "It may mean naught, lass." But what if her fears were founded? What if the lamp's refusal to show her how to get home meant she wasn't going home?

The dismay he expected rose inside him, but oddly muted. Conflicted. He wanted her gone, of course he did. He had no room for a companion in this life of his. And yet . . . he'd slept better last night, with the lass in his arms, than he had in years.

He wasn't sure he wanted to explore the reason for that.

Julia looked up at him, worry sharp in her eyes. "What do you think it means that it won't answer me?"

"I dinna ken." Talon turned to the flame. "Show me where to find the Fire Chalice of Veskin within the castle where it hides."

Still nothing happened.

"Do you see anything?" Julia asked, breathlessly.

He met those pretty, mismatched eyes, and watched the flicker of hope spark in their depths. If the lamp now refused him, too, its lack of answer to her question no longer rang with the ominous knell it had a moment before.

"Nay. I see nothing." He turned back to the lamp. "Show me the whereabouts of the men searching for you."

Again, he waited and again, no scene arose in the flame. Then, as if doused with water from an invisible hand, the flame went out, casting them back into the gloom of the cave.

"Bloody lamp," Talon muttered.

Julia laughed, the sound low and soft, and infinitely lovely.

He turned to her, bemused. "Ye laugh," he said, enchanted. Clearly, his own lack of response from the lamp had doused her fears.

A smile playing at her lips, dancing in her eyes. "Sorry, but your calling it a bloody lamp struck me funny, seeing as that's exactly what it is."

Her smile called to his own, especially when her hand grabbed hold of his arm.

"But it's more than that, Talon. Three wishes. Don't you get it? Just like in all the fairy tales, your magic lamp gave you three wishes."

"The questions," he murmured.

"Yes. Its lack of response to my question didn't mean anything. Magic lamps only ever grant three wishes."

"My three, aye. But what about yours? Should it not have granted you three wishes as well?"

"It was your blood. Maybe if I filled the lamp with mine, it would give me three wishes, too."

"Nay." He took her hand and squeezed, running his thumb across her knuckles. "I'd not have your blood spilt."

Their gazes caught. Her smile faded as something warm sparked to life in her eyes.

With his free hand, he reached for her, unable to resist the temptation. His fingers lifted and played with a silky lock of golden hair. "Yer a bonny lass, Julia Brodie, even when ye frown. But when you smile, you put the sun to shame."

She broke the connection of their gazes, looking away. Yet she didn't pull her hand from his. She didn't leave.

"And when ye laugh . . . I'm thinking the angels in heaven grow quiet just to listen."

He sensed she wanted to reject his words, yet couldn't. Not quite. Could she hear the sincerity in them?

He was a man adept at flattery, yet the words he'd spoken had possessed nothing but the truth. Had she heard it?

She turned back to him, her laughter gone. Her eyes were guarded, yet in their depths he saw a softness, almost a vulnerability, she'd not shown him before. Aye, she'd heard the truth in his words.

With his fingertips, he traced the fine lines of her face. Her cheekbone, her brow, her jaw. Her full, intriguing bottom lip.

He was a man adept at seduction, yet it was he who was seduced. By her beauty. By the fire that burned inside her—prickly and sharp, yet warm and strong. A fire that hid the vulnerability at her core and the sweetness he wasn't certain even she sensed within herself.

She watched him, still as stone, as if transfixed by his touch. Had no one ever touched her like this? Did she ever let anyone get this close? His instincts said no, despite her assertion that she'd known many men.

As he'd held her against the chill and the dark last night, he'd tasted her on his tongue. Remembering their kiss had nearly driven him mad with longing for another.

That need rose fierce and warm inside him all over again.

His hand slid from her face and slipped behind her neck to exert only the tiniest bit of pressure as he slowly closed the distance between them. Beneath his hand, she tensed and he forced himself not to tighten his hold. His pulse raced, his blood heated, and he saw an answering flare in her eyes. He'd not push her this time. If she pulled away, he'd let her go. Because his body sensed the truth he wasn't sure she was willing to confront.

Sooner or later, she'd be beneath him, welcoming him into her body. Whether she was ready to admit it or not.

The first touch of his lips on hers set fire to his blood. Heat surged through his veins, pressure rushing low, filling him. Hardening him.

If need had always been a calm burn, this was a stormy ocean. If lust had always been a fire, this was the sun.

She was sweetness and flame, softness and spice. And he wanted her with a desperation he could barely credit. Yet he knew if he pushed too fast, too hard, she'd only fight to get free. And he wanted her willing.

So he kissed her gently, coaxing this time instead of forcing. Offering instead of demanding as his lips moved over hers with firm, yet soft insistence. It was all he could do not to gather her into his arms and lock her against him where she would never get free.

But his need was nearly out of control. He had to touch her.

Lifting his hands slowly, he gripped her small head, sliding his fingers into her silken hair as he ran his tongue along the line of her lips, seeking entrance to her mouth.

She answered his plea, parting those lips with a soft moan that stabbed him with triumph and desire. He swept his tongue inside her mouth and her lush, sweet taste swamped his senses. As she melted against him, surrendering to the passion that blazed between them, his control all but shattered.

Her tongue met his, sliding against his own, as her fingers dug into his hair. Barely holding on to control, he pulled her into his arms, his hands on her back as he resisted the desperate need to pull her tight against his body, tight against the erection that grew more painful by the moment.

He struggled for control, knowing if he pushed her too far, too fast, he'd lose her. Never had he fought such a battle. She was fire in his arms, honey in his mouth, lightning in his blood. Her breaths tore from her lungs as erratically as his, her heart beating in a rhythm as violent as his own. And he scented the sweet musk of her arousal.

Need slammed into him hard.

Never had he experienced such hunger from a simple kiss. He'd glimpsed it in the kiss he'd forced on her last night, this raging, dagger-sharp desire. But this time he'd gifted her with the reins, coaxing her to join him instead of forcing her to submit. And the effect was beyond anything he'd expected. Beyond anything he'd dreamed.

He felt her passion rising in the tense, needy lines of her body and the fine trembling of her hands as she clung to his neck. He felt her body heating in the way she melted against him, and in the small, restless movement of her hips. Whether or not she realized it, her body begged to be touched, stroked.

Filled.

Dear God in heaven, he wanted to be the one to fill it. Now. Here.

His hand moved from her back to her thigh, rubbing the firm, slender appendage through her skirts. His fingers burned to feel her soft, naked flesh.

She moaned into his mouth, as if hearing his unspoken thoughts.

The last thread of his control snapped. He grabbed a fistful of fabric and pulled, then another and another until he reached the hems, until his palm encountered the soft, warm flesh of her leg.

Need burned through his blood, a need to spread her, to touch her. *To enter her.*

But as his hand began its slide toward her heat, she froze.

Nay. Not now. Not now.

He yanked back his hand, but it was too late. His body tensed for a primal battle, but when she tried to push away, he forced himself to let her go.

"Always the seducer, aren't you?" The words should have sounded shrewish, but her voice was too breathless. Her tone almost sad. Over and over, she'd assured him she was no virgin, yet she acted like one. Exactly like one.

"Julia . . ." He buried his head in his hands, willing the fire in his body to ease back to the point of bearing. "I'll not force ye to give more than you're willing."

"You forced me . . . to kiss you last night."

"Aye. I'll not do it again." His voice sounded pained even to his own ears. And he felt that pain. Jesu, but he felt it.

"Why not?" Her voice was quiet, if unsteady, her question honest. "What changed?"

"I dinna ken." What had changed? He'd never taken a lass against her will, but he was not averse to coaxing that will along a bit. And he knew well how to make a lass long for him to fill her.

Perhaps he was certain there would be no seducing this lass—if he pushed too hard she would bolt. But that wasn't the entirety. If he was honest with himself, he wanted her to come to him willingly, body and mind. He wanted . . . what?

More intimacy than copulating.

Which was ridiculous. What was more intimate than copulating?

Jesu, he didn't know what he wanted. All he knew was he'd not gotten it today. And probably never would. There was nothing for it but to move on. Whether or not she was truly a virgin, her gates were closed and he wasn't certain he had either the patience or fortitude to go through this trial again.

"Are we going to hang around here all day, or are we going to find that chalice so I can go home?" Her tone was tight, her breathing still as fast and shallow as his own. With need, yes. But he sensed something more.

Perhaps a hint of trepidation.

Talon sighed.

He poured the blood from the lamp into the dirt and wiped it off with the linen strip the lass had torn from her shift.

Julia went to stand at the mouth of the cave, hugging herself as if needing to calm her own body as much as he needed to calm his.

"It looks like rain," she murmured. She wasn't angry with him, he was sure of it, which only deepened his conviction that the thought of intimacy frightened her. The question was why?

Did he really want to know?

At the moment, his body still throbbing and aching, he'd prefer to think of anything else. Anything but the myriad ways this slip of a lass was wreaking havoc on his body and his life.

EIGHT

Julia stared out through the branches of the bush blocking the cave's entrance, her arms wrapped around her middle, her hands gripping her waist as if she could force her body to settle down, to release the terrible tension that had gripped her the moment Talon's lips had pressed against hers.

Her body still trembled, still ached, throbbing and contracting low inside. *Wanting*.

Yet she didn't want him at all. Not really. Maybe she'd enjoyed his kisses. Enjoyed? Ha. Died and gone to heaven was more like it.

Maybe, for one brief moment, she'd seen something in his eyes that had made her want ... more. Something she couldn't even explain. A warmth. A need to hold and be held. To stroke and comfort. Something so much more than sex.

But if, on some subconscious level she'd felt he was

offering that, she'd realized her mistake the moment he pulled up her skirt and grabbed her thigh. Clearly his only goal had been to get between her legs. Just like every other male.

Stupid of her to think there was anything more. Yet that brief longing, and its swift demise, had left her with a feeling of such emptiness that she ached.

Why? She'd never needed touch or comfort before. That wasn't who she was. Warmth wasn't in her nature. So why would it matter that the brief glimpse she'd gotten of it was false?

It shouldn't matter. She crossed her arms tighter. It *didn't* matter. She was just tired of this place. Just hungry and sore and thoroughly out of her element.

And Talon was just another man. End of story.

Her stomach growled noisily.

"You're hungry," Talon said.

If she'd been home, in the middle of a meeting, such a sound would have mortified her. But here . . . She gave a mental shrug.

"You could hear it from there, huh?"

"Aye. 'Tis likely the queen heard it from London."

"Very funny." She turned back to him. "You're not hungry?"

"I am. The ring will provide."

She walked back to where he sat wiping out the magic lamp. "You depend on that ring for everything, don't you?"

"And why not?"

She went to sit on a large rock sticking out from the cave wall like a stool. "What if you lost it? Would you even know how to fend for yourself?"

The look he threw her was laced with annoyance. "I'll not lose it."

She leaned forward, resting her forearms on her knees

as she laced her fingers together. "How long until the food arrives?"

"The ring feeds me when it pleases."

"Okay."

As he finished cleaning the lamp, he met her gaze. "I dinna ken *okay*. Ye've said it before. What does it mean?"

She had to think about that for a moment. "*All right*, for the most part. Sometimes I use it instead of *yes*. Just now, I was accepting your words. Maybe *I understand* would have been a more accurate way . . ." Her voice trailed off as the food appeared out of thin air.

A thick loaf of bread and a pair of large, roasted turkey legs suddenly sat in the dirt halfway between them, along with a large pitcher of some kind of liquid.

The heavenly scents of roast meat and fresh bread met her nose, making her stomach growl with need.

"*Nice.*" She reached for a turkey leg, barely fazed about having to brush off a bit of dirt to eat it. "Where does this stuff come from?"

"I dinna ken." Talon reached for the other turkey leg.

Julia took a big bite, finding the roast meat juicy and perfectly cooked. Or maybe she was just hungry enough that her taste buds would have welcomed cardboard.

She was nearly done with the turkey leg when the rain started, a first-class downpour. "Now what?"

"We finish our meal, then we'll set out." Talon tossed his cleaned turkey bone into a corner of the cave.

"In the rain?"

He looked at her with amusement. "The hood of your cloak will keep ye warm enough. Do ye fear the rain in your time?"

"I don't know if I fear it, but I certainly don't walk around in it without an umbrella."

"An um . . . ?"

"Umbrella. It's a portable . . . tent . . . thingie that people carry over their heads to keep them from getting wet. Even when it rains, it's not that big of a problem. I'm rarely out in any weather all that long. I live my life almost entirely indoors."

"Why?"

"I live in a city. A city with buildings a hundred stories tall." Finished with her own turkey leg, she hesitated, then tossed the bone where Talon had, unable to shake the guilty feeling that she'd just littered.

She noted the ring hadn't bothered to send along moist towelettes. Or even napkins. Seeing no other choice, she wiped her greasy fingers on the hem of her dress.

"Stories?" Talon handed her the pitcher and she lifted one side to her mouth and took a long drink, then handed it back to him.

"Levels. Full levels with ceilings even you could walk under with ease."

He eyed her with disbelief. "A hundred, one on top of the next?"

"Yep. Skyscrapers, we call them, though they don't really touch the sky."

He broke off a thick chunk of bread and handed it to her. "How long does it take to reach the top of such a place?"

"Not long, not with elevators. An elevator is like a tiny room big enough for ten or so people to stand up in. A thick cord on a pulley lifts it. It all happens mechanically. And electrically. But that's a story for another day."

If they had another day. With any luck, her time here was almost over.

He eyed her with a wary curiosity. "Much has changed in the future, aye?"

"You can't begin to imagine."

"You can tell me about it as we ride."

"Did the horses come back?"

"Nay, but with a wee bit of cooperation from the amethyst, we'll get new ones."

She shook her head at him. "See, this is what I'm talking about. What would we do if you didn't have that ring?"

He met her gaze. "We'd walk."

"Oh."

They finished eating. When they were done, Talon rose, lifted his cloak off the ground and shook it out, then swirled it over his shoulders, lifting the hood over his head.

As Julia did the same, he picked up the lamp and tucked it under his arm beneath the cloak.

"You're just going to carry it like that?"

"Have ye another suggestion?"

She made a wry twist with her mouth. "Not a one." Nothing went with you around here unless you hand-carried it.

They walked together to the mouth of the cave. Julia stared at the rain with dismay. It wasn't coming down as hard as she'd thought, but still, they'd be soaked in no time.

"Don't you think we should wait until it stops?"

"Och, lassie. 'Tis Scotland. The rain is as common as the sun. If we avoid it, we'll ne'er reach the chalice. And I've vowed to deliver it in less than a fortnight. I've no time to wait. Particularly when I dinna ken where we are going."

Julia groaned. "Great. Just great." The first thing she'd be doing when she got home was checking into the nearest hospital with pneumonia.

Taking a deep, bracing breath, she followed Talon into the rain.

Talon held Julia tight against him, her legs draped over one side of the horse as he kept her from slipping off the bare-backed beast. He'd requested horses of his ring and had to wait nearly an hour, but finally a pair had ridden up, each sporting a bridle. Neither a saddle. He'd helped Julia mount, but she'd slipped off the rain-soaked beast and back into his arms, her horsemanship of last night gone as if it had never been.

She'd wanted to try again, but he wouldn't allow it. Not when she might fall beneath the horse's hooves and be trampled. So he'd pulled her up in front of him, and there she'd stayed, holding the lamp for him, keeping it hidden from sight beneath her robe.

The second mount trailed behind them. He'd be lying to himself if he claimed disappointment over the riding arrangements. The feel of the lass leaning back against him pleased him overmuch.

They'd traveled the morning, seeing few others in the rainy weather. Two men had passed them on the muddy track a few miles earlier. The way one of the men's eyes had widened as he'd glanced at Julia, Talon had feared he'd glimpsed the lamp, but the pair had continued on and he'd seen no further sign of them.

Soon after, the rain had stopped. Once the horses were dry, he would pull into a secluded copse and try begging a pair of saddles from the ring. And perhaps a return of Julia's horsemanship skills.

But not yet. His arm squeezed her against him lightly. Not yet.

The track led them over open moors, pitted and water-logged. Bright yellow tufts of gorse dotted the landscape while overhead the clouds thinned, the sun struggling to break through.

Julia's head tipped back against his shoulder blade.

"Will ye sleep, then?" he asked softly.

"No." She straightened, and he was sorry he'd commented. She glanced back at him. "Does it bother you when I lean on you?"

He met her partial gaze. "Nay, it pleases me. Make yerself comfortable."

She watched him a moment more, then gifted him with one of her rare smiles and leaned back against him. "Do you think the rain's through with us?"

"Och, 'tis an impossible thing to know. The rain comes and goes." He brushed the top of her head with his chin. "If you're not in need of sleep, tell me the one thing that has changed the most in the future, lass. What will surprise me most?"

"Ha. One thing?" She looked back at him with a saucy green eye. "I'm not sure I can narrow it to one. How about the fact that the first thing I'll do when I get back is call my boss in New York . . . in the American colonies . . . and talk to him as clearly as you and I are talking now. Then I'll fly home inside the belly of a huge metal bird and arrive home the same day I leave Scotland."

He stared at her, then shook his head. "You're telling tales."

"Not at all. And that's just the beginning. The Industrial Revolution started a hundred and fifty, maybe two hundred years ago, leading to new technologies that have grown at an exponential rate ever since. For the parts of the world that have embraced technology, life has changed irrevocably."

Technology? Her words made little impact, since he had no conception of the things of which she spoke. Flying in the belly of a bird? Clearly, the vision her words put in his head was not what she meant. Such a thing was impossible.

Yet he listened to her raptly, enchanted by the sound of her voice and the enthusiasm lacing her words. And for mile after mile, he asked her questions, listening carefully, for he soon found that the more pointed his questions, the more pleasure in her voice when she answered.

"You've the same deep enthusiasm for explaining as a man who once tutored me," he told her after a time. All the children of the clan had been expected to read and write. Even the son of the clan drunk. "Have ye never wanted to tutor others? Bairns?"

She was quiet for a moment. "When I was a girl, I thought I wanted to be a . . . tutor . . . when I grew up. We call them teachers in my time."

"The wish left ye?" She'd told him all about her work in finance, which seemed a strange life for a lass.

"Yes." Her tone was colorless, unhappy, all the more apparent in contrast to the richness of her words before.

He squeezed her softly. "Why?"

She sighed, her mood palpably moving to one of reflection. And unhappiness, he thought. He frowned, sorry for it.

He felt her shrug. "Nothing happened. I just changed my mind."

But the defensiveness in her tone told him much. And nothing at all. Something had happened to make her alter her course. An alteration, he sensed, that had been a mistake. A simple change of mind, or something more? He wondered.

The more he got to know her, the more curious he became about her. When was the last time he'd probed a woman for her thoughts or her life's history? When was the last time he'd cared enough to ask?

Without a doubt, this lass was more interesting than any he'd known, her history far, far in the future. That was all it was, he told himself. Simple curiosity. A natural desire to understand her strange world.

Little to do with the woman herself.

But his arm tightened a fraction more around her middle, his chin brushing the soft, silken crown of her head. Deep inside, a part of him began to wish she wouldn't leave him.

Talon judged the sun to be just past its zenith when he led them through a copse and down to a stream hidden from the road. Clouds still blanketed the sky, but the rain showed no signs of resuming, for which he gave thanks.

"What are we doing?" Julia asked, straightening and stretching.

"'Tis time we rested this poor beast and requested saddles, I'm thinking. Are ye hungry?"

"Not really. I'm thirsty, but I see the water fountain."

Water fountain? "Ye mean the burn?"

She threw him a small smile, which he was near certain meant she'd been jesting. He smiled in return. It mattered little that he couldn't share the jest. Her smile was gift enough.

He swung off the beast's back, then grabbed Julia around her slender waist and lifted her down, resisting the urge to pull her into his arms and kiss her again as he had in the cave. At the thought of it, of pulling her into his arms and sliding his tongue between those beckoning lips, his body tightened all over again.

But she'd not welcome his kiss again so soon, he was certain of it. Not when he'd frightened her.

The thought gave him pause. Is that what he'd done? Frightened her?

His conviction remained that she was as skittish as a virgin. And it was high time he treated her as such. Even if it killed him.

Which it well might.

He released her the moment her feet touched the ground,

while his good intentions still held firm. As she turned away and attempted to work the stiffness out of her legs, he pleaded his case for saddles from his ring, then grabbed the reins of the horses and led them down to the burn.

"Are ye ready to ride again?" he asked as she walked beside him.

"I think I lost my skill."

"Mayhap the ring will return it."

She gave him a look that was an odd mix of shyness and excitement. "Could you teach me to ride? For real?"

A smile broke over his face and he had to clench his hands to keep from brushing a loose wisp of golden hair from across her cheek. "Aye. Once we have saddles. If the skill doesna come back to you."

She grinned at him, sending his heart tumbling end over end in his chest. "Okay."

At the water's edge, she knelt and scooped water into her hands as he knelt beside her and did the same. When they'd had enough, they rose and paced while the horses drank their fill.

"Talon, what will you do after you deliver the chalice to your client? Will you go home? To the Highlands?" Her hood was back, her golden head a beacon lighting the dreary day. Bonny, bonny lass.

"Nay. I'll take another job. There are always people wanting the services of the Wizard."

Her head cocked, her eyes gleaming with curiosity and intelligence. "How do they find you?"

"I've a man in Inverness to whom they go. I seek him out, he tells me about the inquiries, and makes the arrangements for the one I choose. Rarely do I meet with the clients directly. The fewer who've seen the face of the Wizard, the better."

"That makes sense, especially when you have to go in

undercover like you did at Castle Rayne. Do they pay you, these clients?"

"Aye. Half the silver when I agree to the work. Half upon completion."

"Do you get a lot of these missions?"

"I always have tasks awaiting me. Most, I turn down, either for lack of time, or because they've offered too little silver."

A glint of respect lit her eyes that pleased him immensely. "You must have quite a reputation, to be so much in demand. Built entirely on word-of-mouth advertising."

"I am the Wizard. The Wizard never fails."

"Never?"

"Never."

"Because of your ring."

Nothing showed in her face, but he felt the prick of her censure and it annoyed him. Clearly, she was implying he'd fail without the magic.

Whispers from his own distant past taunted him, carried on the breeze. *Talon Manure. Ye worthless piece of shite.*

His jaw hardened and he turned away. The horses were still without saddles and still in need of rest, or he'd mount and be gone. He'd no more desire to speak of his ring.

But the lass wasn't through with her questions. "What do you do with your silver?"

At first he didn't answer, but she'd no inkling she'd touched a nerve. And they had time on their hands. "I have it stashed in half a dozen different places. Hidden where none will find it."

"Yet you don't even need it, do you? The ring gives you everything."

Was that ridicule in her tone?

He glared at her. "No man ever has enough silver." But he rarely thought of his stashes. They meant little to him.

Perhaps because, as she said, he needed nothing as long as he had the amethyst.

"Do you ever think about doing something more with your magic? Like feeding the poor or healing the sick, or any of that stuff?"

"Nay." His voice was sharp. He was done with her tedious questions. "I live my life. 'Tis every man for himself in this world." It had always been that way. "Stay here," he snapped, and strode away, trying to regain control over his rising temper.

She didn't know what his life had been like. She barely understood his world at all. How could she when she'd come from a world where she never even had to face the rain?

The ring was his life. Even if Hegarty came for it as he'd once promised, he'd be leaving empty-handed.

The old fear clawed at his innards. Hegarty's return was a nightmare he'd lived with for nigh on twenty years. Though, in truth, he had little doubt the ring could disappear on him even without Hegarty's appearance. Every morning when he woke, the first thing he did was feel for it upon his finger.

Every moment of every day he lived with the ever-present fear that the ring would disappear as surely as his chaplain's robes and his beard had. That he'd be left without his strength, without his abilities. Without his life.

The Wizard dead.

Only Talon would remain.

His jaw clenched hard against the waking nightmare whose dark breath perpetually grazed the back of his neck. The worst of it was there was nothing he could do to stop it. Except avoid home and any chance of running into Hegarty again.

And hoard his silver against that dark day.

NINE

Talon walked off his pique at Julia's tiresome questioning of his life then returned to where she waited for him by the burn.

She watched him return, her expression guarded, her mouth tight with temper and disapproval.

Her temper only reignited his own. She knew little of his world and nothing of his life. It was not her place to judge him.

Neither spoke. He sat on the banks of the burn, where he could watch for the saddles to appear, his temper slowly dying away as it was wont to do. His was not a temperament that lent itself easily to anger. Particularly since the amethyst had entered his life and his beast of a father had left it.

They waited for a goodly time, Julia pacing impatiently, as if unused to idleness.

Finally, she turned to him, frustration ripe in her eyes. "How long does it take a horse to recover, anyway?"

Talon shrugged. "The animals are well-rested."

She looked at him with that same raw impatience. "Then what are we waiting for?"

"The saddles."

"Can't we ride while we wait?"

Talon shook his head ruefully. "I tried that once. Ended up with a saddle on my head."

Her brows drew down in comic disbelief. "You're kidding."

"Nay, I am not. The ring has a vexing sense of mischief. If a saddle appears under the hooves of one of the horses, it could hobble him."

Julia sighed, the sound loud and frustrated. "What if the saddles aren't coming? It doesn't always give you what you ask for, does it?"

"Not always, nay. Though it will usually give me what I need."

She gave him a dubious look. "Maybe it doesn't think we need saddles."

Talon winked at her, suddenly wishing to ease her out of her dudgeon. "The ring's seen ye ride, eh?"

The look she turned on him broke, her mouth turning up on one side in a reluctant smile. It was enough.

Her expression turned rueful. "There is that."

Magic tingled over his skin. Julia's head snapped to the horses expectantly.

As they watched, saddles appeared on the two beasts, causing them to nicker and sidestep with alarm.

Talon rose and went to them, settling them, then helped Julia mount. To his relief, she didn't seem to need his assistance. Her riding seat had returned.

As they set out, side by side, the wind picked up. Talon

had taken off his own robe and folded it beneath him, not needing the warmth. But Julia remained in hers. The stiff breeze had blown back her hood and now blew through her golden hair. He rather liked the way the wind lifted the short tresses, tossing them playfully about her bonny face in a way that would only tangle long hair.

He was beginning to like everything about this lass, he realized. The thought made him frown.

They'd ridden fewer than a dozen miles in silence when they crested a low hill to find a small village in the distance below.

"A town," Julia said beside him. "Is that the one we're looking for?"

"I dinna ken. We'll have to ride into it."

She looked at him, hope bright in the green eye that pinned him. "Any chance we can go inside somewhere and warm up?"

"Are ye cold, then?"

She looked to the front again, nodding. "I'm soaked through."

As was he, but he was more than used to it. Physical discomfort meant little to him and rarely bothered him unless it was extreme. But she was a lass. A soft lass, to be sure, if she lived her life within the confines of walls. And he'd not have her sicken.

If he were alone, he'd stop to rest his horse and eat whatever the ring provided for his meal. But her words came back to him. *You depend on that ring for everything, don't you? What if you lost it? Would you even know how to fend for yourself?*

His pride rose, pricked by her comments. She knew naught. And yet . . . Well, he had some coin in his purse.

"We'll find the tavern, and get a meal and a spot before the fire to warm you. Does that please you?" He asked the question perhaps more sharply than he'd intended, but she didn't seem to notice.

The look she turned on him was one of true delight. Her eyes gleamed, her smile radiated such purity, such beauty, his chest began to ache. His lungs ceased to function. He felt slain.

"Thanks, Talon." Her words held a wealth of warm sincerity as she stole that joyous gaze from him and turned it toward the village.

But his own gaze remained firmly on her, as if she'd enchanted him. Enslaved him.

Jesu, what just happened? As he stared at her decidedly delicate profile, at the golden halo of her hair, he felt under the thrall of magic, but a magic that was hers and not his ring's.

He scowled, fighting against the pull of her. Her time in this century was short. At any moment the ring might snatch her away from him and send her home. To feel anything for her was a mistake. He knew that.

Yet feel he did. Curiosity and empathy. Admiration and protectiveness. Affection and desire. More with every passing mile.

He longed to taste her kiss again with a need that made his hands shake. And he desperately wanted her beneath him as he had almost from the start. But what he wished for most, as daft as it sounded in his own head, was simply to bask in the beauty of her smile.

Daft as a loon.

His anger sparked with frustration. Never had he let a woman turn his head. He'd be the greatest of fools to allow this one to now.

He urged his mount forward, needing to escape his thoughts and the lass's smile before he did something truly stupid.

Like beg her to stay.

* * *

They rode into the village less than an hour later. Though it was similar in nature to the one he'd seen in the flames, he knew at once this one was not the town he sought. But he found the tavern with ease and soon had Julia ensconced in front of the fire, her damp cloak laid out to dry, her golden hair wind-tossed yet lovely around her face.

He wasn't the only one intrigued by her beauty. Only four men shared the tavern with them, but not one had taken his gaze off the lass for more than a handful of seconds since their arrival. He doubted any one of them had seen a lass such as her before. An achingly lovely lass with too-short hair and mismatched eyes.

Julia seemed unaware of the gazes turned her way. Either that or she was so used to such attention, she'd learned to ignore it. Instead, she ate her lamb stew with obvious relish. Her pleasure fueled his own and though he tried to steel himself against her, he lost the fight quickly. She was sunshine and color in a world that had never been anything but shades of gray.

He'd felt more alive in the hours since her arrival than he had in all the years that had come before.

The realization startled and dismayed him, for he knew she wouldn't stay. He resented that his eyes had been opened to what he'd been missing. Companionship. Perhaps even friendship.

He scowled inwardly at his self-absorbed musings. Since when did he need a companion?

Julia's being here was a blight on his peace of mind. She knew things about him no one else knew. Things that could put him in grave danger. The sooner she was gone, the sooner he was alone again, the better.

But his gaze drank in the sight of her and wouldn't let go.

The color had returned to her cheeks and she no longer

shivered, both of which eased his worry that she'd take a chill and sicken.

"You're warming," he murmured, drawing her gaze.

A small smile breached her mouth, lifting his spirits. She looked up and met his gaze. "I am. I feel much better."

"Good." He watched her, seeing the shadows in her eyes. "You appear lost in thought."

Her lips pursed as she nodded. "I need to get home. I have a meeting on Thursday that could make or break my career."

"And what of your family? Will they be missing you?"

A pain sliced through her eyes, sharp and so swift he almost missed it. Yet when she spoke, those unusual eyes held nothing but calm. "I don't have a family. Just me and my career. I like it that way."

"Do ye now? I find it hard to believe no man has asked for your hand."

The thoughtful look she gave him turned slowly amused. "Do you really?" But the amusement quickly fled, the pensiveness back in her eyes. "You told me last night I wore shields and I denied it. But I think maybe you're right." Her expression turned almost shy. "You're the first man who's gotten beneath them. I don't warm up to many men."

He found it telling that she believed she'd let him in, yet she barely let him touch her. Then again, she'd given herself over to his safekeeping in sleep. A gift of immense trust, that.

He doubted she truly warmed up to *any* man, truth be told, himself included. But the fact that she believed herself warming to him pleased him immensely.

"I'm glad you've let me in, then," he said sincerely. "Ye can be a bonny companion when ye wish to be, Julia Brodie."

She flashed him a quick grin that held a sharp edge of knowing amusement. "Thanks. So can you."

He grinned back at her, unaccountably pleased, though why he should be, he wasn't sure. The lasses always found the Wizard to be a bonny companion.

But he'd not always held fast to his Wizard persona with this one. She'd seen Talon. In some small ways, perhaps even gotten to know the true man. Even so, she was warming to him.

Pleasure flowed through him, rich and sweet. Bittersweet, for he had a feeling he'd miss her when she was gone, more than he wished.

The innkeeper joined them and began gathering their empty dishes. He was a thick-waisted, bearded man with a ruddy face and friendly eyes.

"I seek a merchant by the name of Jamie McBean," Talon told him. "Do ye ken where I might find him?"

"McBean, eh? There's a Jamie McBean in Monymusk, little more than a day's ride from here."

Talon's pulse quickened. "And is there a castle near Monymusk?"

"Aye. Picktillum."

"Pink-harled?" Talon described the castle he'd seen in the flames. "Four towers, one of them round?"

The innkeeper nodded. "'Tis Picktillum, true enough. The home of the Viscount Kinross." He gave Talon brief directions and moved away.

Julia's eyes glimmered with excitement. "Sounds like we know where we're going now."

He smiled at her enthusiasm. "Aye." Soon he'd have the fire chalice in his hands. Soon he'd have no more need of Julia's help. Soon she'd be gone.

The knowledge settled dully in his stomach.

They paid for the meal and set out again, each on his or her own mount. The sun had come out while they were dining and now shone brightly over a damp and glistening landscape. Travel was slow on the muddy track but, despite knowing he had less than a fortnight to complete his task, he felt no urgency. Indeed, he found himself loath to reach Picktillum.

For the first time in as long as he could remember, he was enjoying himself. Enjoying the journey. Most of all, he was enjoying his bonny and temporary companion.

He felt the vibration of hoofbeats even before the four riders came into view behind him. They raced along the road, sending mud flying as they bore down on them.

"Off the road, lass," he said to Julia, reluctant to take his gaze off the men behind. "Ride up the hill."

His hand flexed, his instincts telling him to be ready to pull his sword, although logic argued the men would most likely ride right on by.

"Who are they?" Julia asked, urging her mount up the gently sloping hill.

"I dinna ken. I canna . . . *bollocks*." He was about to say he couldn't tell, but that wasn't true. He recognized one of them. Nay, he recognized them all.

"Aren't two of them from the tavern?" Julia asked. "And the other two . . ."

"Are the pair we passed on the road earlier." *Jesu*. That was no coincidence, he was certain.

She looked at him with confusion. "I don't understand."

"I fear I do." He'd suspected the men they'd passed on the road had glimpsed the gold of the lamp. They'd likely circled around and followed them for a time, then recruited two more brigands to help them carry out their robbery.

With only a moment's hesitation, he pulled the golden lamp from the wrappings of his cloak and held it aloft where the sun would glint on the treasure. Then he tossed it onto the ground.

"What are you doing?" Julia exclaimed.

"Ride, Julia. *Quickly*. They'll likely not bother with us

once they have what they've come for, but I'll take no chance." The lass was too bonny by far. And had only one protector.

With a worried nod, Julia did as he commanded, urging her mount into a full gallop. He followed close, keeping an eye out behind.

But his precaution was for naught. The four altered their course to follow them, completely ignoring the lamp.

Bloody hell. They wanted the lass. *Jesu, they'd kill her.*

"Faster, Julia!" His heart lodged in his throat as he prayed her newfound riding skills were equal to the task.

"I don't know how to do faster!"

It wouldn't be enough. The four were gaining on them with alarming swiftness.

He pulled his sword, keeping himself between her and their pursuers even as he knew he was going to have no choice but to take them on.

"Keep riding, Julia. I've no need to tell you what they'll do to you if they catch you, aye?"

Fear clouded her features, but was quickly swamped by fierce determination as she bent low over the horse and held fast.

The sound of beating hooves grew louder and louder until Talon knew he had no choice but to turn and take them on before one of them lopped off his head from behind.

He swung his mount around and charged the short distance, taking two at once. The clang of metal on metal rang over the damp ground. But, as he'd feared, the other two continued after Julia.

Fear for her lent fire to his determination. With a hard, well-timed swipe, he slew one of the miscreants. But the man cried out and Talon's already battle-shy horse reared and stumbled. He had no choice but to leap from its back before the animal went down.

As the slain man's mount took off, Talon faced his second attacker, avoiding the man's steel with leap after leap as he fought to take him. He finally managed to take a swipe at the man's leg, opening a bloody gash. But to his dismay, the brigand swung his horse around, preparing to flee, leaving Talon with no mount. And no way to follow but on foot. Depending on how far they took Julia to do their evil, he might not find her again until it was too late.

A desperate fire burned in his belly at the thought of that fierce spirit quenched. Of that small, perfect body broken and bleeding. *He would not allow this wickedness.*

As the miscreant urged his horse forward, Talon pulled his knife from his belt and flung it hard, burying the blade hilt-deep into the man's back.

With a death cry, the man fell from the horse. Talon leaped forward and grabbed the reins before he lost this mount, too, then retrieved his bloody knife and swung onto the back of the beast.

Heart thudding in his chest, he urged the horse into a hard gallop in the direction Julia had gone, praying he was not too late to save her.

The land rolled and bucked, hills rising in every direction. Empty. His hands tightened on the reins.

Already he'd lost her.

Fear for her lodged beneath his breastbone. A need to protect her rose inside him, stronger than any emotion he'd ever felt. She hadn't the strength to fight them off, yet he knew the fire in her would not be easily doused. She would fight them, tooth and nail.

And they'd kill her.

His teeth ground to dust in his mouth. Fury raged in his blood. They'd taste his blade this day. They'd taste it.

And they'd die.

TEN

Julia white-knuckled the reins, her head down, her heart pounding. Behind her, men chased her on horses of their own, men who would rape her if they caught her. Maybe even kill her.

If only her skills were real! If only she knew the tricks to making a horse go faster, but all she could do was trust instincts that weren't hers. All she could do was trust Talon's magic ring and pray it was enough even though her mind kept screaming *I don't know how to do this!*

Her stomach cramped with fear. Beads of sweat rolled down between her shoulder blades.

"Move, horse, *move*," she begged.

The muddy ground flew by beneath her, the wind tearing the hair back from her face, making her eyes sting. Why had the ride yesterday felt so exhilarating? She couldn't remember. She couldn't even fathom that she'd enjoyed it.

In the distance behind her, she heard the clank of

metal, the clash of swords, and knew at least one of those swords was Talon's. She hazarded a glance.

Directly behind her, much too close, rode the two men they'd passed on the road that morning, their eyes now bright with the excitement of the chase.

Turning forward again, she was afraid she was going to be sick.

She'd seen no sign of Talon, but she'd ridden over a rise and down again, obscuring her view. Two of the men had fallen behind, no doubt to take him on. *Two against one.*

His ring would save him. She had to believe that. *He can't die.*

Because if he did die, then what? He wouldn't come after her? He wouldn't save her?

That sick feeling rolled through her stomach.

Why would he come after her, even if he could? Thanks to the lamp, he now knew where the chalice was. He didn't need her anymore.

Ice wove through her heart.

He wouldn't come. Of course he wouldn't. People in movies and fairy tales might risk their lives for others, but that kind of thing didn't happen in real life. If her own experience was anything to go by, they rarely even *compromised* their lives for others. And when they did, they resented it bitterly.

Why would he come after her? She was nobody to him.

When it came down to it, she was nobody to anyone.

Her hands gripped the reins tighter, the terror and desperation burrowing deep into her soul as she accepted that she was as she'd always been. On her own. No knight in shining armor was going to ride out of the mist to save her.

This damsel in distress was going to have to save herself.

She pressed the horse faster, but when she glanced over

her shoulder, terror stabbed her through the ribs. The men were nearly upon her, one drawing up on either side.

Shit, shit, shit.

Little by little, they drew even with her, then pressed in, crowding her, trapping her between them. They were rough-looking men, unshaven and almost certainly unwashed, dressed in clothes much like Talon wore, except theirs were ratty and badly stained.

The thought of these men, these *bastards*, touching her . . . *forcing* her . . .

The terror welled up, constricting her throat until she could barely breathe. Lights danced at the edges of her vision.

One of the creeps edged closer and grabbed for her reins.

She jerked them out of his reach, glaring at him. "Leave me alone, you asshole!"

"Och, she's got the Brodie eyes, right enough," the asshole shouted to his companion. This time he didn't bother with the reins, but reached for her instead, trying to snag her around the waist.

Julia fisted her hand and threw it back, connecting with his mouth.

"*Witch*," he snarled, and hit her back, his knuckles connecting with her temple in a blinding flash of pain. As she fell back, head spinning, he hooked his arm around her waist and yanked her out of her seat. For one terrible instant, she thought she was going down, doomed to be trampled beneath the hooves of the horses. Instead, she found herself flung across the man's lap, face down, so hard it knocked the wind out of her, sending pain arcing through her ribs.

The ground moved past dizzily beneath her and she closed her eyes against the sickening movement. Flecks of dirt and grass pelted her cheeks. As a tight band of hope-lessness squeezed her chest, panic began to bubble up, tast-ing of horror.

They were going to rape her. They were going to throw her on the ground, push up her skirts, and rape her and there was nothing she could do to stop them.

White-hot desperation burned across her mind. A sob caught in her throat. If only she were taller and stronger. If only she'd studied martial arts or something. Maybe she'd have been able to fight them off.

Who was she kidding? She'd be incredibly lucky to manage to get away from *one*, let alone two of them, even if she were an Amazon. And heaven knew, she wasn't. There was no hope she could get away from them before they hurt her. None.

She swallowed hard against the bile rising in her throat, her body beginning to shake from within.

If she couldn't escape their abuse, then she'd just have to get away after. If she could just survive, sooner or later they'd make a mistake and she'd take advantage of it. And then she'd run.

Run where? By then, Talon would be long gone.

The thought of him made the tears start to roll. Had he fought off the two men, or was he even now lying in a pool of his own blood? She didn't want him to die. He might not be her knight in shining armor, but there was goodness buried inside him even if sometimes she felt like he tried to hide it.

Please don't let him die.

Her stomach spasmed. Her body felt like ice. Deep in-side her skull, her head pounded. Hysteria began to pluck at the edges of her consciousness, but she fought it back, knowing in some dark part of her mind that if she gave in to the fear, she'd be lost.

Instead she fought for strength, for anger. This was her

life, dammit, as bizarre as it might be at the moment. And no one was taking it away from her without a fight.

But the hysteria hovered, on the attack, stripping slices from her soul.

A hand landed hard in the middle of her back, startling a low cry from her throat. High above her, the bastard who'd captured her yelled something in a language she didn't understand. His tone was sharp. Angry-sounding.

He pressed down on her back as he twisted, as if looking behind him. His hand flexed with tension and he kicked the horse, pushing the animal faster.

Her heart gave a hard leap of hope. Someone was coming. Talon?

No. Why would it be Talon? Her captor was probably just trying to outrun one of his companions so he didn't have to share her.

The hysteria crawled closer.

I want to go home, I want to go home, I want to go home.

But the magic stone around her neck ignored her. Talon believed he was the one who'd brought her here, that she'd been meant to do something to help him. But deep inside, she feared she'd never find her way home again.

The way this day was going, it wouldn't matter. She'd be dead before nightfall.

Her trembling intensified.

The clang of metal close by broke through her dark musings, startling her with a jerk. *Swords.* Talon? Or were the bad guys turning on one another, now? She couldn't see, dammit. She was hanging down the wrong side of the horse.

The battle sounds lasted for what seemed like forever, then suddenly went silent. Her captor urged the horse faster. And she knew.

Hope leaped high, filling her body with a heady lightness. A renewed strength. Tears stung her eyes. The hysteria receded to the edges of her mind.

Her captor swung the horse around to face the attack and she saw him. *Talon.* Not the Talon she'd come to know, the con man with the charmer's smile, but a warrior with savage eyes, his lips pulled back over his teeth, his sword running red with blood.

Her civilized self, the Julia Brodie who wore pumps to work and never ran a red light, recoiled at the violence in the man. But the damsel in distress wept with relief. And the cavewoman inside her, the deeply buried primitive with wild hair carrying a spear in one hand—a woman whose only goal was survival—watched in awe and hailed the barbaric strength and power of the man.

As horse and rider, and bloody sword, bore down on her, the hysteria once more flared around the edges of her mind. As the swords clashed inches above her head, she shrieked and cringed, squeezing her eyes closed and pulling her arms over her head. The sound ripped at her courage, reverberating through every cell in her body, bursting through her eardrums.

Steel collided above her, so close she was pelted by the flying droplets of blood. The trembling inside her turned to great quakes as her back arched involuntarily, exposed and vulnerable. At any moment one of the swords might slice right through her spine.

Stealing a glimpse, she opened one eye just as Talon swung hard, his face a mask of fury. His blade sliced through her kidnapper's cheek. Blood sprayed her, a drop landing on her eyelashes, and she recoiled with horror, swiping it away with a badly quaking hand.

The battle roared, Talon in a berserker's rage, his hair swinging as he hacked against her captor's blade.

Suddenly the man above her cried out and reared. He fell back, lifting her with his knees, catapulting her into the air. Something clipped her jaw, slamming her teeth together as she landed in the mud, half-tangled with her captor.

The man kicked her in the ribs as he scrambled to his feet.

Through a haze of pain she saw Talon swing off his horse and the battle resume on foot.

Head ringing, ribs on fire, Julia sucked in a painful breath and pushed herself up, stumbling to her feet, desperate to get away from the swords swinging too close. She backed away from the fight, dazed and hurting, the hysteria clawing deeper and deeper into her mind.

This isn't real. This isn't happening.

Talon swung, the tip of his sword slicing the other man's face, temple to opposite jaw. Blood bloomed, bright red, washing down the bad guy's cheek and jaw. When he reared back, Talon lunged forward, burying his blade deep in the man's gut, then pulled it out again. With an expression of hard satisfaction, Talon watched her kidnapper fall face first into the mud.

Julia stood as still as a rock.

It was over.

He was dead. *Dead.* A moment ago, his hand had pressed into her back. Now he lay unmoving. *Lifeless.*

The hysteria she'd barely managed to keep at bay rushed at her again. Her forehead pounded, her skin turned cold and clammy. Her insides started spinning like the insides of a blender. If she didn't get sick first, she was going to start screaming and screaming and screaming . . .

Talon turned to her, breathing hard, his blood-coated sword still tight in his fist, his expression frozen in that terrifying mask of battle-rage.

He started toward her. Blood splattered his clothes and his face. Even his hair was streaked red.

Shaking violently, she backed away. "You killed him."

Her words sounded accusatory, filled with all the horror and disbelief roiling inside her. But she couldn't control her tone. She couldn't control *anything*. She was shattering inside, on the verge of a monumental breakdown.

No. She was stronger than this. She refused to break. Deep inside, she fought against the hysteria, finding and embracing the only emotion strong enough to battle it back.

Anger.

She clung to it, feeding it, letting it fill and strengthen her.

Talon stopped abruptly and stared. "What would ye have had me do?"

Her lips pressed together, trembling. He'd come after her. He still thought he needed her help to get that chalice. That damned, fricking chalice.

"The chalice is so important to you that you'd risk everything for it? You'd *kill* for it? Over and over, you'd kill for it?"

"I killed for you," he said softly, stepping toward her.

She threw up her hands. "Stay back." Her stomach cramped. She wasn't being fair to him and she knew it, but this wasn't about fairness. It was about survival. And if she gave in to the weakness and flew into his arms, she'd shatter.

"You're hurt." The soft concern in his voice was nearly her undoing. He reached for her.

"*Don't touch me.*"

Talon's eyes turned flat. His mouth compressed and he turned on his heel and strode toward his horse as if he meant to leave her behind.

Would he? After he'd risked his life to get her back? No, he'd take her with him and use her as the ring meant for him to. Why else would he have come after her?

She stalked after him, her quaking legs barely functioning.

As he swung up on his own horse, she grabbed the

reins of the horse she'd been a captive on and struggled to swing into the saddle. Her muscles had turned to rubber.

Talon set off without a backward glance and she followed. They rode in strained silence, Talon glancing back at her every now and again with an unreadable look on his face.

After a short while, he led them off the road and into the woods. Her curiosity about where they were going, or why, was minimal. She was still shaking badly, caught in a battle of her own, a battle for control and sanity, and she was hanging on by a thread. Her ribs and body ached. Her head pulsed with pain. Physically, she felt like she'd gone three rounds with a prizefighter. Mentally, deep inside her civilized mind, she barely kept the screams at bay.

She heard the creek a few minutes before they reached it. Talon swung off his horse, then turned to her, as if he'd help her down.

She shook her head. His jaw tightened and he turned away, walking to the creek.

Julia slid off the animal's back, her muscles quivering, her breaths too fast, too shallow to do her any good.

As she forced herself to follow him, she watched as Talon scrubbed his hands and face with water, washing off the blood. She sank onto the spongy grass at the water's edge to do the same.

The water was frigid and perfect. The shock of it startled her system, turning her mind away from that dark precipice it hovered over. Again and again, she dipped her hands into the stream, rinsing her face, her hands, her hair. Over and over she scrubbed as if she could erase the memory of the blood. As if she could force the cold all the way into her mind, numbing it.

When she finally felt some small measure of control, and could no longer feel her hands at all, she pulled back and dried herself on her blood-splattered clothes. Then she rose and turned to find Talon already mounted, his strong face in profile, his gaze far in the distance.

Feeling beaten, inside and out, she went to where Talon had tethered her horse and mounted.

Without looking back, Talon started off at a sedate pace and she followed. As they rode, she fought not to think, not to feel anything but her aching jaw and pounding head.

But the emotions never ceased circling her, reaching for her through the bars of the cage she'd hastily erected around her. Emotions with sharp, ragged claws that threatened to slice her into shreds, destroying her control . . . her sanity . . . once and for all.

Talon pushed them farther than he should have, farther than the animals deserved, riding well past dusk before he finally sought a room for the night.

Anger seethed inside him, his constant companion since he'd risked everything—*everything*—to save the ungrateful woman's life and was greeted not with relief and thanks, but with horror and disgust. Shadows from his past.

Damn her. Damn her to hell. No one looked at the Wizard that way. *No one.*

He found them a farmhouse with a room available. A matronly woman with a wide, friendly face ushered them up the stairs to the second floor. The room was surprisingly spacious with a bed large enough to sleep two people. Not that he'd get a chance to sleep in it. The way Julia was acting, he doubted she'd willingly share the room with him, let alone the bed.

She'd get no choice with the room. The bed, he had yet to decide. Perhaps sleeping on the floor would do her good, the little shrew.

As the matron started the fire in the hearth, Julia stood looking out the window, her back stiff as a pole.

He'd saved her, dammit. *Saved her*. Had she no concept of the danger she'd been in? Did she really think he could have gotten her from the brigands with a simple *please*? Was she really that great a fool?

He hadn't believed it.

Never before had he risked so much for another. Any other. And in return she looked at him as if he'd turned back into the Talon of old, a creature unworthy of her barest suffering.

The matron stood. "Johnny will bring yer supper in a thrice. Will ye be wanting a bath?"

"Aye," Talon told her.

She nodded. "I'll heat the water and have the bath ready when your supper is through."

"My thanks, mistress."

When she'd gone, he stared at Julia's unmoving form, her back turned to him as if she couldn't even bear the sight of him anymore. As if he were a maggot to be crushed beneath her boot.

Old corrosive anger burned through his blood. He'd been so damned scared he wasn't going to reach her in time, his heart had nearly stopped beating. Yet the violence he'd had to use to save her was the very thing that had turned her against him. The fury of it churned inside him until he was a mass of anger and frustration.

With angry strides, he crossed the room, grabbed her shoulders, and pulled her hard around to face him.

Her face was pale, her eyes glazed. Then anger flared in their depths and she shoved at him.

"*Don't touch me.*"

Something dark and ugly snapped inside him and he pushed her against the wall, trapping her hands and yanking them above her head. Fury steamed from every pore in his body.

"You pretend you canna stand to look at me, that you canna stand my touch, but you're a liar. Your body burns to join with mine, Julia Brodie. There's fire between us and you'll not pretend you're too good, too pure to bear my touch."

With his free hand he gripped her jaw and held her pinned. Then he leaned down and slammed his mouth to hers in a kiss meant to punish, to dominate. She would not look at him as if he were dung on her shoe!

She bit him. He jerked back to find her staring at him with fire.

"*Let go of me.*"

"Admit you want me." The demand came out low and dangerous. He wouldn't hurt her, but by God, she was going to admit she desired him. To both of them.

"Go to hell."

"Och, aye. 'Tis a certainty, that. *Admit you want me.*"

"I don't!"

"Your heart's racing. I can see the vein pounding in your throat."

"If it's pounding, it's in fury that you're manhandling me again."

No, it wasn't. She was furious, they both were, but he could sense the passion rising hot and thick between them as it did every time they got too close.

"Your breathing is shallow. Your eyes are growing dark. And between your legs, you're turning wet. Your body wants mine, Julia Brodie. It's opening, becoming slick, wanting to join with mine."

She struggled against his hold. Almost certainly against his words. "You're wrong. I want nothing to do with you. I feel nothing for you."

"'Tis an easy enough thing to find out." He shifted

both her wrists into one of his hands, trapping them above her head, then reached for her skirt, yanking it up where he could reach the hem. And what lay beneath.

Julia struggled harder against his hold. "What are you doing? Talon, no."

"I'm only going to touch you with my finger. Touch that wetness and prove to us both how much your body weeps for mine."

He found the bottom of her hem and lifted, his fingers brushing against her bare thigh.

"Stop it!" She fought him, struggling to kick him.

But she would cease her claiming she didn't want him. Cease looking at him as if he were beneath her. His fingers slid to the top of her warm, silken thigh. Desire twisted and turned inside him and he grew desperate to touch her, to feel her damp need for himself.

But she'd locked her thighs against him. Her breath caught and turned ragged. Her body began to shake.

He teased the line between her soft thighs with his finger. "Open for me, lass. I'll not hurt you."

"*No.*"

At the sound of the heartbreak in that single word, he stilled. The fat tear that rolled down her cheek stopped him cold.

"Please, don't, Talon. *Please, don't.*" Her watery gaze sought his, wild with desperation and terror. She was shaking. Not from desire. Perhaps not even from anger.

"Julia . . ."

The tears began to roll, sliding down cheeks that were too pale, and she began to cry in earnest. Great hiccuping sobs rose from deep, deep within her, as if from the depths of her soul, forcing their way out with a violence that appeared to be ripping her apart.

"Lass, forgive me." He was suddenly torn between the need to aid her and the certainty he was the one who'd caused her pain in the first place. He feared his touch was only making it worse.

He released her and stepped back, giving her room, watching helplessly as she bent double as if in terrible pain, and slid to the floor, sobbing as if her heart had irreparably broken.

"Ah, lassie, I'm sorry." He didn't know what to do to make it better. "I'm sorry if I frightened you. I was angry, but 'tis no excuse. I willna hurt you. I'll ne'er hurt you, Julia."

The storm had her in its grip, and a storm it was. Curled into a ball on the floor, she tried to speak, but he couldn't make out the words through the crying. Tears ran freely from her eyes. Her pain sliced through him, cutting him with a dozen knives, all the more sharply because he knew it was his fault.

He couldn't bear it.

"Julia." He reached for her, softly stroking her hair as he watched for her recoil. But she didn't pull away, didn't seem to notice.

A rap at the door had him scowling, but he scented supper and rose. He opened the door to the lad, blocking his view of Julia as he took their dinner, then closed the door in the lad's face. Setting the tray on the table, he returned to Julia, who continued to cry as if her heart had broken and would never mend.

He sat beside her, his back to the wall, and stroked her arm as her sobs quieted, turning to great trembling gasps for air.

"Julia-lass?" he asked quietly.

Slowly, she turned her head to look up him, her eyes red and broken, her lashes spiked with the misery of her tears.

"I took no advantage of ye last night and I'll take none now. But ye need a shoulder to cry on, and I'd have ye use mine."

He braced himself for her rejection, fully expecting her to turn away. Not only had he frightened her, but she'd already made it more than clear she wanted naught to do with him any longer.

But to his deep relief, she nodded. As she began to lever herself up, he scooped her into his arms and settled her sideways on his lap. To his surprise, she turned and pressed her damp face against his neck, her arms tucked tight between them.

His arms went around her and he gathered her close as a second storm of tears overtook her, but not as violently as the first.

"I . . . I . . . was so . . . scared." The words trembled out of her between sobs.

"Ah, lassie, I'd not have hurt you. I'll never again hurt you."

"I . . . know. Not you. *Them*."

And suddenly he understood. His hold on her tightened and he pulled her closer as the bands around his heart and mind loosened some of their terrible grip. He remembered the glazed look in her eyes and the terrible paleness, even before he'd forced his kiss upon her. A shattered look not caused by him, perhaps. Not caused by what she'd seen him do, but by the terror she hadn't known how to settle.

He understood that feeling, had known it numerous times. Wasn't he guilty of it, even now? Jesu, but he'd been terrified when they had her. Terrified he'd lose her to them and be too late finding her again to save her. And when he'd retrieved her and she was once more safe, he'd let that fear transform to anger.

Now he was beginning to wonder if she hadn't done the same.

In silent understanding, he held her tightly as the storm finally ran its course. Slowly, she quieted, her head pressed to his shoulder, her body releasing the last of the misery on hard shudders that shook through them both.

He slid his hand up and down her arm as he had a hundred times. "You're safe now, lass. You're safe."

She straightened, slowly, like an old woman, and he pulled his arm from around her and let her go. But she didn't move from his lap, only wiped at her face with her hands, sniffling, then curled up against him again, gifting him with her trust and her forgiveness more clearly than if she'd spoken.

"Now that you know where the chalice is, I didn't think you'd come." Her voice was soft, almost broken.

It took him a moment to understand her meaning. "Ye thought I'd let them have ye?" he asked incredulously.

"I thought . . . you didn't need me anymore. And there were four of them."

He stroked her head, pressing it against his heart. "I couldna forsake ye."

"Why not?"

His fingers slid into her hair, playing with the soft, golden strands, uncertain of his answer. If she'd been any other lass, would he have gone after her?

Of course. He'd have left no lass under his protection to such a fate. The difference was no other lass would have been under his protection.

"I brought ye here. I'll see ye home safe, aye?" He felt her arms slide around his waist.

"Thank you. For saving me."

Something warm and fine moved inside his chest, filling it. Filling him. He stroked her head, his thumb tracing gently down her damp cheek.

"You're welcome." He pressed his lips to the top of her head. "Are you well enough to eat? Our supper is here."

She nodded and he rose and lifted her to her feet. But when he would have released her, his hands said otherwise and he tugged her into his arms. She came with little coaxing, burying her face in his chest and wrapping her slender arms around him once more, with surprising strength.

As she clung to him, his arms tightened around her protectively.

He would keep her safe. If it was the only good thing he did in his life, he would keep his promise and see her safely home. Even if the thought of never seeing her again was beginning to feel like a blade to his heart.

ELEVEN

As Talon ate his dinner with obvious relish, Julia pulled off a small chunk of bread and nibbled on it halfheartedly. She felt like she'd been tumbled and spun by a washing machine and hung out to dry. Her eyes were swollen half-shut from her crying jag, her jaw, head, and ribs all ached from the beating she'd taken this afternoon. Emotionally, she felt as flat and lifeless as the nearest rock.

She was warm now, at least, but she still felt rubbery and shaky. And the shakiness wasn't entirely the result of the day's ordeal. In part, it was due to her rescuer himself.

Talon flustered her on the most fundamental level. How could one person make her feel awkward and off balance, yet utterly grounded all at the same time? Her body reacted to his nearness, her emotions where he was concerned were nothing short of bipolar. Yet she felt comfortable around him, as she never had around another man. As she rarely felt around anyone.

Picking up her spoon again with a hand that still shook, she stirred the stew, no longer interested in it. What she'd managed to swallow was delicious, but her stomach remained a tangle of knots and refused any more.

She'd let him hold her, comfort her, as she'd cried in his arms. Why? She'd never needed anyone to hold her or coddle her and she didn't need anyone now. Yet she couldn't deny how sweet it had felt to accept Talon's strength and gentleness, even if only for a matter of minutes.

He was a good man even if he was a con man and a thief. And the truth was she liked him. As they'd ridden this morning, sharing the same horse, she'd told him about the future. He'd listened to her and heard more than her words. He'd heard her love of teaching, a love she'd all but forgotten over the years.

Talon saw past the face she showed the world—the petite blond with the bad attitude. For the first time since she was fourteen, she was starting to let her guard down around a man.

Maybe it was inevitable, given their current situation.

She stirred her stew thoughtfully. No, not inevitable. Talon had gotten beneath her skin in a way she was pretty sure no other man could have.

"Are ye not hungry?" Talon asked, quietly.

She shook her head, meeting his blue-eyed gaze.

"Ye need a dram of whiskey, I'm thinking." His voice was low and kind. "Give me yer hand."

Her eyebrows lifted, but she did as he asked, placing her hand in his open palm. His fingers closed around hers, his thumb brushing over her knuckles.

"Ye tremble still. I've tried different ways over the years to settle myself after a day like this. Sleep rarely comes until I do."

"What ways? Other than whiskey?"

A hint of that boyish smile curved his mouth and brightened his eyes. Dimples peeked out, then retreated. "A good fight is one."

"More violence."

"'Tis a man's way."

"What's another?"

His eyes took on a gleam that was a little brighter, a little hotter. "Can ye not guess?"

She could. It was written all over his face. Her pulse began to speed. "Sex."

"Aye."

She tensed, certain he was going to try to talk her into it, or try to force the issue again.

Instead, he released her hand and leaned back in his chair. "Which is why I suggested the whiskey."

She stared at him for a long moment, waiting for him to continue, before she realized that was all he'd intended to say. No pressure. No seduction.

"Thank you." Her words were simple, yet sincere. "I'm not up for another fight with you."

"I ken that." He banked the heat in his eyes and smiled at her gently. "Ye've been through much this day. I'll try not to make it any worse than I already have."

She smiled, feeling something build in the silence between them. A connection—an understanding that grew and warmed. And a feeling that she'd known him forever, that she'd been waiting for him forever.

The thought startled her.

Talon pushed to his feet. "Let's get those baths first, before they get cold."

"I thought she was going to bring the bathtub up."

"Nay, they'll not be carrying the water and tub all the way up here. The bath will be waiting in the kitchen, where it's warm. We'll wash down there."

She stared at him in dismay. "In front of everyone?"

He smiled kindly. "Behind a screen. You'll undress, then dress again before you step out from behind it."

"Oh." Of course, with only one set of clothes, she'd have to put her bloodstained duds right back on when she was through.

As if reading her mind, he said, "I'll see what I can do about talking the ring into fresh clothing." His mouth twisted into a grimace. "We could both use some."

A half hour later, they were back in the room, hair wet and smelling of heather soap. On the bed were a dozen items of clothing—a beautiful gold brocade skirt and matching top, a good-quality silk shift, a pair of hose of some kind. A pair of pants and a ruffled shirt for Talon, along with a dark green jacket and a deep gold velvet vest. Also on the bed were wool-hooded cloaks far nicer than the Jedi robes, and wonder of wonders, the navy blue one was half the size of the deep brown one.

Julia fingered the fine fabric of the skirt. "This is expensive stuff."

"I asked the ring for the clothes we'd need to breach the gates of Picktillum. Apparently, we're not to go in as servants."

She looked up at him. "What story will you give them that will get us into the castle?"

Talon shrugged, dimples flashing. "I dinna ken. The ring will give me something to say when the time comes."

She lifted an eyebrow at him.

He answered her unspoken question. "Aye, I trust the ring for nigh on everything." His eyes grew serious. "But I didna trust it to save you today. I never asked it for help."

"Why not?"

Talon looked at her thoughtfully, his mouth tensing. "I dinna ken." His voice turned low and pained. "All I could think of was reaching you before they hurt you."

Julia bit her lower lip and looked away, back at the clothes, feeling warmed and . . . awkward. She stroked the skirt again. "The ring gaveth and didn't taketh away this time." Last time Talon asked for clothes for her, the old ones, her own clothes, had disappeared. It still annoyed her that she'd lost them.

"Yet," Talon said.

Her gaze jerked to his as his meaning sunk in. Their clothes could disappear at any moment. Her eyes widened. "How long do you think we have?"

A gleam of humor lit his eyes. "The ring has a mind of its own, aye?"

"So we'd better change." She frowned. "I hate to lounge around in such nice clothes." What she needed were a pair of sweats and a T-shirt.

"Ye needn't wear more than the shift." He sat on the edge of the bed and pulled off his boots. "'Twill be all ye wear to bed." He looked away, but not before she'd seen the heat flare in his eyes.

This shift was silk, not threadbare cotton, but the silk wouldn't cover her much better than the one she had on. Still, the sooner she got out of these grimy, bloodstained clothes, the better. Especially if they were about to disappear.

She glanced at Talon, about to ask him to turn around. But as he pulled his shirt off over his head, revealing a hard, well-defined chest, a perfect six-pack, and thick well-muscled arms, she forgot what she'd been about to say. He was breathtaking.

As she stared, he untied his pants and let them drop without a moment's hesitation. He wore nothing beneath.

She was no connoisseur of the male form, but his was . . . perfection. There was no other word for it. Trim hips, strong legs, and . . .

Oh my. Her cheeks heated. She knew she should look away, but she was caught, trapped within the spell of his male beauty. As she stared at him, his male parts, which hadn't started out particularly aroused, grew. And grew. Longer, thicker, until he was fully, gloriously, horrifyingly erect.

Her pulse began to race. Her body melted, turning warm and soft. And damp.

He didn't move. She couldn't breathe. And it was minutes before she realized he was watching her watch him. Her gaze shot to his face, her cheeks flaming.

His eyes were at once warm as a summer sky and hot as flame.

"All I have is yours, Julia," he said softly. "If ye want it."

She jerked her gaze away. "I-I'm sorry," she stammered. "I shouldn't have stared."

"Your staring pleased me. Dinna be sorry." Out of the corner of her eyes she saw him pick up the pants. "Do I frighten ye?"

"No. God, Talon, we are *not* having this conversation."

"What conversation would that be?" A hint of humor lightened his tone.

"I'm not going to stand here discussing the merits of your penis with you."

His soft laughter stole some of her embarrassment. Out of the corner of her eye she watched him pull on the pants, hiding that eye-catching bit of anatomy. When she was certain he was covered, she glanced at him, careful to look only at his face.

"Will you please turn around while I change?" She marveled at the steadiness of her words even as she wondered where the old Julia had gone. The old Julia would have demanded and expected her demands to be obeyed. Not that Talon obeyed anyone but himself.

He did as he pleased. And he saw too much. What had he said to her last night? *I do what you are too stubborn and prideful to admit you want, lass.*

Arrogant man.

The worst of it was, he was right. Sometimes. She'd needed to be held last night even if she hadn't realized it. What if he tried again to give her what her gaze had probably told him—wrongly—that she wanted? Him.

No, he wouldn't. She had to believe he wouldn't. Beneath the sometimes caveman-like manners, he really didn't want to hurt her. She'd learned that, too. He might steal a kiss or two, and he might try to seduce her. She wouldn't put that past him at all. But in the end, he'd never force her.

He'd killed four men to save her from that fate.

She met his gaze. "Please turn around."

"Ye may need help."

"I got out of everything downstairs. I'm pretty sure I can do it again." At his boyish look of disappointment, she smiled. "I promise to ask for help if I need it."

That intriguing mouth of his kicked up on one side, but he turned.

With hands that were far more unsteady than they'd been downstairs, she untied the laces on the jacket and fought with it to get it over her head. The skirt was more cooperative. The moment she untied the string, it dropped to her feet. Lastly, she yanked off the shift, glad to have the dirty clothes off her newly clean body.

Even with his back to her, Talon's presence filled the room. She couldn't shake the memory of his nakedness. Of his exquisite male beauty. And she remained intensely aware that a quick pull of the string on his pants and he'd be as naked as she was all over again.

The thought should have revolted her. But she felt only warm, liquid heat.

With a shuddering breath, she grabbed for the clean silk shift and pulled it over her head. Looking down, she saw her nipples poking through plainly. She reached for the skirt, but couldn't bring herself to put on such finery to sit around in.

The cloak might do, except she wasn't cold and she'd roast in the thing inside. She eyed Talon's vest and grabbed it, pulling it on over her head. It was miles too big, yet perfect, falling just below her hips, covering her breasts and all her important parts without adding too much warmth.

"I'm done."

Talon turned back, eyeing her with amusement. "Ye could start a new fashion."

"I have a feeling this one might not take off. Now . . . about that whiskey?"

He nodded toward the table, where a lovely crystal carafe and two glasses sat. Had they been there when they walked in the room and she just hadn't noticed?

The way things popped in and out, there was no telling. Nor did she care.

Talon poured them each a glass and they sat at the table, each lost to their own thoughts as they sipped at the surprisingly smooth drink. The ring knew its whiskeys.

Talon refilled his glass. "Tell me something, Julia-lass."

Julia met his gaze. Her body was beginning to feel the relaxing effects of the alcohol. "What's that?"

"Did any of the lads ye've known . . ."

Julia stiffened, her relaxation flying out the window.

"Did any of them break your heart?"

She looked down into the amber liquid in her glass. "I don't want to talk about them."

"I dinna wish to know about them. I wish to know about you."

Julia took a small sip of her whiskey then met his gaze. Nosy man. The whiskey slid down, warming her insides.

How would he feel if she probed into his private life? The thought had her cocking her head at him with interest. "I'll tell you what, Braveheart. A truth for a truth."

He lifted a single brow at her in question.

She leaned forward. "For every truth I offer you, you have to give me one in return."

The corner of his mouth quirked up, but his eyes held no gleam. Slowly, he nodded. "Aye. A truth for a truth."

Julia ran her thumb up and down her glass. "None of the boys I . . . knew . . . broke my heart. None of them meant anything to me at all."

His brows drew down thoughtfully and she realized she'd given more than a single truth. She'd told him more than she'd meant to.

"My turn," she added quickly.

Talon nodded.

"How long have you had that magic ring?"

"Since I was a lad of fifteen. How long ago did ye know . . . your last?"

Julia groaned. "Are all your questions going to be about my sex life?"

"I wish to understand you, lass, and I sense these lads were important. Ye may not have thought so at the time, but they've made ye who ye are now."

"A whore?"

His eyes tightened at the word, but he shook his head. "Nay. Skittish. Uncertain of your own worth."

"My worth?" She kicked back half the whiskey in a single gulp, then reached for the carafe. "I'm worth plenty, dude, and don't you forget it."

That intense, disconcerting gaze of his pressed into her, weighing her down. "If you ken your worth, then why did you think I wouldn't try to save you today?"

This was all getting way too personal. The carafe clinked

against her glass as she poured, her hand refusing to steady. She set the crystal in the center of the table and settled back in her chair, forcing herself to meet his gaze.

"I know what my worth is to *me*. I care what happens to me. I don't expect anyone else to."

"Because ye have no one?"

"Because I've never had anyone."

"Yer parents?"

"Didn't want me." God, why was she telling him this stuff? "I've answered a bunch of your questions, Talon. Now it's my turn. Where did you get your ring?"

"A wee little man gave it to me."

Her mouth twisted ruefully, uncertain whether he was playing with her. But the look in his eyes was serious. And she supposed his answer made as much sense as any other under the circumstances.

"Why do you think your parents didn't want you?" he asked softly.

His question pinched and she shook her head. "I get more questions. You're ahead of me."

"Aye, but answer this one first. 'Tis a simple one."

She frowned, then shrugged. "I guess it is pretty simple. My parents didn't want kids. My mom had her tubes tied . . . an operation to make sure she never got pregnant. But it didn't work. She got pregnant with me when she was thirty-seven. She wanted to terminate the pregnancy, but my dad talked her out of it. He didn't want me either, but he didn't believe in abortion . . . in terminating pregnancies. I think he regretted that decision after my mom left us when I was six months old. He used to tell me I'd ruined his marriage and his life by being born."

Talon leaned across the table and took her hand in his. "I'm sorry for that. 'Twas a terrible thing to tell a bairn."

"Yeah, well, it was the truth. Kids need the truth, right?" She shrugged. "I paid him back. I was a rotten kid."

He squeezed her hand. "I dinna believe it. Headstrong, mayhap, but never rotten."

"Oh, no, I was pretty bad, believe me. I was always getting into trouble." She shrugged, the memories of those days leaving a sour taste in her mouth. "It was the only way I could ever get his attention." She straightened and took another healthy sip of whiskey. "Your turn. Tell me something about your family."

"I have no kin." The harsh way he said the words had her looking at him sharply.

"None? I thought Highlanders had clans and stuff. Aren't there any other MacClures?"

He twirled the glass between his hands, looking down into the liquid. "I never knew any MacClure but my da. He was a broken man—a man without a clan—when he married my mum. We lived within the protection of her clan, but were never truly part of it. My da was not . . . the kind of man others took to."

"I'm sorry. Are your parents gone, too?"

"Aye." He looked up at her, pinning her with that pair of Carolina blue eyes. "Now 'tis my turn. How old were you when you took your first lover?" he asked softly.

She met his gaze and saw no judgment in those eyes. Only gentleness. Perhaps even understanding.

She didn't want to tell him. God, she was so through with this conversation. She shifted in her seat restlessly. But the soft snare of that gentle gaze wouldn't let her go.

With a sigh, she looked down into her glass. "Fourteen."

"How old were ye when ye took the last?"

For no reason she could understand, her eyes began to burn with tears. Her jaw tightened. "That's none of your business."

Talon leaned forward and captured her hand again, his thumb tracing light circles over the back of her hand. "Aye. But I would know. I wish to understand."

She pulled her hand away, leaving her glass on the table and pressing her fingertips to her closed eyelids as old misery clawed at ancient wounds. "I knew all of them within a space of four days." Despite the press of her fingers, tears began to leak out beneath her eyelashes and she brushed them away.

She heard him move and a moment later felt his warm hand on the back of her head, his other on her elbow. "Come, Julia-lass. I wish to ken what happened, but 'twill be easier to tell me if ye dinna have to feel my gaze on ye."

The feel of his hand sliding beneath her legs startled her, but before she could object, he lifted her off the chair and into his arms as if she were seven, not thirty. Then he settled onto her chair, cradling her on his lap.

"Talon . . . I'm a big girl. I really can sit by myself."

"Aye." He pulled her close and tucked her head beneath his chin. "But ye fit so neatly upon my lap. Stay, Julia." He stroked her arm and her hair with a gentle touch. "Tell me what happened."

What was the matter with him? What was the matter with *her*? Because she couldn't bring herself to fight him. She liked sitting on his lap too much. She enjoyed letting him pet her. She should probably give some serious thought to why. But not now. Not tonight. Not when she was starting to feel enough of a buzz that the knots of tension from the awful events of the day were finally starting to loosen.

But as comfortable as she felt on his lap, she still didn't want to tell him her story. At the time everyone had known. Everyone.

His big hand ran slowly up and down her arm. His chin rubbed the top of her head. She could feel him waiting for her to speak, but he didn't push her. If he'd demanded, she might have fought him out of sheer stubbornness if nothing else. But he just waited for her to spill her heart.

Finally she did, closing her eyes against the ugly memories.

"I don't know why I did it. We'd just moved to Los Angeles. A city in . . . the Colonies. Kind of. It's probably hard to imagine cities in the New World, but they'll build them. My dad and I were always moving, the whole time I was growing up. Every six to nine months. I was never very good at making friends, but I learned early how to make my mark everywhere I went. Mostly by making trouble. I was the kid who did the things none of the others dared. When I was young, I'd make faces behind the teacher's back or pull pranks on her. The kids, at least the bad kids, all wanted to be my friend."

"And when ye were fourteen, ye found another way to make them like ye," Talon said softly, stroking her hair. "The boys, at least." It was the raw ache in his voice that made her turn and press her cheek against the base of his throat, drinking in the warm comfort of his clean, masculine scent.

"The first time was after school the second week of class. I'd been up to my usual pranks to get attention, but the boys in high school were smarter. One of them figured out that a girl who liked to cause trouble might like trouble of a different kind. He told me to meet him in the parking lot after school. I did."

The arms around her tightened. "He forced ye?"

"No. He kissed me and I let him. Then he opened the back door of his car . . . his carriage, I guess you'd call it . . . and I got in. I let him, Talon. I laid there and let him while three of his friends stood guard around the car to make sure no one came and caught us. I saw them turning around, peering into the windows excitedly, watching us.

"The next day, another of those boys asked me to meet

him in the parking lot and I did it again, with him. By the third day, I was the most popular girl in school. All the boys watched me. They all tried to talk to me. And each afternoon for four days I spread my legs for one of them. Then my father found out." He'd never loved her, but the look he'd turned on her that day had been so cold that even all these years later, she shuddered at the memory. "He told me he was sending me away."

All the time she was growing up, all she'd wanted was his attention. The thought of losing it, of losing *him*, completely devastated her. He'd told her that she had a good brain, that she could be president of a company someday. Or she could get herself pregnant and throw it away, like she was trying to do.

"I begged him to keep me. He was all I had. I promised to change if he'd give me another chance and he agreed. We moved a few months later and the boys all watched me in the new school as if they already knew what I was, but I ignored them. I had to get good grades, perfect grades, or my dad was going to throw me away.

"I studied hard and got accepted into both of his alma maters—his colleges. Princeton and the Harvard School of Business. I don't know if women get educated in this time, but we do in mine. I think I was hoping . . ." She stopped, raking her upper lip with her teeth as comprehension flowed through her clearly for the first time. In talking about it, she was starting to understand.

Why had she never talked about it before?

But she knew the answer all too well. She'd never had anyone who wanted to listen.

Talon cupped her shoulder. "Ye were hoping?"

Julia sighed. "I think in a secret part of my heart, I'd always hoped to make him proud of me. But I never did."

"Perhaps ye will. Perhaps he'll come around."

"No. He won't. He died last September. I hadn't seen

him in seven years. The day I graduated from Princeton, he washed his hands of me."

"I'm sorry for your pain, Julia-lass. But 'twas his mistake, not yours. His loss."

"Thank you for saying that."

"'Tis the truth."

She fell silent as Talon's strong hand gently stroked the misery away.

"You've been pushing the lads away ever since you were fourteen," he murmured. "Trying to please your da."

"I guess. But I could never have a boyfriend or a husband, Talon. I hate sex. I *hate* it."

"Aye, I imagine ye would when you'd no feelings for the lads. I imagine it was painful, too. Lads that young can be rough in their enthusiasm."

"It always hurt."

"It doesna have to be that way. Not with a man who kens how to bring ye pleasure. Done right, it can be a fine experience. For the lass as well as the lad."

She heard the shift in his tone, the way his voice moved lower, his words slow and full.

"I'm not having sex with you, Talon."

He didn't reply, just continued to pet her, easing away the misery, and calming her soul.

He stroked her head, weaving his fingers through her hair. "Your da doesna sound like he was much of a father to ye," he said after a time. His fingers lifted a strand of her hair and tugged gently as if he were wrapping it around his finger.

"He provided for me. Nothing more."

"Who loved ye, lass? When ye were a wee bairn, who loved ye?"

"The nannies took care of me."

"But they changed with every move, aye? Every six to nine months."

"Yes."

"Who loved ye?"

"Nobody. I don't need anyone to love me."

"Your parents couldna see past their own selfishness to ken ye well. To see your worth. 'Tis why ye didna think I'd come for ye today, aye?"

Her breath left on a shudder. She didn't want to think about today. "If the people who were supposed to love me the most barely cared if I lived or died, then no. I didn't expect a stranger to care."

She pulled back and looked up at him. "I'm still not sure why you risked so much to come after me."

He met her gaze, his eyes gleaming. "Because I do see your worth."

She frowned. "As the tool sent to help you find your chalice."

"Nay, more than that. You've a quick mind and a courageous heart, Julia Brodie. And a bonny smile that lifts my spirits like a bright summer's day."

"I could have used someone like you in my life when I was growing up." The whiskey was making her feel comfortable and lazy. And just buzzed enough to say whatever came into her head. "Are you my friend, Talon?"

"Aye, lass. Mayhap even more."

He smiled and she returned it, then leaned back against him. "Who loves *you*, Talon?"

He kissed her ear. "My ring."

Julia laughed. "We're two of a kind, aren't we?"

"Aye. I'm beginning to think we are." His hand slid to her hip, rubbing gently against the silk of her shift, sending languorous warmth flowing through her blood. "Let me kiss ye, lass."

Without waiting for her reply, he eased her away from his shoulder and lifted her chin, forcing her to look at him again.

He wanted to kiss her. No, he was *going* to kiss her. The intent was clear in his eyes.

As his face dipped to hers, it never occurred to her to resist. She wanted his mouth on hers. She longed to taste him again.

His head tilted as he slanted his mouth across hers in a deep, drugging kiss, more potent than any whiskey. Her limbs felt heavy, her body hot and tingly. A low moan escaped her throat as she gave herself up to the familiar yet surprising joy of his kiss.

His fingers slid into her hair as he tilted her face this way and that, deepening the kiss, demanding her total surrender. His tongue swept inside and she nipped it with her teeth then stroked it lavishly with her own.

Desire swirled inside her, spinning lower until she throbbed and ached deep down, wanting more. Need tightened as his mouth left hers to trail kisses down her neck.

His hand caressed her shoulder, then moved lower to cover her breast. She stiffened.

Talon lifted his head, but not his hand, as he looked into her face. His eyes were heavy-lidded, his mouth damp. "Easy, lass. I only wish to touch ye. To pleasure ye."

"I'm not having sex with you." But her voice sounded as breathy and sexy as some porn queen's. Heat swirled inside her.

"I'm not asking ye to. Just let me show ye a taste of what it can be like, hm? Just a wee bit of pleasure."

If she'd been fully sober, she would have said no, she was sure of it, but he was so gentle and his touch felt so good . . .

His fingers slipped inside the neck of her shift, sliding over sensitive flesh to close around her nipple. A gentle squeeze made her gasp and arch into his touch.

The air tore in and out of her lungs in harsh, noisy breaths as she struggled against the rising tide of pleasure.

A tug at her shift and he dipped his head and took her bare breast deep into his mouth.

Julia cried out with the pleasure, her hands rising into his hair, holding him tight against her. "Talon," she gasped. It was too much. How was she supposed to handle so much sensation? What was she supposed to do?

He tugged again and her second breast was bared and sucked into his mouth. Again, she cried out and arched into the pleasure while his hand kneaded her damp breast, plucking at her nipple. Every tug of his mouth and fingers pulled at the sensitive flesh between her legs as if a physical cord joined them.

The heat rose inside her until she was damp and throbbing, and rocking with restless need.

"Talon."

As he sucked on one breast, his fingers abandoned the other. She felt the heel of his hand at her knee, felt him pulling her shift up her legs.

Julia jerked upright. "Talon, no."

He released her shift, his hand rising to her face, his warm palm cupping her cheek as he turned her face to him again. "I'll not hurt you. I just want to touch you, to see your eyes darken with pleasure."

"So you can take advantage."

"Nay." He kissed her cheek. "So you can heal."

"I'm not broken."

He lifted his head and met her gaze with those blue, blue eyes. "Nay, you're too strong for that. But there's pain in you. I see it in your eyes. I feel it when I touch you. Let me bring you pleasure with my finger, Julia. Just that. I vow, just that."

Her pulse was racing now, her legs growing damp from the thought of where he wanted to touch her. Her body clearly wanted the same. But she didn't.

"I don't want anything inside me."

"I won't put it inside you. Just a simple touch that won't enter you at all."

Crazily, she wasn't pushing him away. Insanely, she trusted him.

He smiled, that charmer's smile that tightened things inside her even when she wasn't half under his thrall. "Say *aye*, Julia."

Oh God. The unfamiliar word slipped from her lips. "Aye."

He kissed her forehead as his hand brushed her knee, then he gently lifted the hem of her shift.

She stiffened. She couldn't help it. The memories of those other times had all run together in her head, one big, wretched memory.

"Shh, lass," he murmured against her temple, as if he could hear the doubts in her head. "Relax. And feel."

But as his hand crawled up her thigh, she grabbed it. "Talon, I can't do this. I don't want it."

His hand retreated to her knee, her own still clinging to his wrist. "Just a touch, lassie, nothing more. I'll not enter ye." His mouth covered hers, his tongue sliding along hers, stoking the flame doused by her fear. "You're no coward, Julia. 'Tis only a touch."

She wasn't a coward. Dammit, she wasn't.

She forced herself to lift her hand from his. "Then touch me, but it won't change anything. I'm still not going to want you inside me."

He kissed her temple even as his hand began to move up her thigh.

She wasn't a coward, but to her mortification, she was beginning to tremble. Her eyes were starting to feel hot.

"I don't want this," she said miserably.

His hand stopped moving, inches from the top of her thigh. "Kiss me."

With a shaky breath, she pulled back to where she could

meet his gaze. In his eyes, she saw a tenderness unlike any ever directed at her. A promise to keep her safe.

He leaned forward and pressed his lips against the corner of her eye, then pulled back.

"Kiss me."

With trembling hands, she pressed her palms to his cheeks and slowly leaned forward, covering his mouth with her own. His arm curled tight around her, holding her with a gentle firmness that had tenderness welling up inside her. A single tear slid down her cheek.

His mouth moved gently over hers, teasing and coaxing until she opened and let him in. Passion swept through her all over again, eliciting a low moan from her throat.

And when his fingers curled around her upper leg and tugged, spreading her thighs, she didn't fight him. Not until she felt the first brush of his finger against her swollen, private flesh did she jerk and pull her mouth from his, stunned by the jolt of pure pleasure.

"Easy, lassie. All I wish to do is this. Just this."

Her hands slid around his neck, her forehead pressing against his cheekbone as he brushed her again and again, each slide of his finger a shock. A wonderful shock of incredible, intense pleasure.

Over and over, he stroked her, each stroke turning her into a woman she didn't know, a woman whose hips rocked with growing need, whose throat filled with small gasps and low moans. A woman whose already bare breasts ached for a man's mouth and whose body heated and wept and *wanted*.

Pressure rose deep inside her, a wildness she knew to be a building orgasm even if she'd never had one.

"Don't stop, Talon. Please don't stop."

She felt his chin brushing her hair. "Not for all the silver in Christendom."

His finger was magic, pressing and touching and rubbing in exactly the right spot, at just the right speed and pressure until . . .

With a cry, her body tightened, cresting and careening into a long, rippling run of pure bliss. Talon continued to touch her, continued to milk her release until she was a boneless mass in his arms.

Slowly, he slid his palm down her thigh, then away, pulling down her shift to cover her legs again.

"I didn't know . . . my body could do that," she said when she could speak again.

"Aye, it can." His arms tightened around her, cradling her. Beneath her, she felt the hard ridge of his own thick arousal.

She shuddered, utterly sated, yet painfully aware he wasn't. That he'd want to be, too. And she couldn't . . . she couldn't . . .

"Are you in terrible pain?" she asked, softly. Guiltily.

"Dinna fash yourself."

"Dinna *what* myself?"

He chuckled. "Dinna worry. I'll be fine."

She buried her face in his neck. "Are you sure? I . . . I can't help you, but I don't want you to be in pain. Not after . . ." Words were failing her.

"Did ye like it, then?" he asked, his voice as full of anticipation as a kid's.

"It was . . . *amazing*. Better than I ever believed."

His hand slid up and down her arm. "Watching you rise, feeling your pleasure break over you moved me, Julia. I may have gotten as much pleasure out of that as you did."

"Now you're just making fun of me."

"Nay, I am not." His hand stroked her hair. "You've a rare passion in ye, lass. Dinna be afraid to give yourself to the right man."

She lifted her head and met his gaze. "And you're the right man?" For once, her tone didn't hold any exasperation. Because she felt none.

"Nay, lass. I am not."

She eyed him with surprise. "You don't want to have sex with me?"

He smiled at her, but the charmer was missing. Sadness lurked in the blue depths of his eyes.

"Aye, I wish to know you like that, more than you ken. But you deserve more than I can give you, Julia. You deserve a man who will love you, lass. Who will marry you and give you bairns. A man of your own time and world." He stroked her head. "You're deserving of that. Of love."

"And you would never love me."

He watched her with that sadness, and then placed a soft kiss on her forehead. "I have no love in me to give any woman. And it wouldna matter if I did. Our lives were never meant to cross."

TWELVE

Talon awoke instantly and completely to the sound of a rap at the door. The room was still dark but for the glow of coals from the hearth, coals that told him they'd been sleeping for nigh on three or four hours. It was still several hours until daybreak.

He slipped out from beneath the blanket and Julia, laying her head on the down pillow instead of his shoulder. Then he rose from the bed, a knife in his hand, and went to open the door.

Before him, reaching little higher than his waist, stood the red-haired dwarf who had given him his ring all those years ago.

"Hegarty." Talon's fist clenched around the knife in his right hand, his ring hand. "You canna have it," he growled.

To Talon's consternation, the dwarf dodged beneath his arm and slipped into the room. "You've called another of the stones, have ye, laddie?" He turned his weathered face to him, eyeing him with surprise. "I sense the magic."

"I dinna ken what you're saying, troll. Now leave me."

"Troll, is it? I'll not be a troll, laddie. Ye can call me a dwarf, right enough. Though Hegarty will do."

Hegarty spied Julia lying on the bed and headed straight for her. Talon cut him off before he reached the bed.

"Leave her be."

But Hegarty ignored him, pushing past his knife as if unconcerned by the blade, or disbelieving Talon would actually attack him.

And truth to tell, he wouldn't. Not unless he hurt the lass. Then he'd kill him.

Julia had rolled onto her back when Talon got up. As he watched, Hegarty's hand shot out and snared the small jewel she wore around her neck, lifting it. With a grunt, he dropped the necklace and shook her shoulder.

"Wake up, lassie." But Julia had downed a goodly amount of whiskey and would not be waking soon. "I'll need my stone."

Talon's gaze jerked to Hegarty as understanding dawned. "You had *two*?"

"A sight more than two." Hegarty shook Julia's shoulder again. "Lassie, wake!"

"She's not . . ."

"From this time?" Hegarty finished for him. "I ken that well enough. The garnet brought her here."

"Nay." Talon shook his head. "The ring brought her to me."

Hegarty looked at him thoughtfully. "That may be. Ye asked the amethyst for something and it called her to fulfill yer wish. Because it could. The amethyst has the power to call all the stones . . . and their wearers."

Talon stared at him. "There are others?"

"That's not your concern, laddie, but you'll give me my ring now." He shot out his stubby hand, palm up.

Talon took a step back. "Nay, I will not. I'll not part with it." He lifted his knife in the dwarf's face. "Ye'll be leaving now, and ye'll not return."

"Not without my ring."

Talon shoved his knife into its sheath and grabbed the back of Hegarty's jacket, yanking the dwarf up and off his feet.

Hegarty kicked and flailed. "Ye'll be putting me down!"

"Aye. Beneath the moon."

Hegarty swung out, catching him hard in the jaw, but Talon was not to be dissuaded. He bodily carried the dwarf out of the room, down the stairs, and out the front door, finally depositing him in the grass.

Hegarty whirled on him, straightening his coat with a scowl. "Ye were more agreeable when ye were a lad."

Talon snarled at him. "This is my life you're trying to take."

The dwarf stilled, eyeing him sharply. "If ye've built yer life around the ring, laddie, ye've built yer life on a lie."

"Go! And never cross my path again, dwarf."

"I'll go, lad. For now. But I'll be back, mark my words. I'll have the amethyst. As I will the garnet. Sooner or later, I'll have them both."

"Nay, you will not." Talon whirled and stomped back into the house and up the stairs, throwing the bolt on the bedchamber door. He stood with his back to it, his heart thundering in his chest.

He'd always known Hegarty would return someday, demanding his ring. But now he wanted Julia's necklace, too. He stared at her as she slept. Julia, who wore one of Hegarty's jewels, just as he did. Did she know? And how on God's earth had she come by it?

So many questions. Too many. His head was beginning to ache even as his stomach soured.

Julia had another way home now. For the price of her necklace, he had no doubt Hegarty would send her. Just like that. No need to discover what use the ring had for her. No need to wait for the ring to release her.

If he told her she had a way home, she'd be after the dwarf in a thrice.

His jaw clenched. His sour stomach told him what he must do, but the ache in his chest denied it. He wasn't ready to let her go.

Pushing away from the door, he returned to the bed and pulled her into his arms, lest the dwarf try to call her to him in another way. Julia turned to him, sliding her arm around his waist with a soft purr, easing some of the tension that twisted through him like a rope coiled too tight.

He couldn't lose her. Not yet. Not so soon. He still needed her.

Heaven help him, he didn't want to let her go.

They rode through the day, Julia enjoying her pretty new gown even though she had to ride with it hiked up to her knees, her Frye boots showing. Talon had promised that when they got closer to the castle, he'd ask the ring to provide a coach, but so far that request had turned into a pumpkin. In the distance, she could see the castle they'd seen in the flames sitting high on a hill above the village. Picktillum Castle, glistening in the sunlight with its one round and three square towers, was a sight to behold.

Julia glanced at Talon, riding tall and proud beside her, dressed in the trappings of a gentleman. But the finery did nothing to diminish the impression he gave of strength. Of danger.

An impression only heightened by the silence in which he'd ridden all day. A silence that was gnawing at her. She'd spilled her guts to him last night, telling him everything. And he'd barely spoken to her since.

He'd convinced her he wanted to know the truth—that he could handle it.

Apparently, they'd both been wrong.

As they rode up the track to the castle, Talon turned to her. "Say little or naught. If ye must speak, tell them you're from the Colonies. You're my wife. With bairn."

She grimaced. "*Pregnant?*"

"Aye. 'Twill give us an excuse to seek hospitality."

"Great," she muttered. "And what are you?"

She expected him to shoot her an annoyed glare. To her surprise, he lifted one hand airily. "Why, I am an Irishman, of course," he said in a surprisingly good Irish accent, a full octave above his usual.

Julia laughed and Talon grinned.

"You are such a con man."

"A con man?"

"A . . ." Her smile faded. "An untruthful manipulator."

His smile dimmed along with hers, his eyes turning serious. "They mustn't ken who we are or why we're truly here, lass. 'Tis the way of it."

Julia sighed. "So we're both con men now."

As they approached the gates, two armed men stepped out to meet them, watching her with more curiosity than they did Talon. They were both nice-looking young men dressed in decent seventeenth-century rugged casual, as she was beginning to think of it. Snug-fitting pants, boots, long shirts that fell to mid-thigh, vests, and a belt laden with knives and other things.

"State your business," one of the men said evenly, his voice neither friendly nor unfriendly.

Talon looked down his nose at them, his hand flicking out dismissively. "I'll speak to your laird."

One of the men scowled, but the other nodded and called to a lad watching nearby. "Fetch Kinross."

"Aye." The boy took off toward one of the towers.

"Come," the man said. "Leave your mounts here."

Talon swung off his horse without his usual grace, then moved to help her down, groaning as if she weighed a ton. But when she looked at him askance, she caught a quick wink.

Talon was totally in character now. Whatever that character might be. And she was intensely uncomfortable with it all. He'd thrown her into the middle of a dangerous play, without lines or any idea of the story. All she knew was she was supposed to be this character's pregnant wife. And if they were discovered to be the imposters they were?

She didn't want to think about it.

They followed the two tall Scotsmen through a courtyard that looked much like the one she'd looked down on in Castle Rayne, then up a full flight of twisty stairs and into a great hall even more beautifully decorated than that of Rayne. The walls had been painted a rich cream and were covered with neat groupings of paintings. Like Rayne, the furniture sat in conversational groupings. Unlike Rayne, there were rugs on the floor beneath them, plump throw pillows, and even coffee tables with books. Other than the lack of electricity, the room could have come out of a twenty-first-century castle decorator's book.

"Have a seat," one of their escorts said. But they'd barely walked three steps when the boy who'd been sent to fetch Kinross returned. With him strode a tall, ruggedly handsome man with the palest eyes Julia had ever seen. His clothes were basically the same as those of his guards, but there was an air about this man that spoke of authority. And power.

A shiver of unease went through her as she feared what would happen if he realized they weren't travelers, but thieves.

As he drew near, his pale gaze hit her and clung, his step almost faltering. She felt Talon's arm go around her shoulders as he pulled her against him, protectively.

"I am Rourke Douglas, the Viscount Kinross," the man said, recovering quickly. But his gaze made only a cursory glance over Talon before returning to her.

"I am Patrick O'Grady, Lord Hertford," Talon said in that Irish accent, releasing her to make a funky bow. But the moment he straightened, his arm went right back around her and he pulled her against him. "This is my wife, Julia. We are on our way to Aberdeen, but our carriage lost a wheel and my lady is with child and in need of a decent bed for a day or two."

The viscount dipped his head, but his gaze was still fastened on her. "From whence do ye hail, my lady?"

Julia swallowed, remembering Talon's coaching. "The Colonies."

His eyes narrowed. "Ye've had quite a journey."

Julia nodded.

"Which colony?"

"New York." Oh hell, was it called New York in 1688? What was it called before that? New Holland? New Amsterdam? That was the problem with being a transplant. You never learned this stuff unless you grew up there. "That's what we call it. It's in New Amsterdam." *I think.*

The viscount's mouth twitched. Was he laughing at her? Those eyes of his got a strange look in them. A flicker of warmth, she thought. And something else that made little sense. Excitement.

She gave a mental groan. If he was interested in hearing all about the Colonies, she was sunk.

The viscount turned to one of his guards. "Angus, ask Brenna to meet us in the solar."

"Aye." The man turned and hurried away.

The viscount motioned them to follow, then led them across the Great Hall to yet another of those blasted tight, turny stairs. Talon kept firm hold of her hand as they climbed. At the first opening, Kinross exited onto a hallway and led them into another room that was as warmly decorated as the Great Hall, but on a much smaller scale.

"Your home . . . your *castle* . . . is lovely," Julia told him.

She half expected him to ignore her, but she found him watching her again with that disconcerting interest.

"Ye find it pleasing to your eye." He nodded, as if satisfied with her answer.

An odd response.

Moments later, a woman walked into the room and stopped, staring at her much as Kinross had. She was lovely, dressed in a vibrant blue day dress that set off her auburn hair to a tee. Auburn hair that wasn't swept up or hidden behind some mobcap or something, but hanging loose around her shoulders with distinctive, expensive layering. Like hair growing out from a good cut.

Goose bumps ran over Julia's arms. The woman gave Kinross a startled look, then turned back to her, meeting her gaze, her eyes suddenly twinkling as if she knew all Julia's secrets and couldn't wait to let her know.

She strode toward Julia, thrusting out her hand in a way Julia had seen no one else do in this time. "I'm Brenna Cameron . . . Douglas," she amended with a small shake of her head, her voice . . . *American.* "The Viscountess Kinross. But call me Brenna."

Julia stared fully now, taking the proffered hand and shaking it numbly as her mouth opened, then closed, then opened again.

"You . . . sound just like I do."

Brenna's face split into a grin. "I knew it! That's a seventy-dollar haircut if I ever saw one."

Julia just continued to stare, her head spinning. "A hundred-dollar haircut. I'm from New York."

Brenna gave a small grimace and glanced at Talon. "Maybe we should talk in private."

Julia let out a long, shuddering breath, feeling the weight of all the deception tumble from her shoulders to fall in a heap at her feet.

"He knows. But . . ." She couldn't wrap her head around it. "*How are you here?*"

The viscount came to join his wife, wrapping his arm around her shoulders. "You're another of Hegarty's lost bairns."

Julia shook her head, confused. "Who's Hegarty?" Out of the corner of her eye, she saw Talon move, standing back from the small grouping, but moving fully into her line of sight. He didn't appear nearly as relieved as she felt. If anything, he seemed more tense than before.

As she wondered at that, Brenna stepped forward and reached for her necklace, lifting it lightly between her fingers. "Where did you get this?"

The question confirmed her suspicions. "This is how I time-traveled, isn't it?"

Brenna nodded. "Probably. You don't remember being here as a child? In this time?"

"I wasn't. But I think my cousin was. She's the one who gave it to me, right after her wedding a few days ago. She wanted me to take it back to New York with me." Julia grimaced. "She told me not to touch it before I got home, but I put it on during the drive back to Glasgow."

Brenna winced. "Oh. Bad move. And, poof, here you are." She cocked her head, her gaze immensely sympathetic. "So you're here by accident."

"Yes. But you're not?"

Brenna shook her head. "Hegarty sent me into the future when I was five to save my life. I didn't remember. I thought I was from your time. So when he called me home last year, it was a bit of a shock." She shot her husband a sharp look wrapped in deep, loving layers. "Especially since no one told me I belonged here for quite a while."

Rourke looked up and away, a flash of guilt on his face even as he stroked his wife's hair. But when he looked down and met his wife's gaze, his eyes were filled with as much love as Brenna's were. "Aye, but ye forgave me."

Brenna smiled at him, something warm and loving and private passing between them.

Rourke turned back to Julia. "Apparently Brenna wasn't the only bairn Hegarty helped with his magic stones. The wee scamp willna say much, but he's let slip that there were other bairns sent to the future about the same time as Brenna. Twenty years ago."

Julia nodded. "That was my cousin Catriona. She was thirteen when she arrived out of nowhere looking like a barefoot street urchin."

Brenna's brows drew down. "Okay, I'm confused. If Hegarty called you back, why wasn't he there to take the stone? Or send you home when he realized he had the wrong woman?"

Julia glanced at Talon, uncertain how to answer that. Uncertain what the right answer *was*. Had Hegarty called her back? Or had Talon's ring?

She watched, dismayed, as Talon joined them with that affected walk, carrying one hand in the air. Why did he feel like he had to maintain the charade? These were friends.

Weren't they?

It occurred to her it was only her own charade that was no longer needed. She didn't have to pretend to be from this time. But Talon still meant to find and steal the chalice from this castle. From Brenna and her husband.

The thought settled like a stone in the pit of her stomach. How could she have forgotten lying was his life?

Talon launched into a tall tale with a flare worthy of an Oscar. "I was traveling to visit my sister in Aberdeen, I was, when a leprechaun, a wee little man, popped out of thin air and told me a bonny lass would soon appear. He could not wait for her himself and bade me take her to Picktillum Castle to await his arrival. If I granted him this boon, he would share his silver with me."

A leprechaun? She noticed that neither Brenna nor Rourke seemed surprised by the description. Wait . . . hadn't Talon told her something about a *wee little man* giving him his ring when he was a kid? *Seriously?* A leprechaun?

But okay, now she was sure the two stones were tied together in some way.

Talon nodded toward Julia, warmth in his eyes. "'Twas a vision that appeared. The beautiful lass at my side."

"Where'd you get the dress?" Brenna wanted to know.

Julia glanced down at the brocade gown, hoping Talon had a reasonable answer, because she was clueless. She couldn't exactly say she ran by the mall on her way to the castle.

"'Twas my sister's," Talon said with an overly dramatic sigh. "I was taking the trunk to her, but had to leave it behind when the wheel on the coach broke. Thieves will have stolen the rest by now, I'm certain." He shrugged, his gaze going back to Julia. "But one gown was put to fine use."

Brenna took Julia's hand, her eyes at once excited and

sad. "I'm sorry you won't be staying. I could use a friend who doesn't think I'm talking about archery when I say I miss *Target*. But you're here now and I'd love to hear everything that's happened since I left."

Julia's mind was spinning. Brenna believed Talon's story. That he'd met Hegarty and that Hegarty intended to send her home. Every word had been a lie. And yet . . .

Could the leprechaun send her home? Excitement set up a fast thrum in her veins. She looked at Talon, then back to Brenna. "What if Hegarty doesn't come back for me?"

Brenna squeezed her hand, then released it. "We know how to get in touch with him. Old Inghinn in the village has some connection to him we don't quite understand. But he's told us if we ever need him, she's the one to go to."

This was it. The way home. All she had to do was ask them to call Hegarty for her and he'd send her home.

Her gaze flew to Talon. Though he didn't break character, she could tell by the tightening of his jaw and the lack of a gleam in his eyes that he wasn't pleased.

For an unguarded moment, warmth lifted inside her at the thought he might miss her. Then she remembered why he'd called her in the first place. To perform some task.

Except . . . God, she was so confused. Who had really called her back here and why? Talon's ring? Catriona's necklace? Hegarty? Or a combination of all three?

Was she here to perform some task for Talon as he'd believed? Or had she simply, accidentally, punched Catriona's return-trip ticket?

The viscount rescued her from the swirling whirlpool of her thoughts. "You're welcome to stay at Picktillum as long as you wish, Julia." He smiled. "If ye wish to delay your departure and learn a bit about the past, I'm sure Brenna would enjoy the company of someone from home."

Brenna grinned. "You have to meet our son. He's almost a month old, but I think he's going to look just like his dad. I thought he was going to have blue eyes, but every day they get lighter."

Julia smiled, unable to resist Brenna's warmth. "I'd love to see him."

The viscount turned to Talon. "I thank you for bringing her here. For helping Hegarty, whatever your reasons. You're both welcome to stay until the wee blighter arrives."

Julia noticed the difference in their invitations. Hers for as long as she wished. Talon's only until Hegarty arrived. But if Talon noticed, and she knew he had, he didn't react. Again he gave that ridiculous bow.

The viscount started toward the door. "Come, Hertford. We'll allow the women time to talk."

Julia's gaze leaped to Talon's, unspoken questions in her eyes. When was he going to steal the chalice? And after he did, would he leave her here, disappearing from her life once and for all? Or would he take her, too, in case he still needed her?

The gaze that met hers possessed a sharpness she couldn't read. A promise. Or perhaps a warning for her not to betray his true mission.

She sent him back a message of her own. *We need to talk. Please don't leave me before we talk.*

She knew she had to go home, but it was all happening too fast. Had she really talked to Talon alone for the last time? Had she already kissed him for the last time without knowing?

The old Julia laughed at her caustically. So what if she had? It wasn't like she'd ever wanted him to kiss her. It wasn't like she'd *wanted* him to hold her.

She didn't need anyone in her life. She never had.

But those old, defensive thoughts no longer worked. She knew better now.

She needed someone in her life, someone to hold her. Someone to care about her.

And God help her, she wanted that someone to be Talon.

Thirteen

Talon stole through the passageways of Picktillum, the light from scattered oil lamps flickering on the walls, lighting his way. Julia had only recently gone to bed, but the time had come to take the chalice and leave and he'd not go before he saw her one last time.

It was her chambers he sought now.

He knew where to find the chalice. The ring had given him another vision of it during dinner, which had proved a wee bit awkward. He'd excused himself as having a headache, but Julia had understood the truth. He'd seen the unhappiness in her eyes.

All evening he'd watched her natural diffidence slowly melt beneath the friendly regard of the viscountess. She'd lit up when she'd realized Brenna was from her own time, clearly feeling a kinship with Brenna and her husband that he'd envied. He'd felt . . . apart. Even jealous.

But then he'd watched the way Julia's eyes had lit with

laughter at something the viscountess said. Her sweet laughter had fallen over him like gentle rain, soaking into his heart, making his chest feel as if it were shrinking and filling at the same time, tightening until he feared his heart would soon cease to beat.

How in the name of all that was holy was he supposed to leave without her?

Yet he would not take her against her will. Even if he still needed her, dammit. She'd come to him for a purpose, and until he knew what that purpose was, he didn't want to let her go.

He needed her.

His life would be so lonely without her.

Finding her bedchamber, he slipped inside.

The fire's embers still burned, illuminating the small, golden-haired beauty sitting up in bed, her arms wrapped around her knees.

At the sight of him, she didn't move, but watched him, something deep and raw in her eyes.

"I was hoping you'd come," she said quietly, her voice tight. Unhappy. "Who are you now? Hertford or the Wizard?"

He crossed to her and slowly lowered himself onto the edge of her bed. Though he wanted nothing more than to pull her into his arms, he did not touch her.

"Who do you want me to be?"

"Talon. Just Talon." She watched him with pensive eyes. "I need to know the truth. Did Hegarty call me back? Or did you?"

"'Twas me. 'Twas my ring."

"But Hegarty gave you the ring all those years ago, didn't he? The amethyst."

"Aye."

"And he gave Catriona the purple garnet. And Brenna the sapphire. I know Brenna was in trouble. Presumably

Cat was, too, though she never said." Her head cocked. "Why did Hegarty help you?"

Talon opened his mouth, then closed it again and rose, moving to stand before the fire. His past was just that . . . past. And he'd no desire to discuss it ever again.

But a need rose past that hard lump of old misery in his chest, a need to give her a glimpse into that darkness. To give her something he'd never given another.

But not this. Though she claimed she wanted him to be merely Talon, she was wrong. The true Talon was a man she would not wish to know.

The truth was nothing he would ever give anyone.

"It was a bad winter," he told her without turning around. "Hegarty's magic helped me to survive."

"He didn't send you to the future?"

"There was no need to. The ring protected me."

"Why won't you tell Rourke and Brenna you were another of Hegarty's bairns? Because they know Hegarty, right? And you don't ever intend to give the ring back to him." The censure was thick in her voice. "And because you don't want them to know you're the Wizard, the thief who intends to steal from them."

The last came out harsh, cutting him. As he suspected she'd meant to.

His temper pricked. He returned to the bed to sit where he'd been moments before, and reached for the jewel that nestled between her breasts, lifting it to rest on his fingers. "You knew all along this was the true means by which you came to me, yet you never told me."

She watched him warily. "It turned hot and started to glow right before I time-traveled. I've been confused about what role it played, especially after I saw the magic your ring could do. But, yes, I suspected it played a role in bringing me here. Especially when I figured out Catriona, who had given me the necklace, had probably come from this time. But I didn't know anything for sure."

"Why didn't you tell me?"

A single brow lifted, the displeasure in her eyes sharpening. "I'd already figured out you were a mercenary in Castle Rayne under false pretenses. Looking for something you intended to steal. Why would I tell you I suspected I was wearing a powerful, magical stone? I was afraid you'd take it from me. And I'd already suspected it might be my only way home."

Talon dropped the stone and lifted his hand to scratch his jaw with a frown. His stomach soured. "Ye think little of me."

She looked away, her gaze going to the hearth, the coals glowing softly in her eyes. For minute upon minute, she was silent.

He waited for her to speak. Waited for . . . what?

"Julia-lass," he began quietly, then stopped, uncertain what he wanted to say. Unsure what needed saying. He ached to hold her again, yet she'd made it more than clear that even the Wizard was beneath her contempt. His instincts told him to pull her into his arms and kiss her anyway. She would melt for him as she always did, whether she wished to or not.

But he didn't want to feel her resistance this time. Even knowing what she thought of him, he wanted nothing more than to pull her against him one last time and bury himself in her sweet, warm scent.

He'd known her but a few days, yet already she'd sunk into his skin, into his blood, as no woman had before her.

His chest cramped and he surged to his feet. He was being a fool to let a wee slip of a lass turn his life upside down. The sooner he was free of her, the better.

"Good-bye, Julia Brodie. Good journey to ye."

He turned toward the door and had taken only two strides when her soft voice sounded behind him.

"Talon."

He stopped and slowly turned back to her, steeling himself against the fierce pull she had on him. She watched him. He stared at her, wanting to turn away, yet unable to break the hold of her velvet gaze. And when she reached out to him, he was helpless to ignore her. He took her hand, the brush of her flesh against his fingers like a soft whisper against his heart.

Lifting his hand to her mouth, she placed a kiss in the center of his palm. His heart contracted. Warm need rushed through his veins. A need to kiss her. To hold her.

Her eyes glistened with unshed tears. "I'm going to miss you." The truth shimmered in her eyes. Turning her face, she pressed her cheek into his open palm as if seeking a comfort only he could give.

"Julia." When she looked up at him, he cupped her face with his hands. Something thick and warm passed between them.

Sinking onto the bed beside her, he pulled her into his arms, crushing her soft breasts to his chest as his mouth covered hers, as his tongue swept inside. *Home.* The word reverberated through his head, singing in his blood. This was where he belonged, with this lass in his arms. The only place he wanted to be.

He tasted her sweetness, sliding his tongue across hers as his hands pressed her closer. With a desperation born of knowing their time together was almost over, he wanted to feel her against him. Skin to skin. Flesh to flesh. His hands shook to know the feel of her satin skin. He'd touched her, but not enough. Never enough.

Tearing his mouth from her sweet lips, he tasted her cheek and her eyes, grazing his lips across her eyebrow, her forehead, her temple. He longed to taste every inch of her, to suckle and lick and tease.

With a growl, he swept her into his arms and deposited her in the middle of the bed.

"Talon." She tensed, but he grabbed her around the waist, holding her to the bed while he situated himself on his stomach beside her and kissed the lobe of her ear. Her shiver shook them both. As his mouth moved lower, teasing the tender skin of her neck, the tension flowed out of her and a low moan rose from her throat, making him smile with fierce satisfaction.

His hand slid to cup the side of her neck as he looked down into her passion-drugged face. Jesu, but he wanted to make her his.

"Let me love you, Julia. This one time. This last time." His hand slid down her shoulder, his thumb grazing the side of her breast. "Let me show you what it can be. What it's supposed to be."

Her gaze pierced his. "Are you going to steal from them?"

He felt the question like a douse of cold water. "Dinna ask me that," he begged.

A look of disappointment tightened her features.

Talon sighed. "The Wizard never fails, Julia. Ye ken that."

She sat up, forcing him to do the same.

"Screw the Wizard, Talon. You don't have to do this."

"Screw?" He shook his head. "I must complete my task. I've been paid good silver to fetch the chalice. It belongs to my client. I dinna ken how it came to be here, but it must be returned to its rightful owners."

Her mouth compressed. "How do you know who it belongs to? What if the guy who hired you was lying? What if he simply wanted you to steal it?"

Her questioning annoyed him. "It doesna matter. The Wizard made a commitment. The chalice must be delivered and so it shall be."

"I won't condone this. You can't steal from them."

He gripped her shoulders. "If ye tell them why I'm here, they may kill me."

"Rourke wouldn't . . ."

His fingers contracted. "Are ye so innocent? Thieves are executed. Or their hand's cut off." He shook her. "You cannot tell them."

She stared at him with a deep, bitter disappointment that made him feel ill.

He released her and rose. "I hope ye get home." Then he turned and walked to the door.

"Talon . . ." Her voice sounded of regret. But not of compromise. "You can be a better man than this."

She had her own ideas of right and wrong and they had no place in his world.

"Good-bye, Julia."

He was the Wizard. And if he was not, he was nothing.

Julia lay on the bed, watching the firelight dance across the exposed rafters crisscrossing the ceiling. Chilled and miserable, she'd put another log on the fire, but still couldn't sleep.

She swallowed back the lump of tears in her throat, refusing to cry. As she'd believed when she'd first met him, Talon wasn't one of the good guys. He stole. He killed. He was a mercenary through and through, doing whatever he was hired to do.

How pathetic was she that the thought of never seeing him again was crushing her heart?

She finally had what she'd been looking for from the moment she arrived here—a way home. From what Brenna had said, Hegarty would surely send her, taking the necklace as payment. But even if Hegarty showed up right now, she wouldn't be able to get back to New York in time for her presentation in the morning. In her time, it was already Wednesday night and Brenna had confirmed that time moved evenly in both centuries.

She wasn't sure she cared anymore.

After all she'd been through, that presentation no longer seemed very important. Maybe they'd let her give it later. Maybe not. For years, she'd been working toward this promotion to investment banker. Yet the thought of it no longer excited her. If anything, it left her feeling hollow.

She adjusted her hands behind her head and stared at the ceiling as she thought about Talon's comment that she seemed to like to teach. He'd asked her why she'd changed her mind about becoming a teacher.

Why *had* she?

It had happened in high school. Right around the time . . .

She remembered now and it all made a horrible sense. Up until that awful day when her father learned about her sexual adventures, she'd wanted to be a teacher. But when he threatened to send her away, she'd vowed to both of them to make him proud of her. The only way she'd known to do that was to try to follow in his footsteps.

Fisting her hands, she pulled them around and pressed them against her forehead. God, she hadn't even realized what she'd done. She'd followed him to Princeton and Harvard, not to major in education, like she'd always dreamed, but in finance, like he had. She'd done it for him, not for herself. And all the years since, she'd busted her butt to succeed. Worked long hours to climb the ranks.

In the hopes that just once, *just once*, he'd look at her and say, *I'm proud you're my daughter, Julia. I'm glad you were born.*

But he was dead now. She would never make him proud, no matter what she did.

Maybe it was time she started living for herself.

She sat up and crossed her legs in front of her, staring at the coals. If she could do anything she wanted, what would she do?

A small rush of excitement fluttered in her chest. She'd be a teacher, just as she'd told Talon. High school. She'd teach math. And, if the high school was big enough, economics or accounting. She'd always been good with numbers.

A small smile pulled at her mouth at the thought of it. She glanced at the door, wanting to tell Talon. Wanting to share her revelation.

But the well of elation drained out of her.

Talon was gone. Out of her life.

Her heart twisted with regret. And gratitude.

For all his faults, he'd given her more in the past few days than anyone else had in thirty years. Not only had he risked his life to save her, but he'd helped her see herself in a different light. He'd helped her understand the lonely girl, desperate for attention, that she'd been at fourteen. And, perhaps, to forgive her.

He'd seen inside her and then opened her eyes to what she really wanted from life. To teach. And to have some-one in her life who cared about her. Because deep down she was beginning to realize she was still that lonely girl.

She pressed her palm against the ache in her chest. If only Talon had come into her real life, and not this strange detour to the past. He had faults, heaven knew he had his faults, but there was goodness inside him, too.

He was so much more than a thief and she knew it. He'd made a promise to procure the chalice and he didn't go back on his promises. Which was honorable, wasn't it?

And there was no doubt he was courageous. He'd fought and killed four men to save her when she meant little to him. Most men would have shrugged helplessly and let them have her, but he hadn't done that. He'd saved her. And held her when she'd desperately needed a comforting touch. He'd wanted to make love to her, and while he might have tried to talk her into it a time or two, he'd never pushed her too far. He'd never hurt her.

Without a doubt, Talon MacClure was far from perfect, but deep down he was a good man.

She wondered if he knew that.

With a sudden, pulsing pain, she knew she would never get the chance to tell him.

He'd told her good-bye.

A cold emptiness swept through her, leaving her feeling like a lonely, hollow shell.

The tears began to roll.

Talon waited for the castle's inhabitants to find their beds before he slipped from his chamber to retrieve the chalice.

As he stole through the castle now, spiraling deep into the bowels of the fortress, his feet felt like lead, his chest heavy as stone.

He'd seen Julia Brodie for the very last time. She should matter to him no longer. Yet her final words would not cease their incessant echo in his head.

You can be a better man.

But she was wrong. He was who he was and he could not change. He didn't want to change! He was the Wizard. The Wizard was his life.

Though for a few short days, he'd had something more. Companionship with a bonny, difficult, darling lass. A lass who couldn't stay in this world, and wouldn't stay with him even if she could. Even the Wizard wasn't good enough for her.

She'd told him she wanted him to be Talon. Just Talon. But she didn't understand what that meant. And she'd turn away from him if she knew the true man, the man who'd grown from that miserable, useless boy. A boy who'd killed his own father.

No, Julia would not want him in any form. She would never be his.

If only he could get her voice out of his head.

At the base of the stairs, he slipped out the door and into the castle courtyard, sliding into the shadows before he was spotted. The night was cool and still, the air stirring lightly around him. The smell of the stables carried to him pleasantly, but the horses he and Julia had ridden here would have to remain at Picktillum. He'd find another way out, an escape without the ring's help, for he'd not risk the ring choosing a fire for its distraction again. He would not risk Julia's safety. Not even for his own.

Staying to the shadows, he began the search for the cellar he'd seen in his vision.

On his third try, he found it. The moment he slipped in through the heavy wooden door and saw the stacks of barrels, he knew. The scent of damp earth and dried spices teased his nose as he moved, unerringly, for the low crevice along the back wall. He knelt and reached his hand inside. His fingers brushed against cool metal. Triumph sought to flare within him, but managed only a flicker before winking out.

He'd found what he'd come for.

But all he could see in his mind's eye was Julia's look of disappointment. In him.

You can be a better man.

Bollocks. He was who he was.

Curling his fingers around the base, he pulled the chalice from its hiding place and slipped it into the waist of his pants, careful to cover the golden treasure with his waistcoat. Rising, he turned and made his way back to the door, then slipped back out into the night.

And discovered he was not alone.

Rourke Douglas, Viscount Kinross, stood waiting for him, his arms crossed over his chest. Two of his kinsmen flanked him, one on either side.

Talon pulled his knife.

Kinross's men pulled knives of their own while Kinross himself just eyed him coldly.

"What were you doing in there, Hertford?"

Too late, Talon realized his mistake. He shouldn't have turned defensive. He should have claimed he was seeking out a lass or some such rot. His thoughts of Julia had him dangerously off balance.

Now that he'd pulled his knife he had no choice but to fight his way out. To kill or be killed.

Rourke held out his hand. "You'll return what you've stolen."

Talon's muscles tensed for the fight. But he hesitated as he'd never done before. Three against one were not the best odds, but he'd managed with worse.

The problem was Julia.

She would never forgive him if he killed Brenna's husband. Jesu, but she'd never forgive him if he killed any of these men.

Deep inside him, the Wizard scowled. *Use the ring to even the odds. Then fight. All that matters is fulfilling the mission. It's all that's ever mattered.*

Until a few days ago, that had been true. Until Julia Brodie dropped into his life and flipped it end over end.

He stared into Rourke Douglas's pale eyes and imagined the bitter anguish in Julia's own if he killed the man. The disappointment he'd already seen in those bonny mismatched eyes had nearly driven him to his knees.

You can be a better man than this.

The Wizard muttered angrily in his head. *She doesn't*

matter. You'll never see her again. Take the damned chal-
ice and do whatever you must to escape Picktillum. What-
ever you must. Sometimes men must die.

But even absent, Julia's presence hovered, sharp and warm beside him, drawing a fierce need in him to be the man she wanted him to be.

With a hard release of air, he shoved his knife into its sheath. He pulled the chalice out from under his waistcoat and held it out to Kinross.

Kinross took the chalice. "Tie him."

Talon bit down hard on his pride as he put his hands behind his back and allowed them to truss him up like a pig for slaughter. Everything inside him railed against giving in. Giving up. But he did it for Julia.

"Wake Brenna," Kinross told one of his men. "And Julia. I'll await them in the solar."

Talon's stomach turned ill. "Leave Julia. She had naught to do with this."

Kinross met his gaze with eyes as cold as frost. "We shall see."

Two of the men grabbed his arms and steered him up the stairs and along the passages like a common criminal. Talon's insides knotted and twisted as he forced himself to submit instead of fight. As his forehead burned with equal measures of anger and shame.

He'd allowed them to take him without a fight. Yet now he was to be forced to stand before Julia, caught and tied, at his lowest since that day twenty years ago when Hegarty first found him.

The disappointment he'd seen in her eyes would take on the hard disgust he'd lived with for the first fifteen years of his life.

In trying to live up to her expectations, he'd become the very thing the world—himself in particular—reviled.

Talon MacClure.

FOURTEEN

"Julia?"

Julia woke to the sound of a soft, feminine query and pried open her gritty eyelids against the weight of too little sleep. A woman stood in the doorway, her face shadowed, but familiar.

"Brenna?" Julia levered herself onto her elbow. "What's wrong?"

"I'm sorry to wake you, but I think you'd better come." Her new friend's words were troubled. Maybe even wary.

Something had happened.

"*Talon.*"

"He's okay, if that's what you're thinking. Rourke has him in the solar."

Has him. The implied *against his will* was left unsaid. He'd been caught stealing the chalice. That was the only explanation.

As Julia climbed from the bed, Brenna crossed the room

to her, holding out what appeared to be a velvet bathrobe. "I thought you might need something to put on. I remember what it's like to have no clothes but the ones on your back."

Brenna's tone lacked the warmth of before, but fell short of actually being cool. As if she'd yet to cast the blame on Julia, too. For now.

Julia pulled on the robe, tied the sash around her waist, and followed Brenna out of the room and down to the solar. Brenna entered first, Julia close behind.

When Julia saw Talon, she stopped, a hard fist tightening around her heart. He was kneeling on the floor, his hands tied behind his back, two of Kinross's men standing on either side of him, pressing his shoulders down, though Talon didn't seem to be struggling. He stared straight ahead, not meeting her gaze, his face a hard, inscrutable mask.

Rourke paced in front of the hearth, his jaw tight and hard. On the table sat the chalice.

The friendliness of before had vanished. They knew Talon for what he was now.

A thief.

Julia looked unhappily from Talon to Rourke, and back again, feeling the weight of her secrets, her earlier silence. Rourke must know she was involved, too, otherwise why would he have had her brought here? Was he intending to tie her, too?

No, he knew she was from the future. He'd know that whatever her involvement, it had been recent and likely unintentional.

"Why did you come to Picktillum?" Rourke demanded, turning to Talon.

Julia looked away, knowing he'd lie and not wanting to hear it.

"I came to find the chalice. To take it back to the man who claims he's the rightful owner."

"And who is that?"

"Niall Brodie, the chieftain of the Brodies of Loch Laggan."

Julia's gaze jerked to him in surprise. "The Brodies of Loch Laggan?"

Rourke's gaze pinned her. "That surprises you?"

"I'm descended from the Brodies of Loch Laggan. My father was the youngest son of the laird. In my . . ." *Time*, she finished silently, her voice dying as she remembered the other men in the room. Men who didn't know she'd come from the future.

The viscount's pale eyes narrowed, but his gaze turned to Talon. "How much of what you told me is the truth? About Hegarty? About Julia?"

Talon turned and met her gaze. Trying to silently warn her not to tell the others the truth, no doubt, though she saw nothing that looked like a warning in his eyes.

No, the look in his eyes didn't feel like a warning, but a plea. A promise.

He turned to look at Rourke. "I'll tell you want you wish to know, but I'll have no audience but you and your viscountess. And Julia."

Kinross looked at him long and hard. "You'll stay on your knees or I'll kill you." The look in those pale, pale eyes promised he'd make good on his word.

Talon nodded.

The viscount motioned his men to the door with a sharp move of his head. "Ye'll be leaving us."

When the door closed behind the two men, Talon met the viscount's pale gaze. "Little of what I told ye was the truth." His eyes swung to Julia.

Again, she felt that promise. As if the words he meant to say were for her and her alone.

"I wear Hegarty's ring," he said quietly. The truth. He'd given Rourke the truth. As a gift, his eyes said. A gift for her.

A sweet warmth fluttered over her skin. Soft emotion caressed her heart and made her eyes ache as she held his gaze.

Dear God, he'd *let* himself be captured, she realized. He hadn't fought them.

For her.

What if they killed him?

"You came into my house to steal from me?" Rourke asked coldly.

"Aye."

Rourke motioned to the chalice. "How did you know where to find that thing? How did you know it was here?"

"As I said, I wear Hegarty's ring."

"Magic," Brenna said softly. "Were you in the future, too?"

"Nay."

"Then why did he give it to you?"

Talon shrugged. "I was a lad."

Brenna nodded. "Hegarty seems to have a soft spot for children in need. I'd assumed he'd sent them all to the future."

"The ring provided the things I needed. I've learned to make it help me . . . find things."

"What things?" Rourke demanded coldly.

Talon met his gaze, his mouth hardening. "Whatever I'm paid to retrieve."

Rourke stilled, his eyes widening with understanding. "You're the Wizard." A small, humorless laugh escaped his throat.

"Aye."

Silence reigned for another minute, then the viscount swung that pale gaze to her.

"How did Julia get here?"

Talon took a deep breath and let it out in a single harsh

rush. "The ring called her. Apparently the amethyst has the ability to call the other stones. Why it called her to me, I've yet to discover. I ask the ring for something and it gives me a clue. Or a tool, which it takes away again when I'm done with it. I believe the amethyst will send her home when she's performed whatever task it brought her here for."

Brenna made a sound of disbelief. "I can't believe Hegarty hasn't come for your ring yet. He's already taken my sapphire."

"He's come for it." Talon met Julia's gaze again. "He's come for both of our stones."

Julia started. "When?"

"Last night. In the inn. You were sound asleep. He couldna wake you and he couldna take the stone from you without your consent."

"If I'd been awake . . . he would have sent me home?"

Talon nodded. "Aye." He swallowed and looked away, breaking the bond of their gazes. "He knows you dinna belong here. He'll send you home."

"He didn't try to take your ring?"

His gaze swung back to her. "He tried. I kicked him out of the inn." His face grew hard. *"He'll not take my ring."*

Brenna frowned. "So you didn't know our connection to Hegarty when you came to Picktillum?"

"Nay," Talon said. "The ring told me this was where I would find the chalice I've been sent to find. And it was."

"Seems massively coincidental, doesn't it?" Brenna asked.

Julia looked at her. "What do you mean?"

"Hegarty's ring sends you to Hertford—"

"Talon."

Brenna nodded. "Hegarty's ring sends you to Talon, then

the two of you to us. Maybe it really is just a coincidence, but it seems unlikely, doesn't it?"

Rourke picked up the chalice and ran his thumb across the inch-long etchings around the rim. "I've never seen this thing before."

"Then how did it get here?" Brenna asked.

"I dinna ken." Kinross handed the chalice to Brenna, then pulled out a long, wicked-looking knife and turned to Talon.

Julia froze.

Brenna gasped. "*Rourke*."

But while Talon watched him carefully, he didn't seem concerned.

Rourke scowled. "I'm just going to untie him." When he'd cut Talon's ropes, he said, "Have a seat."

Talon nodded once and rose. "Niall Brodie claims the chalice, the Fire Chalice of Veskin, is theirs, stolen sometime within the past twenty years. He doesn't know when it was taken or by whom. The Brodies didn't realize it was missing until recently and don't know how long it's been gone."

"So, when you were hired to find it, your ring told you to come here?"

Talon snorted. "In a roundabout, pain-in-the-arse way. The ring does as the ring does."

"Sounds like a Hegarty ring," Brenna muttered.

"Can I see the chalice?" Julia asked, intensely curious about the thing now.

Brenna handed it to her. Julia expected to feel cool metal. But as her fingers came in contact with the gold, shock ripped up her hands and into her arms, an electrical current that short-circuited her brain.

Her vision went black.

And suddenly she wasn't in the castle anymore, but a

dark, firelit cave. A cave that smelled of copper and ex-crement and fear.

Shadows danced on walls splattered in bright red paint.

No, not paint.

Blood.

Talon lunged for Julia, grabbing her before she fell. As he swept her into his arms, the chalice fell from her fingers to land with a thud on the tapestry that adorned the floor.

"*Julia.*"

Her lashes fluttered up, her eyes dark against a face as pale as death. Eyes filled with horror. But she was alive and he could breathe again.

"What happened?" she asked, her gaze catching his and clinging.

"'Tis what we all wish to know," Rourke said.

Talon felt a shudder go through her. "Easy, lass. You're safe." He lowered himself to the sofa, holding her tight against his chest.

Julia hooked her arm around his neck, making no move to leave him. "I saw something. A cave. Blood."

"Do you get visions like this often?" Brenna asked.

"No. Never." She was shaking even as perspiration dampened her brow.

"Do you think it was the chalice?" Brenna asked. "Or the necklace? Or maybe the combination of the two? We *are* dealing with Hegarty's magic, after all."

Julia sat up straighter, her fingers going to the jewel at her throat as she looked at Brenna. "Do you think if I take it off, I won't see the blood?"

Brenna shrugged. "I have no idea. I was just wondering out loud."

Julia's fingers closed around the small stone—the thing

that had sent her through time and would send her home again. Her thumb brushed over the smooth surface. Taking a deep breath, she pulled it off over her head.

Talon held out his hand, wondering if she would trust him with it this time. Without hesitation, she dropped it into his palm, then made a move as if to rise off his lap to retrieve the chalice.

He held her fast, unwilling to let her go.

As if reading his mind, Brenna picked up the chalice and handed it to him.

Julia reached for it, then stilled, her arm tightening around his neck as if afraid to touch it again.

"You don't have to do this," he told her softly.

She glanced at him, meeting his gaze with troubled eyes. "I need to know." With another deep breath, she reached for the chalice. The moment her fingers touched the gold, she jerked, then froze. Her eyes started to roll back into her head.

Talon yanked the cursed cup out of her hands and dropped it to the floor, gathering her tight against him. Her head fell to his shoulder, but she groaned, telling him she remained conscious.

"Julia?" he asked worriedly.

"I saw . . . the cave again, only . . ."

When she didn't immediately reply, Talon gently ran his fingers into her hair, pushing it back from her face. "What, lass? Only . . . what?"

"It was different. Daylight instead of firelight."

"No blood this time?"

She shuddered and he pulled her closer. "Lots of blood, the same as before. But something else this time. A foot. Just . . . a severed, bloody foot. A girl's, I think."

"Perhaps some kind of animal got to her." Talon pressed her head to his shoulder and stroked it gently as her body began to tremble violently.

"Did anyone else see it?" Julia asked softly.

"Nay. Only you. You've a gift, lass. Mayhap the chalice is the conduit."

"More Hegarty magic," Brenna muttered.

"A gift?" Julia snorted. "Where can I return it?"

Talon rubbed his chin over hair. "Perhaps you're seeing the future. Or the past."

Julia made a sound of dismay. "Do you think this is why the ring called me? Because I'm supposed to see something in the chalice?"

"I canna say. But you needn't touch it again if ye dinna wish to."

She shuddered. "I don't. Ever."

"I'm with you," Brenna said softly. "Do we really need this thing, Rourke?"

"Nay." The viscount shook his head. "Take it with you when you go, Wizard. I dinna ken why that thing is in my home, but I want it gone. If the Brodie wants it, the Brodie can have it."

Talon nodded. Finally, he had what he wanted. What he'd come for. Yet he felt no satisfaction. No elation.

It was time to go. Time to take the chalice and leave Julia behind. Hegarty would see her safely home. He believed that.

But his hands refused to loosen their grip on the woman in his arms. He met Rourke's gaze. "May I remain until first light?" He stroked Julia's hair. "Until I'm certain she's recovered?"

Rourke studied him for a moment, then nodded.

Talon rested his chin lightly on the top of her head, feeling as if his chest would cave. How was he to leave her behind?

"You'll see that Hegarty sends her home?"

Rourke nodded. "We will." His gaze swung to Brenna. "We'll go to Old Inghinn on the morrow."

Brenna's face fell, but she gave a nod that quickly dissolved into a yawn. "I'd love to stay up and chat, but I'm nearly asleep on my feet. Julia, do you want me to stay with you tonight? Or . . ." She met Talon's gaze.

Talon's grip on Julia tightened.

Julia raised her head. "I'm feeling better. I'll be fine, Brenna. Thanks." But as she started to rise from his lap, Talon caught her tight against him and rose. "I'll carry ye back to your chamber, lass."

"You don't have to do that." But she hooked her arm around his neck and held on.

"Aye, I do."

Rourke picked up the chalice. "I'll put this somewhere safe tonight and give it to you in the morning."

Talon nodded his thanks. He didn't want the thing anywhere near Julia, but he refused to release her to take it. Not until he had to.

As Talon carried Julia back to her chamber, he felt her fingers in his hair, the sweet touch stealing a measure of the chill that had come over him when she'd walked into the solar to find him on his knees.

The press of her soft lips to his temple dispelled the rest of the cold. "Thank you for telling them the truth. It meant a lot to me that you did that."

"Aye. 'Tis the reason I did."

He felt her smile, and felt her head brush his own. "I know."

When they reached her door, she lifted her head and met his gaze. "Come in with me." Her eyes glowed with a softness that wove through his heart and a heat that had the blood pumping hard through his veins.

Her cool fingers trailed down his cheek. "If this is our last night together, I want . . ." She looked away, a shyness stealing over her features. Finding her courage, she again met his gaze. "I want you to teach me what it can be like. I want . . ."

She pressed her cheek to his and whispered in his ear. "I want you to make love to me. Stay with me, Talon."

As his body caught fire, he squeezed her close to his chest, wondering how he was ever going to live without her.

FIFTEEN

Julia clung tightly to Talon's neck as he carried her into her room. All her life she'd told herself she didn't need anyone. All her life she'd lied.

Sadness swept over her as she pressed her head against his, filling her lungs with his scent, a scent that had become increasingly familiar. Increasingly dear.

How was she going to stand it, knowing she'd never see him again? Knowing that the moment she returned to her own time, he'd be long dead?

Her arms tightened around his neck. In the morning he'd leave and she'd stay, waiting for Hegarty to come and send her home.

She'd never see Talon again.

Talon pushed the door closed with his shoulder, then strode with her to the bed. She looked up at him in the dim glow of the hearth embers. A shiver tore through her at the thought of giving herself to him totally. Was she sure she wanted to do this? The thing was, she knew *he* wanted to. And the thought of giving him this ultimate gift—her body and her trust—filled her with a sweet pleasure all its own.

A gift. To the man who'd shown her caring and friendship, loyalty and tenderness, when no one else ever had.

A gift. To the man she'd come to care for beyond anything that was wise.

She'd never thought of sex as a gift. There had never been anyone she'd wanted to give herself to. It didn't matter that she wouldn't enjoy the act itself. Holding him in her arms as he found pleasure and release in her body was enough.

Talon laid her gently on the bed, then turned away.

"Talon . . ." Was he leaving? Hadn't he understood? But as she sat up, she realized he was only going to the hearth to put on another log.

He tossed the wood on the embers, sending sparks leaping and flying, then rose and returned to her, his walk strong and sure, his face in shadow. But when he reached the bed, he didn't take her into his arms. He didn't try to undress her . . . or himself. Instead, he sat on the edge of the bed, facing her, his thigh brushing hers.

When he lifted his hand it was only to trail his knuckles softly down her cheek. "You're so beautiful, Julia-lass. I don't ever want to forget you."

She reached up and took his hand, then pulled it to her mouth and kissed his knuckles. Her heart began to flutter in her chest like a trapped bird. She was as inexperienced at seduction as a virgin.

"Make love to me, Talon." She couldn't quite force herself to meet his gaze, but she felt him watching her intently.

He made no move to comply, and she was suddenly afraid he didn't want her after all. With his free hand, he slid his fingers into her hair, cradling her head.

"Look at me, Julia." When she forced herself to, his gaze bore into hers as if he were trying to delve into her mind. "Why, lass? Why do ye want me?"

She watched him uncertainly. "You don't want me?"

"Aye, I do. More than anything. But what do you want?"

Her gaze fell to his chest. "I want . . . to hold you. While you find pleasure."

His thumb traced soft circles on her cheek. "And what of your pleasure?"

"I'll find mine, too," she added hastily, suddenly remembering all the talk in movies and magazines about women faking orgasms to spare their partner's pride. Could she do that? Fake an orgasm? Probably. She'd seen *When Harry Met Sally* three times.

The problem was, Talon had made her come for real last night in the inn and she'd been so out of control, she didn't have any idea what sounds she'd made, or how she'd acted. She had no way of knowing how to duplicate that.

Would he know the difference? Could guys tell these things?

Talon continued to stroke her cheek, watching her as if reading her thoughts. If he didn't make a move soon, she was going to lose her nerve. Shoving through deep layers of inhibitions, she reached down between his legs and slid her fingers along the thick ridge of him. The thick, *huge* ridge of him.

Talon sucked in a hard breath.

Julia's hand recoiled at the thought of that thickness pressing painfully inside her.

"Lass, ye needn't . . ."

"I want to."

"Julia." He framed her face, looking deeply into her eyes. "I think ye do. But I think ye don't." His thumbs stroked her cheeks. "Ye can stop it at any time, aye? Tell me to stop and I will."

"I'm not a virgin, Talon."

He continued to hold her face, touching her as if he held a rare orchid in his hands. "Aye, ye are. In all the ways that matter, you are."

His words made her chest ache and her cheeks burn. He understood more than she had herself. That she was afraid. That those early sexual experiences had been too much, too young.

"We'll go slow, lass," Talon said quietly. "'Twill be unlike before. I vow it. This will be your first time." He gave her an impish grin. "If ye want your maidenhead back, I'll ask the ring for it."

Despite his grin, she realized that if she asked him to do that for her, he would.

She smiled softly. "No thanks. That first time was the worst."

"It always is." His eyes turned serious and he slowly leaned in to kiss her, a featherlight brush of lips on lips that sent pleasurable shivers tripping through every cell in her body. For long moments he kissed her, nothing more. As if that was all he wanted, as if that was all sex was about. His mouth on hers, plundering, sweeping, stroking. A simple touch that lit fires in her limbs, her chest, her abdomen, and deep down low until she felt the tension building, her body turning restless. Needy.

Unhurriedly, his hands began to roam. Into her hair, over her shoulders, down her back, avoiding the critical zones, taking it slow. Building the heat and the excitement, without triggering her natural defenses. On a purely logical level, she understood he was deliberately easing her along, intentionally not pushing too fast.

His approach was masterful. His patience and gentleness melted her, strengthening her wish to give him anything. Everything. She'd been prepared to take nothing in return. Instead, he was the one giving to her.

His mouth dipped, his lips claimed her neck, and all thought fled. With a gentle tug of his fingers, her bathrobe fell open. Her shift slipped. His mouth covered her bare shoulder and desire skyrocketed.

She felt his fingers at the ties of her shift, loosening the neck further. Then cool air slid across her bared breast. As his thumb brushed her sensitive nipple, she sucked in a trembling breath, loving the feel, even as she watched his head dip.

Just as he'd done last night, he took her breast deeply into his mouth. Her head fell back as she absorbed this intimate and wonderful touch.

"Talon," she said on a gasp. "You don't have to do all this if you don't want to. You can take your pleasure."

He lifted his face, peering into hers with a heavy-lidded, lazy grin. "This is my pleasure." He planted a small, sweet kiss on the end of her nose. "There is nothing more exciting to me than watching your passion rise, hearing your breathing change, listening to your quick gasps and low moans as I touch you. As I lick you."

He pressed a kiss to the curve between her neck and shoulder and she tilted her head away, giving him full access.

"The only thing I would ask, when you're ready, is that ye allow me to undress you. I wish to see you, Julia. All of ye."

His voice throbbed with such carnal pleasure, she felt answering pulses all the way to her womb.

"Undress me, Talon."

A smile broke across his face, a smile at once sweet and dangerous and oh so hot. He pulled off his shirt first, revealing that beautiful body once more. He pulled off his boots, then turned to her.

His expression, as he pushed the robe from her shoulders, was fiercely tender. He tugged the sleeves off her arms, then rose to his feet and pulled her to hers. The bathrobe pooled on the bed behind her. Talon lifted her shift up and over her head, baring her to his sight with one quick movement.

Julia stood before him as she'd never stood before a man. Naked. And strangely, amazingly, comfortable in that fact.

His eyes roamed her body, lighting fires everywhere his gaze caressed her. "So bonny." He gathered her to him then, pulling her tight, flesh to flesh.

With a low sound of impatience, he swept her into his arms and deposited her in the middle of the bed, then followed her down. His lips were everywhere, grazing her shoulder, her neck, the hollow between her breasts.

He took her in his arms and rolled her to her side as he kissed her, his hand sliding over her hip and her buttocks. His fingers stroked her flesh, digging in firmly, tensely, as if he wanted to do more but was determined to take it slow. His deeply sensuous ministrations sent the pressure building inside her.

Slowly, his hand began to move again, sliding down the back of her thigh, sending her heart soaring and her body weeping with excitement.

His fingers curled around her knee and he lifted her leg, pulling it to rest on his hip, opening her. Little by little, as her breathing grew ragged, his fingers slid the length of her inner thigh toward the aching, throbbing source of her heat.

The first brush of his finger along her swollen lips made her jump, then moan with pleasure, even as her body tensed for what was yet to come.

But Talon, she was beginning to realize, had infinite stores of patience. Over and over, he stroked her heated flesh, flicking the nub of her clitoris, moving away, then flicking it again. Each finger stroke along that open line moved easier. Slicker. Every stroke of her clitoris made her arch and gasp until she feared she'd forget how to breathe.

And all the while he kissed her—her throat, her forehead, her cheek.

The first dip of his finger inside her sent sensation exploding outward from her core in a brilliant arc, eliciting a harsh groan and sending her hips thrusting to meet him, to deepen his claim on her body.

"*Talon.*"

"Ye like that."

"Oh God, yes. More."

His finger dove deeper, stroking her sensitive inner walls, then circling around and around, sending her into a swirling mass of pleasure and need.

As his head dipped to pull her breast into his mouth, his finger pulled out of her, only to return, thicker, fuller than before. Not until it moved in two directions at once, fluttering insanely, wonderfully, did she realize he'd pushed two fingers inside her this time. Pleasure danced deep within her with the fluttering of his fingers until she lost control, gasping and rocking against his hand. Deep inside, she felt things tightening. Rising.

"Talon, I want more. I *need* more."

He released her breast and lifted up to look down into her face. In his eyes she saw a deep, tender satisfaction. On his mouth a small, devilishly sweet smile.

"Do ye want me inside you?"

"Yes. You. Only you."

He pulled his fingers from her depths and stood, shucking his pants, revealing a long, hard erection. She'd expected the sight of him to fill her with dread, as the feel of him had initially, but as aroused as she was, the sight of him had the opposite effect. Amazingly, the thought of that length and breadth spreading her, filling her, only excited her more.

He came to her and she opened her arms and thighs for him, sliding her hands around his broad shoulders as he settled between her legs.

But he didn't enter her right away. Instead, he took her head in his hands and stared down into her face, his own a tense mask of barely leashed passion and precious gentleness.

"Now, Talon. Come to me."

He kissed her, capturing her mouth even as she felt the hard press of silken flesh against her slick opening. He pressed forward, the pressure building, building, millimeter by millimeter, but she felt no pain. Only unimaginable pleasure.

He took her slowly, with infinite care, then pulled out and repeated the process only slightly faster than before. As he pressed all the way into her, his tongue sliding against hers, a feeling of profound rightness enveloped her. She'd always known the others had been a mistake, but she hadn't realized just how big a mistake. Until now.

And yet, it wouldn't have mattered if she'd been older. Or if she'd cared for them. Deep inside, she knew Talon was the one she'd been waiting for. The only one who would ever matter.

Over and over, he pulled out and pushed into her again, faster and faster, filling her, delighting her, driving her toward that bright, spectacular release he'd brought her to last night. She met him thrust for thrust, the desperation building inside her to join with him on the most fundamental level, to become one with this man who was beginning to mean everything to her.

Her chest swelled with emotion even as her body rose.

His thrusts grew faster, harder, and she urged him on, rocking to meet him, groaning every time with the pure, exquisite joy pulsing through her. The pressure started up again, building and twisting, up and up until the orgasm tore through her, a cataclysm that unraveled her and knit her back together again in a different pattern than before. Whole, as she'd never been.

As Talon groaned with his own release, she felt reborn.

For minutes on end, they lay there, joined, their breathing and pulse rates slowly falling back to normal.

Finally, Talon pulled out of her, then rolled onto his back, taking her with him. He held her cradled against his chest, his hands sliding from the nape of her neck, down to her thighs, and back again.

"Ye felt pleasure this time," he said softly. It wasn't a question.

Julia lifted her head and grazed her lips along his jaw. "Amazing. Incredible." She nestled her head on his shoulder, too spent to keep it lifted. "I didn't know it could be like that."

Deep inside, she knew it would never be again. Because never again would it be with Talon.

The stab of pain was sudden and harsh. The thought of leaving him pressed down on her, a terrible weight on her chest. She curled her arm around him, clinging to him, feeling devastated. And painfully confused.

She had to get home. And she knew the way now. All she had to do was stay here and wait for Hegarty.

But the thought of leaving Talon filled her with a dull, aching grief. "I wish I could take you back with me."

His hand slid down her bare back. "Nay. I dinna belong in that place." His words held no spark of interest. Nothing but aversion. Even if Hegarty agreed, and there was no reason to think he might, Talon would never want to leave this place for one where he was a complete and total outsider. Where he was powerless. Without understanding or knowledge. Over his head.

No, that wasn't Talon, she was certain.

Besides, only Hegarty could send him there, and he

would certainly demand the amethyst in return. A thing Talon would never agree to.

When she went home, she'd be going alone.

If only she could delay that inevitability a little longer. A few more days. A few more nights.

Her body went very still.

Why *not* stay a little longer? What difference would it make at home? She was already missing. And she'd already passed the point of being able to make it home in time for her presentation.

What did she have to rush home to anyway? An empty apartment? A job she was seriously considering quitting?

Why not stay a few more days? By then, she'd be sick to death of this place and more than ready to go home. Maybe by then, she'd be ready to leave Talon. And even if she felt the same as she did now, she'd have a few more memories to take out and replay during those long, lonely nights at home.

"Talon?"

His hand sifted through her hair. "Hm?"

She lifted her head, needing to see his eyes. "If I go with you to deliver the chalice to Loch Laggan, will you bring me back here afterward?"

His hand stilled in her hair. "Ye dinna wish to go home?" His voice was thick with confusion.

"I do. Just . . . maybe not yet. I was thinking . . . the ring brought me to you for a reason, right? Yet we don't know what that reason is. You may still need me. What if you still need me?"

Slowly, he rolled her off his chest and back onto the bed, then rose and walked to the hearth. His naked body in the firelight was a sight to behold, but the tenseness of his walk had her wishing she hadn't said anything.

"I dinna think it's a good idea." His voice was flat.

That horrible, all too familiar feeling of rejection sliced

through her and she clenched her jaw tight against the ache.

"It was just a thought," she said diffidently, and climbed from the bed to retrieve her shift, keeping her back turned to him as she fought against the crushing emotion she couldn't bear for him to see.

As the shift slid down around her hips, she felt Talon's hand on her arm. He tugged her around, the expression on his face at once soft and oh-so-serious.

His hands curved around her shoulders. "It's not that I dinna want ye to come, Julia-lass. I do. More than ye ken, I want ye by my side for a wee bit longer. But ye react to that chalice and I dinna care for it. There's more going on here than I ken, and I will not have ye harmed."

The tight band of misery began to loosen. "The fact that I react to it, or it to me, is all the more reason you need me to stay. It's all the more reason I want to stay. I'm a Brodie, Talon. A Brodie of Loch Laggan. This is my family's history we're talking about, my clan's. I want to understand it."

"Have ye forgotten your own cousin fled that place twenty years ago? Hegarty wouldna have sent her to the future if she'd not been in need. Most likely, in danger."

"That was twenty years ago. The danger could have been anything." She met his gaze. "I have to go home. We both know that. And once I do, I won't be coming back." She lifted her hand to his cheek. "I'm not ready to leave you." She smiled at him faintly, impudently. "Besides, I'm not sure I have the hang of the lovemaking. I need a little more practice."

His mouth kicked up, his dimples flashing. "I'll have no quibbles about giving ye that practice, though you've proved to be a fine pupil." As his expression turned once more serious, he cupped her jaw in his hand. "I'm a selfish man, Julia. I always have been." His thumb brushed her chin. "I should make you stay here where you'll be safe. But nay, I want you to come. If you want to be with me longer, I want you to come."

He lowered his head and kissed her, and she kissed him back. Then he lifted her into his arms and put her to bed, climbing in with her and holding her close.

As his arm went around her, it occurred to her she didn't know how far Loch Laggan was from here, or how long a trip they were talking about. With a mental groan, she accepted that she was looking at more days of riding horses and sleeping on lumpy mattresses. Or hard ground. More days of relieving herself behind bushes and forgoing all but the basics of personal hygiene.

But she'd be with Talon, spending her nights lying with his arm tight around her. Welcoming him into her body and knowing the most exquisite pleasure and rightness.

Yes, she was nuts. But it was only for a short while, then her life would return to what it had been. And all she'd have of this time would be the memories.

"Are you sure you want to do this?" Brenna asked Julia the next morning. "So many things could go wrong. Highwaymen, disease. Drunks who'd rather stab you than look at you. Sometimes I think they kill one another just to relieve the monotony of their lives. I'm tempted to invent the game of soccer just to give them something better to do."

Julia smiled softly, then sobered. "I've seen the violence, Brenna. I get it."

Why did she feel so close to this woman she barely knew? No doubt because she was the only one in the entire world who understood the place she'd come from. But it was more than that. She genuinely liked Brenna and wished she could have the time to get to know her better. It would be nice to have a friend.

Julia shrugged. "I know I'm taking a risk. But I'm not quite ready for this experience to end."

Brenna eyed her shrewdly. "You're not ready to leave Talon, are you? You've fallen in love with him."

"No, I just . . . Oh God." She stared at the other woman. "Maybe I have."

Brenna took her hand and squeezed it, her eyes filling with sympathy. "It's a terrible position to be in, isn't it? I thought I was going to have to leave Rourke." She shrugged. "I thought he was going to leave me. I was wrong on both counts."

"But you belonged here all along even if you didn't know it."

"Yes."

And she didn't. The unspoken words hung between them.

Brenna squeezed her hand again and released her. "I'm sorry, Julia. I understand why you want to spend a little more time with him, just . . . be careful, okay? And when you get back, I'll treat you to a Mexican feast."

The twinkle in Brenna's eye had Julia smiling. "Mexican? In seventeenth-century Scotland?"

Brenna laughed. "The entire time I was pregnant I craved Mexican food, so I worked like a fiend to replicate it here and I've done a pretty decent job, I have to say. The problem is no one else has acquired a taste for it." She looked at her hopefully. "Do you like Mexican food?"

Julia grinned. "I love it."

"Good. I'll start gathering my spices so I'll be ready when you get back. It's a plan." Brenna reached for her, giving her a big, heartfelt hug.

Julia surprised herself by returning the hug in full measure. She usually wasn't the kind of person anyone wanted to hug. But Brenna . . . Brenna was special.

Julia smiled. "I'll be back soon."

"Be prepared, I fully intend to talk you into extending

your vacation even longer, and spending some time with me."

"I'd like that." And she meant it.

As they walked together to where Talon waited with Rourke and the horses, a small thrill of excitement fluttered within her. Excitement at the thought of seeing Castle Ythan in its prime. Of meeting her ancestors a dozen generations back. Of possibly discovering the reason the ring had called her to help Talon.

And the warm, pleasurable excitement that being with Talon always brought her.

Talon smiled at her, his dimple flashing as he took her hand and helped her mount. As his hands slipped from her waist, Rourke stepped forward and handed Talon something wrapped in cloth.

An unpleasant sensation prickled her skin.

"The chalice," Rourke murmured, his gaze swinging to her with concern.

Talon nodded. "My thanks." He moved to his own horse and mounted.

"Are you sure you won't take a couple of my kinsmen?" Rourke asked.

"My thanks, but no." The old charmer's smile spread across Talon's face. "My methods havena failed me yet." He was speaking of his ring, Julia knew.

Rourke didn't look convinced, but nodded.

With a backward wave, they said good-bye to the Viscount and Viscountess Kinross and headed for Loch Laggan.

As they started across the open moor, Julia looked back at Picktillum Castle and wondered if she was making a mistake by leaving the one place she had friends, the one place she was safe. The one place from where she was certain she could get home.

Instead, she rode into the unknown.

But as her gaze met Talon's and something infinitely warm, infinitely deep passed between them, she knew those other reasons paled in comparison to the main one. With a certainty born of all the days she'd spent alone, she knew she simply wasn't ready to leave the man with whom she'd fallen in love.

SIXTEEN

Within three hours of leaving Picktillum, the wind picked up, the temperature dropped, and the rain started. Julia began to have serious second thoughts about this journey, wondering if she'd made a mistake in coming with Talon. By the time they found a room and stopped for the night, she was sure of it.

Not only was she cold and wet, but she was hugely out of sorts. She'd been in such a good mood as they'd prepared to ride out from Picktillum. But her mood had begun to deteriorate almost at once and hadn't gotten any better all day. If she didn't know better, she'd think she was PMSing, but she'd finished her period only a few days before the wedding, thank God. What in the hell would she do about her period *here*? Although, maybe she *was* PMSing. How did she know the time traveling hadn't screwed up her cycle, too?

Then again, they'd done the deed last night with no

protection whatsoever. For all she knew, she could be pregnant.

Hell. That's all she needed.

At least she knew *that* wasn't the cause of her bitchiness. Even if she were pregnant, it was way too soon for her body to be reacting to it.

Talon ushered her into the room he'd paid for in the hovel-sized farmhouse in the middle of godforsaken *nowhere*. He pressed against her, his hand at her back.

"In ye go, lass."

"I'm in. Jeez, Talon, it's the size of a closet." A low-slung, tiny bed sat against the far wall—a wall she could practically reach out and touch from the doorway. A tiny hearth sat in the corner beside an even smaller shuttered window. Tucked behind the door was a washstand. And that was it.

Julia slid toward the hearth to allow Talon room to enter.

He closed the door behind him and shrugged. "'Tis this or sleep in the rain."

Julia scowled. "And they don't even have a bathtub?" She'd made a point of asking while Talon paid for the room.

"They've a burn."

"A creek. A freeze-your-ass-off, fishy-smelling creek."

Talon gave her a hard look, then pulled the cloak over his head and laid it on top of the washstand. "Take off yer wet garments, Julia," he said coolly, clearly not enjoying her foul mood any more than she was.

Which only annoyed her more.

"Can you at least get us some food? I'm starving."

"Aye." Without a backward glance, he left her.

With a growl of frustration, she pulled off her soaking-wet cloak and laid it on top of his. They would still be soaked in the morning this way, but there was nowhere to hang anything up. Not in this mouse hole.

She took a deep breath through her nose and let it out slowly. The tension inside her started to unwind a bit and she squatted in front of the small hearth, seeking whatever warmth it had to provide.

Coming with Talon had seemed like such a good idea at the time. One night in his arms and she'd forgotten all about the horses and the cold rain and the miserable sleeping arrangements.

How were they ever going to sleep in here? There wasn't room for two people to stretch out even if they removed all the furniture.

But she sighed, no longer feeling like hitting someone over it. This, too, shall pass. Eventually. Not until midafternoon had she thought to ask Talon how long a trip she'd signed up for. Five days, he'd told her. Each way.

Good grief.

Talon pushed back through the door, two bowls in his hands and a small loaf of bread under his arm.

Her skin prickled with annoyance, though what she was annoyed about, she couldn't begin to guess. It was as if the sight of him was beginning to set her off.

Great.

It was going to be a damned long ten days.

They ate the tasteless gruel perched on the edge of the bed, in silence, her annoyance growing for no discernible reason. If she got her period, she was going to be royally pissed.

"That was the worst meal I've ever eaten." She ground her teeth together, but the anger wouldn't be contained. "Where in the hell are we supposed to sleep, anyway?"

"Ye'll take the bed and ye'll not worry about me."

"You're just going to play martyr?"

"Would ye rather take the floor?"

"You can't sleep on the floor." Her hand swept out, nearly hitting him. "There isn't enough of it."

Talon took the empty bowl from her fingers and set the pair of them atop the cloaks on the washstand. Then he turned to her. "What ails ye, Julia?"

She scowled as she looked away. "I shouldn't have come. I wish I hadn't come."

Talon sighed. "I've no time to take ye back. I vowed to have the chalice to Loch Laggan in a fortnight. We'll barely make it if we press on. I'll lose two days if I return ye to Picktillum first."

"Why is it so damned important to deliver that thing on time?"

"Would ye have me break my vow?" He looked at her intently. "Would you break you own?"

She gave him a baleful stare, then looked away. "No. If I make a commitment, I move heaven and earth to meet it."

"Aye."

"What if I stay here, God forbid? Or find my own way back?"

"Have ye already forgotten what can happen to a lass? Even a lass with a man at her side. Ye'll not travel alone, Julia. I'll not allow it. Ye'll be staying with me."

She glared at him. "Who in the hell do you think you are . . . ?"

He grabbed her shoulders and hauled her against him, kissing her, stealing the words from her mouth. She stiffened, his high-handedness only exacerbating her already foul mood, but at the taste of his mouth, desire rushed through her, sweeping away the frustration that had built within her during the miserable day.

With deft hands, he divested them of their damp clothes, setting atop the pile the chalice that had been tied to his belt all day. Then he took her into his arms, his body heat stealing the last of her chill. The restlessness that had plagued her all day took another form, turning her needy and impatient. She pressed her hips against him, against the thick, hard erection trapped between their bodies.

"I want you, Talon," she said fiercely against his mouth.

"Aye, Julia-lass. And ye'll have me."

Their bodies smelled rain-damp and earthy, but she found she didn't mind the smell at all. Talon's hands caressed her back, one sliding into her hair, the other diving lower to cup her rear. He pulled her hard against him, rubbing himself against her stomach, letting her feel how badly he wanted her.

Heat gathered low in her body. Moisture dampened her upper thighs.

"Talon, *I need you.*"

He pressed her down onto the bed, but instead of following her down as she'd expected, as she wanted, he knelt on the floor beside her and took her breast into his mouth. She felt his hand slide between her legs, pulling her knee outward to open her for him. Then his fingers were playing in her wetness, burying themselves inside her body.

She arched into his intimate touch, lifting her hips to deepen the penetration as she buried her fingers in his hair. Her body was on fire, desperate for his touch, desperate to be filled.

All day, she'd done nothing but snap at him and complain, yet he touched her with hunger and tender care.

"I'm sorry I've been such a bitch today." She gasped as his fingers fluttered inside her. "Such a shrew."

His mouth released her breast. "Wheesht, lass," he said softly. "'Twas a trying day." He licked her nipple, then lifted his face to look down into her own. His thumb brushed her clitoris, making her jerk and moan as he watched her. A devilishly satisfied smile lit his eyes and lifted his mouth, making one of his dimples peep. "And ye'll forget the day now. Ye'll forget all but me."

He lowered his face to hers and kissed her thoroughly, his tongue sweeping inside her mouth as his fingers continued to play. The tension between her legs built, her hips grinding restlessly against his hand, seeking the release he was driving her toward.

Without warning, he pulled his hand away and covered her body with his.

"I want ye, Julia-lass." His blue-eyed gaze bore into hers, holding her captive as he slowly slid inside her, filling her. Making them one.

Over and over, he thrust into her as she lifted her hips to meet him. All the emotion she felt for him welled up, pressing against the inner walls of her heart until she thought it would burst.

"I love you," she said softly against his shoulder. The release broke over her and she cried out with pleasure, arching into him, pressing him deeper.

Moments later, she felt his body tense as he pressed harder, thrust faster, then shuddered, a low sound of deep satisfaction rumbling from his throat. He'd found his release, but instead of holding her as he had last night, he pushed off her and reached for his pants.

Julia watched in confusion as he turned his back to her and pulled them on, then tied the chalice at his belt, as it had been all day, and reached for his shirt.

"What are you doing?"

He pulled the shirt over his head and down over the chalice. "I'll be back. Sleep." Without another word, without meeting her gaze, he left.

She stretched languorously, her body feeling sated and wonderful, even as she glanced at the closed door. Was something wrong? Had he heard something that had spurred him to investigate?

She sat up slowly, a vague disquiet niggling her brain.

Everything had been normal between them, perfect, until he'd come. And bolted.

Right after . . .

Oh, no.

Right after she'd told him she loved him. Was *that* why he'd left like that? Surely not. He knew she didn't mean to stay here. It wasn't like she was going to try to trap him into marriage or anything.

But she was suddenly sure it was those three words that had sent him running.

A sick feeling curled in her stomach, a deep and painful hurt. Because clearly he didn't feel the same.

Damn him.

Never before had she told someone she loved him. Her father hadn't wanted the words and no one else had ever mattered. Why couldn't Talon have pretended? Or just said thank you or something.

Why had he had to make it so blasted obvious he hadn't wanted to hear the words?

She rose and pulled on her shift. It didn't matter whether he loved her back, dammit.

But the pressure in her chest intensified until she could barely breathe around it.

Nine more days of this hell, then she'd be back at Pick-tillum. She'd be going home.

Then maybe this miserable feeling would finally go away.

Talon stood in the dark, the cool wind blowing his hair back from his face, doing nothing to ease the turmoil inside him. His head pounded, his belly ached. His ribs felt as sore as if he'd been pinned beneath a horse.

She loved him.

And he was naught but a lie.

His body still thrilled with the aftereffects of their love-making, a joining sweeter even than last night's. Sweeter than any he'd ever known, for it had been more than merely a coming together of two bodies. A melding of person, of spirit. Of being.

He felt changed. Reborn. As if, for a few bright moments, he'd become the man she wanted him to be.

For a brief few moments, his heart had sung, his spirits had soared before crashing to the dirt like a bird with a damaged wing. Battered. Splintered.

The man she thought she loved didn't exist.

He clenched his fists at his sides and arched his back, pulling the damp night air into his lungs and exhaling hard, as if he could free himself from the confusion within him.

In a handful of days, she'd upended his world.

He should have left her at Picktillum, where she'd have been safe. Where he wouldn't have had to worry that every traveler who saw her would try to steal her from him as the brigands had done two days ago, or that at any moment she'd lose her riding skill and tumble beneath the deadly hooves of her horse. Or that with every mile she was becoming more necessary to him.

Even her ill-temper and sharp tongue this day had done nothing to quell the ache inside him at the thought of saying farewell to her once and for all. At the thought of never again kissing her sweet lips or sliding deep inside her body.

He strode out into the yard feeling the need to escape these feelings that wove through him, snaring him in emotions he didn't want to feel. An aching need to hold and protect. To cherish and never let go.

Emotions that had no place in his heart or mind. Nor in this gypsy-like existence of his.

For most of his life he'd been on his own, with no one

to look out for but himself. He liked it that way. He was better on his own. Without a lass to worry over. Without this damnable ache in his chest, this constant fear that next time danger closed around her, he wouldn't be in time to save her.

Aye, he should have left her behind where she was safe, but there was little help for it now. He hadn't the time to take her back.

She would remain at his side another handful of days until he delivered the chalice, then he would see her safely back to Picktillum and leave her with the Viscount and Viscountess Kinross. He'd long ago learned to take a quick measure of a man and he trusted Kinross to fulfill his promise to call Hegarty to send her home.

In fewer than a dozen days, she would be out of his life.

A relief.

Even if the thought of never seeing her again felt as if his heart were being ripped from his chest.

Julia gripped the reins with one hand as her palm slid across her chest, uselessly trying to ease her miserable, and growing, discomfort. Though the day had dawned clear, her clothes were still damp from yesterday's rain, and had turned painfully itchy. If Talon had tried to get them a change of clothes, he hadn't said. And the ring had clearly ignored him.

And if that weren't enough, emotionally she felt beaten. Bruised.

She'd told him she loved him and he'd run.

The jackass.

For nearly an hour, they'd ridden without speaking this morning, but she was tired of the quiet. Tired of trying to give him some space and privacy with his thoughts.

She was tired of hurting in silence.

"Forget I said the L-word last night, Braveheart." She tried to sound offhanded and casual, but her voice sounded tight. Angry. Well, hell. She *was* angry. "It didn't mean anything. It just came out in the heat of the moment. My mistake."

He didn't answer. He didn't react at all, as if he hadn't even heard her.

She was in no mood for this shit. If she was going to try to smooth things over, he was going to help. "Why does the L-word bother you so much, anyway? It's not like you're in any danger of getting trapped into marriage with me."

He eyed her with impatience. "Must we discuss this?"

"Yes. Indeed, we must. Find the words for your emotions and start talking, dude. It's not like we have anything else to do."

Talon turned away, but his frustration was palpable, which gave her hope he was feeling the pressure to come up with something. Anything.

His hand shot out in a wide, impatient arc. "Ye've known me a handful of days," he snapped. "'Tis foolishness to believe ye love me."

Okay, she'd probably asked for that. "Thanks so much for calling me a fool."

"I didna call ye a fool."

"Close enough."

"'Twasn't love ye were feeling, but pleasure. Many lasses make that mistake."

Julia snorted. "Right. Silly me. I keep forgetting my heart isn't located between my legs."

"'Tis a shrewish tongue ye have today, lass," he said quietly.

She opened her mouth to offer some cutting retort, but he was right. He didn't deserve this. Any of it. She wasn't usually like this. Yes, she could be a first-class bitch when she wanted to be, but she didn't *want* to be with him. She wanted to be laughing and smiling and making love every time they gave the horses a rest.

Instead, her skin was crawling as if she'd been rolling in an anthill and it was driving her nuts!

"I know I've turned into a shrew, Talon. *God*, I know. And I don't know why. It's not your fault. I mean, I hate that you ran off when I told you I loved you, but . . ." She shook her head. "Tell me this. If I'd known you for six months when I said the words, would you have believed me?"

This time he simply didn't answer. Which was an answer in and of itself.

"You wouldn't, would you?" She watched that hard profile. "Why not? I mean, I know I'm the last person who should be talking about love. I wouldn't recognize it if it bit me, which is why I know I was just caught up in the moment. But I still want to know why you don't think I could ever love you."

She frowned, an ugly thought worming its way into her scattered and tumbled mind. Talon saw her a little too clearly.

"Have you seen into my heart? Is that it? Is it as barren as I think it is?"

He turned to her, his tight expression yielding only a fraction. "I dinna ken love, Julia. I have none inside me. And I wouldn't recognize it if I saw it in you."

"So if you wouldn't recognize it, why are you so sure I can't feel it?"

"I didn't say you couldna feel it. I said only that you do not feel it for me."

"Why not?"

"Because ye've never seen me. Ye see only the Wizard."

She blinked with surprise. "I don't even particularly like the Wizard. He's a thief and a liar and he only cares about fulfilling his missions. It wasn't the Wizard who saved me when those thugs came after me, Talon. You said yourself, you didn't even think about using your ring."

His profile remained stony and closed as she studied him. "You really think I only know the Wizard, don't you?"

"Aye."

"Then tell me who the real Talon is. Show him to me."

He ignored her.

"You can't, can you? Because you already have. He's you, Talon, whether you know it or not. You, when you're not lying or conning someone. He's the man who risked his life to save me. The man who understands me better than I understand myself."

But Talon's mind was locked against her; she could see it in the stiffness of his back and the hard line of his jaw.

"Deep down, you're a good man, Talon MacClure. A strong, brave, good man. You don't need the ring. You'd be a better man without it."

But his stony profile didn't change and she wondered if he even heard her. It was pretty clear he didn't believe her.

Over the years, his identity had gotten twisted up with that of the Wizard. She wondered if he even knew who the real Talon was anymore. She suspected he could no longer tell one from the other. But she could. She definitely could, and he was wrong. It was Talon she'd fallen in love with.

Even though, in two weeks' time, she'd be back in her own life. And how they felt about each other would no longer matter.

SEVENTEEN

"Julia-lass. Wake now."

Julia came awake with a start to the sound of Talon's low voice and the firm hand on her shoulder. She was shaking, sweating, her heart thundering in her ears.

"What happened?" she asked groggily.

She sat up, the scents of the forest rich and damp in her nose. There'd been no house to beg a room off of tonight and they'd wound up having to sleep on the ground.

"Ye had a dream."

Images flashed in her mind and she shuddered. Blood. Death. The details eluded her, but the images and the re-membered horror remained, chilling her to the depths of her soul.

"The chalice. I must have touched the chalice." Though how, she wasn't sure. They hadn't made love tonight. They hadn't slept together at all.

"Nay. Ye did not. The chalice was not near ye."

She shivered again, but this time with that same itchy, crawling sensation that had plagued her since they set out on this misbegotten journey. Only worse. God, how could it be worse? Did she have fleas? Or lice?

Gross.

She jumped to her feet and paced away.

"Julia."

"I'm not going anywhere," she said testily. The moon was out, the forest shadowed, but lit well enough for her to avoid running into a tree or tripping over a bush. She needed to walk, to move. To get away from . . .

From what? Her mind couldn't finish the thought. Yet as she walked, the itchiness dulled. The crawling sensation began to fall away. She stood in a pool of moonlight letting the scents and sounds of the night sink into her, calm her body and mind.

She was nearly asleep on her feet when the crawling sensation returned. Slowly at first, then stronger and stronger until it was nearly as bad as before.

"Dammit." She'd thought she'd finally gotten rid of it.

"Julia," Talon said quietly.

She hadn't heard him, but she opened her eyes to find him nearly upon her.

"Talon." That overwhelming need to escape slammed into her again. "Stay here."

As she hurried back the way she'd come, the discomfort eased again, then began to rise and she knew he was following. She turned to him as he reached her.

"What is it, lass?"

"I think I'm allergic to you." The golden base of the chalice peeked out from beneath his shirt, glinting in the moonlight. "No, not you. The chalice."

"I dinna ken . . ."

"It's bothering me, Talon. Even when I'm not touching

it, it's driving me crazy." And suddenly everything made sense. "I'd bet money the chalice is the reason I've been in such a bad mood."

"Even when ye dinna touch it."

"Yes. Ever since we set out on this trip I've been feeling off. Out of sorts and restless." She eyed the cup-shaped bump beneath his shirt. "I don't like that thing."

Talon grunted. "Mayhap your necklace is part of the cause."

Julia's hand went to her throat, gripping the gem protectively. "I took it off at Picktillum. I still got the visions when I touched the chalice."

"Aye."

But she wondered. Both the chalice and the jewel had magic. And more than likely, something to do with Hegarty. With reluctant fingers, she pulled the necklace off and dropped it into Talon's waiting palm.

Almost at once, the irritation drained away again.

"You're right. The necklace is catching the chalice's magic. The stone is the problem." She looked at him questioningly. "You're not feeling anything? You wear one of Hegarty's stones, too."

"Nothing, but neither do I share your visions. You're connected to the chalice in a way the rest of us are not."

"Great." She held her hand out for the necklace.

"Ye dinna wish for me to keep it?"

"No." She snatched the necklace from his hand and dropped it into her boot. "It might be my only way home."

A strained moment of silence stretched between them.

"I'll not steal it from you, Julia, if that's what you're thinking."

Her mouth tensed. "I know." But did she? She trusted Talon. But she had no illusions about the Wizard. He was a liar. A thief. A con man. When it suited him. When he needed to be.

And though she saw no reason why he might need her necklace, she was taking no chances.

As if he heard her thoughts, Talon turned his back and walked away.

They were being followed.

"Find us a place to hide, ye worthless piece of rock," Talon muttered to his ring two days later.

Talon glanced behind him through the rolling glen, seeing no sign of the riders amongst the hills and trees, but they were there. His instincts had picked up the distant sound of horses nearly two hours ago, not long after they'd set out after their midday meal. The sound had not veered away in all that time. It was possible the riders simply traveled the same path, of course, but after the last time, he couldn't help but expect the worst.

Especially after what had happened as he'd bought their midday meal.

In the five days they'd been on the road, the ring had become more and more fickle as if it, too, reacted poorly to the magic of the chalice. Only twice had it provided them with a decent meal. The rest of the time, he'd been forced to spend good coin to buy oatcakes, cheese, or strips of beef from a farmer or farm wife.

A couple of hours ago, he'd done just that. He'd been watching the farmer as Julia joined him. He'd seen the startled look on the man's face. And watched the speculative gleam enter his eyes.

He'd not liked the look at all.

"That thing is driving me nuts, Talon." Julia rode closer to him than she had in two days, ever since they'd realized the necklace reacted to the chalice. Ever since she refused to trust him with her stone. Though she'd taken to carrying it in her boot, her mood had not improved overmuch. The stone remained too close to her person. "Just a little more distance?"

"Nay. There are two riders behind us."

"Couldn't they just be following the same route?"

Her voice was sharp with annoyance, but he ignored her shrewish tone, knowing now it was caused by the magic.

"Aye. But I'll not be surprised again."

She met his gaze, the memory of the last time shimmering in her eyes, and sighed. "What are we going to do?"

"I've been asking my ring for fresh horses for two hours now without success. It doesna like the chalice any better than you do."

"Will you know if they start to gain on us?"

"Aye, and they're gaining."

Her gaze jerked to his. "Shouldn't we go faster?"

He shook his head. "The horses are already tired. And the riders are still a fair distance behind us. As soon as we come upon a likely place, we'll stop."

"A place to hide?"

"A place to protect ye while I confront them." They'd not much time. He could feel the riders behind stepping up their pace.

"Over that rise," he told Julia. Then he'd have no choice but to face their pursuers. But as they crested the rise, he found not open glen before him, but ten armed and mounted men awaiting them, guns pointed at his chest.

His blood went cold. Behind him, the sound of hoofbeats grew louder as the two who'd followed them closed the trap, blocking their escape.

His muscles tensed. If he'd been alone, he'd have made a run for it. But Julia's skills weren't enough for such mischief. And he'd never leave her to them.

He'd die before he let anyone harm her again.

As one, he and Julia pulled up.

"This can't be good," she said softly.

One of the men broke away from the group and rode forward, a large man with meaty hands wearing a green plaid and bonnet upon his light-colored hair. "We mean ye no harm," he began in Gaelic. "But the lass is one of our own."

Talon replied in English. "And who would ye be?"

"Angus Brodie from Loch Laggan," the man replied in kind. "The lass is ours. She has the Brodie eyes."

Julia scowled at him. "How did you know we were coming?"

"The farmer," Talon told her. He'd undoubtedly sent word. He addressed Angus. "We are on our way to Loch Laggan. Niall Brodie awaits my arrival."

The big man's gaze narrowed. "And who would ye be, then?"

Talon hesitated, his grip tightening on his reins. He'd no desire to share his identity with this lot. But his life might well depend upon it. And if he was dead, who would protect Julia?

"I am called the Wizard."

Angus's eyes widened with surprise. He leaned forward eagerly. "And have ye brought what ye promised him?"

"I have."

A grin split the big man's face. "Och, aye. Niall will be most pleased. We'll be accompanying you back to Ythan Castle, we will."

The twelve men pressed around them, forming an escort.

And a threat.

Why he was so certain they presented a threat, Talon wasn't sure. But he'd long ago learned to listen to his instincts. And those instincts were shouting with warning.

* * *

The sun had almost set as Ythan Castle came into view, the home of the chieftain of the Brodies of Loch Laggan. It wasn't much, as castles went, nothing like Picktillum. Instead, it sat on a hill, a single square tower rising four stories among a small village of thatch-roofed stone huts.

Still, Julia couldn't help but stare. Goosebumps raced over her skin. As a child, she'd been to this place. Her father used to bring her to Scotland every couple of years to visit his relatives. Her uncle, the chieftain, had lived with his extended family in a mansion house not far from here. On a road that passed right by the ruin of the old castle.

On a couple of occasions, she'd joined the cousins on an exploration of the old ruin, which in her time was little more than a stone shell open to the sky.

Ythan Castle, in 1688, was no ruin, but a thriving stronghold and home.

"I always imagined wooden towers built around this stone one, but there's nothing more here," she murmured to Talon, who rode close beside her.

"'Tis a keep, nothing more."

Her fingers held fast to the reins. "What's a keep? I've heard the term . . ."

"It's the last line of defense. The most secure part of a castle. In this case, it's the only part of the castle. The Brodie chieftain and his family live here, along with their retainers. The other clan members live in the village, or elsewhere, scattered around the heaths and moors. If the Brodies come under attack, those who can will retreat to the keep for protection."

"Won't they starve to death?"

"In a siege, aye. Few clans have the money to build grand castles. But if an enemy comes a-warring, he'll not kill the laird without a battle."

She'd been asking Talon questions for the past couple of days and he didn't seem to mind. As they'd reached the lower Highlands, he'd explained that the Highland line was one demarcated less by topography than culture. The Highlanders were the last of the Gaelic-speakers and the poorest, least educated, and least civilized of the Scots.

Future generations might turn the rough and often violent Highlanders into the stuff of legend, but from what she'd seen so far, being one in the seventeenth century meant living in the dark ages.

It had occurred to her a few miles back that, although about half the Brodies accompanying them wore plaids, not a one wore the black-and-red plaid she'd always been taught was the true Brodie plaid, nor anything like it. Instead, most of their plaids were dull shades of green and brown and gray, few alike. And not one wore a kilt. These plaids weren't neat little pleated skirts, but looked more like blankets belted haphazardly around their waists with one thick end draped over their shirts, across their shoulders.

"Why don't they wear the Brodie plaid?" Julia murmured when her curiosity finally got the better of her.

Talon glanced at her. "And what is the Brodie plaid?"

Her eyebrow lifted. "I thought . . ." She sighed. Had nothing of history been recorded right? "I was always taught that each of the clans has their own distinctive plaid."

Talon's eyebrows rose in amusement. "Everyone wearing the same? 'Twould be muckle boring, would it not?"

She made a wry twist with her mouth. "I guess it would." She glared at him, but there was no heat in her pique this time. "This trip is really killing the fantasy."

As they entered the village, people stopped what they were doing to look up. Their gazes skimmed the riders with little interest until they landed on her. One after another, she watched as interested eyes fixed on hers and widened. As hands flew to faces to make the sign of the cross.

"Why are they doing that?" she hissed at Talon.

"I dinna ken. 'Tis possible they think ye Catriona returned from the grave."

"Not likely. Other than the eyes, we look nothing alike."

Even at thirteen, Cat had been tall, and her hair dark as night. No, they were reacting to her mismatched eyes. The Brodies were making the sign of the cross because of her *Brodie* eyes. How much sense did that make?

"How certain are you that you didn't come from here, too?"

"Positive." Her earliest memory went all the way back to four or five, seeing the Eiffel Tower with her father, as they took a taxi through Paris after picking up her latest nanny.

"You canna remember all the way back, Julia. None of us remembers our infancy."

Her frustrated gaze snapped to his, but he was looking elsewhere. She hadn't come from this time. She knew it.

Didn't she?

How could she be 100 percent certain? Talon was right—she didn't remember anything before the age of four or five.

A cool perspiration began to dampen the back of her neck. A cold fear worming its way into her heart.

Fear that she wasn't who she thought.

Fear that she should never have come here.

Her hands tightened on the reins. She didn't like this one bit. But as her gaze once more scanned the hard, closed faces of their escort, she knew there would be no escape.

As they reached the castle, the massive oak-and-iron doors swung wide. Half of their escort dismounted, then swung the muzzles of their guns at them, motioning them to do the same.

Talon dismounted with his natural, fluid strength, then reached for her, gripping her around the waist as he lifted her down.

"If this is the way they greet family," she muttered, "I'd hate to imagine how they welcome unknown strangers into their midst."

"Mind your tongue," Talon said quietly, sharp warning in his tone.

They were ushered up the stairs and into a great hall that looked like a medieval castle should. The air inside was far cooler than that outside, and smelled of smoke and garbage. Torches hung in sconces on walls that appeared to have been whitewashed at some time in the distant past, but were now stained with smoke and God knew what else.

No grand hearth warmed the room. No fire at all, which was probably a good thing, since the only place she could see where they might have lit one was an open fire basket sitting in the middle of the hall. No wonder the walls appeared smoke-stained. There was nowhere for the smoke to go. It would fill the room.

The furniture—what little there was—appeared rustic and rough-hewn. A long trestle table ran the entire length of one wall; a second, much smaller one sat in the middle of a slightly raised platform. The dais? Crude wooden chairs accompanied the smaller table, while only benches had been paired with the longer one.

Ythan might technically be called a castle, but it was a long way from being anyone's fairy tale.

On the walls, out of reach of the torches, were a couple of tapestries. Her stomach clenched as she recognized one—a battle scene from a long ago Brodie victory. In her time, the tapestry had hung, ancient and fraying, beneath glass in the living room of her uncle's manor house.

As their escort ushered them into the middle of the Great Hall, a pair of women bustled in through one of the interior doors. Both were middle-aged and dressed simply, yet carefully, giving Julia the impression they were part of the laird's family and not servants.

"Angus?" one of the women asked.

"Aye," the big Highlander replied. A response that sounded more like a confirmation to her ears.

Apparently it was.

"Praise the Virgin," the woman cried, hurrying to Angus's side as her gaze slammed into Julia's. "'Tis a glorious day."

Who do you think I am? Julia asked silently. Had another girl gone missing with the Brodie eyes? A petite blonde they were clearly mistaking her for?

A man strode into the room from still another door—a tall, good-looking man dressed in a clean linen shirt over rough-looking pants, his hair dark and graying lightly at the temples. A man with Catriona's features, with her high forehead and long, straight nose.

Which made all too much sense, since Julia was all but certain Cat had fled this place twenty years ago. Was this man Cat's brother, then? Or maybe her cousin?

The question that lashed at Julia's mind was why Catriona had fled. What danger had she run from? And did that danger still exist?

The possibility of that incident twenty years ago having anything to do with today had seemed remote in the warmth and relative civility of Picktillum. But Ythan was part of a different time, a different world.

And her Brodie kin, a dozen generations back, were acting way too strangely to give her any measure of calm.

As the laird—for Julia had no doubt he was the man in charge—approached them, his gaze zeroed in on her and held. In his eyes, she saw emotions that made no sense. Joy. Triumph. Maybe even relief. As if he knew her. As if he'd been looking for her.

Oh God. *Was* she one of Hegarty's lost ones? Was it possible?

As the man reached them, he tore his gaze from her and turned to Talon, rough power etching his face.

"The chalice?" he demanded.

"Niall Brodie?" Talon countered, his own tone as hard.

"Aye. And ye'll be the Wizard."

"I am." Talon untied the golden cup from his belt and handed it to the man.

The chieftain took the cup and held it high, eyeing it with almost the exact same look he'd turned on her. Triumph. Recognition. Deep relief.

"Ye'll come with me, Wizard. I'd a word with you as I fetch your silver."

Julia found herself suddenly surrounded by women. "Come, lass," a booming female voice said behind her. Julia turned her head to find a large, severe-looking woman with huge breasts looking down her nose at her. She reminded her of a prison matron. "You'll be having a bath, I'm thinking," the big woman practically shouted.

A pair of hands clamped around her upper arms. Julia's gaze shot to Talon, but he shook his head. "'Tis where ye belong."

"No! You're wrong." She wasn't simply accepting this. Even if she'd started out part of this world, she wasn't part of it now. She struggled against the hands that held her firmly, but the women towered over her, closing around her as they ushered her away. "Talon!"

"Wheesht!" the prison cow bellowed.

The hands on her arms bit into her flesh painfully. As the

group pushed her into yet another narrow, twisty stairwell, she felt the last thread of control she'd held over her life disappear.

Talon.

Surely he didn't believe she really belonged here. Surely he wouldn't leave her.

But the Wizard had been offered his silver. His mission was complete. And while he'd risked his life to save her from rape and death, he knew these Brodies were her kin, whether present or past. She ought to be safe enough here.

She'd offered him her love and he'd pushed it away.

Now that he'd accomplished his task, would he wash his hands of her?

She wanted to believe he wouldn't. *Talon* wouldn't. But the Wizard, she was much less sure of.

Would he leave her here?

She was all too afraid he would.

EIGHTEEN

Talon watched the women sweep Julia through the far doorway, her voice echoing in his ears. *Talon.*

But he said naught, made no move to free her. He'd already come to the conclusion now wasn't the time. And if he'd had any doubt of that, the tip of the Brodie dirk pressing silently into the skin of his lower back assured him of the fact.

For a reason he could only guess at, Niall Brodie had claimed Julia. One of theirs, aye. With her mismatched eyes, there was no doubting it. Yet there was more going on here and he intended to get to the bottom of it.

He would not forsake the lass.

As if reading his mind, Niall raised his hand. "Search him."

The look in the man's eyes told Talon he'd welcome a reason to slide a blade between his ribs. And every man around him had one at the ready, he'd no doubt. Including the one behind him.

Talon lifted his hands and gathered the Wizard's persona around him. He threw the chieftain of the Brodies a self-deprecating smile. "I've delivered your treasure as promised. I've no quarrel with ye. I'll be getting my silver and be on my way."

The Brodie eyed him sharply. "Aye, ye'll forget the lass. She's no longer yer concern."

Talon scowled. "That one's been naught but a pain in my arse."

Niall Brodie's eyes narrowed. "How did you come by her?"

"I found her in Aberdeenshire. At Castle Rayne. Where I found the chalice," he lied. "She'd been thrown from a horse and remembered not how she'd come to be there. She still remembers naught of who she is or from whence she hails. All she knows is that she's a Brodie. Since I was coming here anyway, I brought her to ye. To her kin."

Niall watched him keenly, his thoughts hidden behind hard eyes the same green as the one of Julia's. After a silent moment, the chieftain nodded.

"Ye've done well, Wizard. Ye've returned me my chalice and my kinswoman. Angus, fetch him his silver, then take the lads and see him to the burn."

Talon's instinct for trouble flared anew. Something in the man's eyes, in his tone, held an ominous ring.

The lads would see him off, would they?

He had a bad feeling he wasn't going to enjoy this send-off. Nay, he wasn't going to enjoy it at all.

Julia struggled against the tide of women and the surprisingly strong hands that gripped her. She was going to have bruises, no doubt about it.

They pushed her into what appeared to be a dark and shadowed storage room filled with buckets and brooms and all manner of crates and jars. A single candle flickered, sending shadows dancing over the walls. In the middle of the space sat a flat, shallow pan with lips that rose only about six inches on each side. Surely *that* thing wasn't the tub?

A dozen hands began plucking at her clothes.

"Hey! I can undress myself." Which was probably a lie.

Out of nowhere, a meaty hand slapped her hard across the face, knocking her back, sending pain slicing through her head and setting bells to ringing in her ears. Tears burned her eyes as she stared at her assailant, the stern-faced matron, in shocked silence.

"Wheesht!" the woman said, her too-loud voice doing nothing to quell the pain in Julia's head.

This wasn't funny anymore. She blinked back the tears of pain as she let them strip her of her clothes, her heart thundering, her stomach cramping with disbelief and outrage. And no small amount of fear. But as one woman knelt to tug at Julia's boots, the necklace slid, tickling Julia's foot, and she feared it was about to fall out. There was no way was she losing her ticket home. She struggled free of the hands holding her and bent to snatch the necklace before it fell on the floor, then rose and slipped it over her head.

As rough hands latched on to her again from every side, one of the women grabbed for the jewel. The thief tried to lift it, but it wouldn't go even when she yanked hard enough to make Julia cry out with pain.

The woman grunted. "It willna come off."

"Leave it," the cow yelled.

Julia swallowed hard, trembling with equal parts fury, outrage, and fear. She had to get out of here. She had to find a way back to Picktillum. Back to Hegarty.

If only Talon would come for her.

The thought of him nearly made her lose the last of her precarious control. *Talon, you bastard, how could you leave me here? I love you, dammit. I love the man I know you are, the man behind the Wizard's mask.*

But that man wasn't here, was he? Had he taken his silver and ridden off? A few days ago, she wouldn't have expected him to risk anything for her. She'd believed no one would.

Talon had proven her wrong. He'd made her believe she was worth saving.

But what if he didn't think she needed saving?

The cow grabbed her arm and jerked her, stumbling, over the lip of the pan and held her while another woman picked up a bucket of water and poured it over her head.

The shock of cold had her gasping and trying to pull away.

A hard slap to the back of her head had her stopping.

No wonder the woman couldn't hear anything. How many times had *she* been hit? As a child, no doubt. Good grief.

Hands and rags scrubbed a harsh-smelling soap over her skin—skin she was pretty sure was a lot cleaner than most of theirs.

Julia shivered, standing naked in the tub, as cold water doused her head and body. Her cheek stung, her ears still rang from the cow's assault.

"I'm not who you think I am," Julia growled between chattering teeth.

"Yer a Brodie," the cow replied, nearly roaring the words in her ear. The woman had to be deaf.

Julia closed her eyes, shivering with cold and misery, willing herself away from the here and now. A plan. She needed a plan.

And what kind of plan was she going to come up with when she didn't know *anything*? All right, then, what she needed now was patience. And courage, because God knew, she could be in for anything.

The fear slid through her veins, doing nothing to dispel the bone-deep cold.

Another wash of ice-cold water dumped over her head and then scratchy wool surrounded her and she was once more yanked out of the pan, stubbing her bare toes.

As the women dried her, she opened her eyes and caught the gaze of one of the oldest women, a woman who had to be at least sixty. The woman looked away quickly, but not before Julia caught the unhappiness in her eyes. Sorrow. Maybe even pity.

God, what did they have planned for her? Was she being prepared for some bastard's bed? Or, heaven help her, more than one?

As if in answer to her silent question, the cow yelled in her ear. "Ye'll be dining with the laird."

Catriona's kin. The man with cold, hard eyes.

Why hadn't she stayed at Picktillum? If only she'd stayed with Brenna.

A thick woolen shift went over her head, followed by a plaid skirt and matching shawl. The skirt and shift fell to the tops of her feet. Feet they apparently meant to keep bare. She considered demanding her boots, but figured she'd just get hit again and probably still not get her boots, so she remained silent.

The women ushered her out of the storeroom, her damp hair cold against her chilled and aching head.

As they pushed and prodded her up yet another twisty stair, she wondered just how much she was going to have to endure before she found a chance to escape. Because she would, eventually, escape. She had to believe it.

Once again, she was on her own.

Talon stumbled to his feet, his lip swollen, the taste of blood and grit in his mouth. His ribs ached and his thigh felt twice its normal size. He'd taken a hell of a beating by those lads before they'd left him beside the burn some four or five miles from Ythan, his bag of silver dropped upon his aching head.

"Julia's in danger, ring," he said through clenched teeth. "She needs me."

He rolled onto his side, struggling to rise onto his knees.

Much was going on that he didn't understand. Too much. The chalice and its magic. Brodies making the sign of the cross at the sight of Julia's eyes—Brodie eyes. Niall Brodie claiming her as kin. Which she was, of course, just not any kin he would possibly know.

Nay, he didn't know what was going on, but he knew Julia needed him. He would not forsake her.

He wiped the blood from his mouth and looked up at the sound of horse's hooves racing over the ground. A riderless horse.

"I'll be thanking ye, ring. Glad I am to have ye back." Hurting all over, he stumbled to his feet, then caught his breath against the pain and swung into the saddle.

He turned the beast toward Ythan Castle and urged it into a fast run. He didn't know what they'd stumbled into, but his instincts roared that Julia was in danger. And his heart . . . God help him, his heart was crumbling beneath the weight of his fear and the need to keep her safe.

The past days between them had been strained, what with her telling him she loved him, then refusing to trust him with her necklace after he'd told her she couldn't love him because she didn't know him at all.

He'd hurt her and she'd pricked his pride in return. But none of that weighed against what, in a few short days, she'd come to mean to him.

Everything. She'd come to mean everything. Her absence left a hole inside of him—a cold, empty darkness he suspected had always been there until she'd stumbled into his life and filled it with light and warmth. And love.

Love.

He hadn't thought he had it inside him. He'd not believed he'd recognize it if he did. But emotion filled him, warming and squeezing his heart, feeling as if his chest were not large enough to contain it all. And he knew it in his bones.

Jesu, he loved her.

And she was in danger.

He urged the horse faster, gritting his teeth against the pain. All that mattered was reaching Julia before it was too late.

The cow's beefy hand dug fresh bruises into the flesh of Julia's upper arm as she pulled her down the hall, through an open doorway, and into a masculine, if sparely appointed, room. A large rustic dining table sat in the middle, a throne-like chair at the head and long benches on either side. The whitewashed walls had been covered by a vast and rather disturbing assortment of weapons.

"The lass," the cow shouted, then released her and backed away, leaving Julia standing before the chieftain, Niall Brodie, and three of the men she recognized from the ride.

She lifted her chin, her eyes telling them she wasn't giving in without a fight, even if deep inside, she started to quake. With a start, it occurred to her that any one of these guys could be her great-great-grandfather half a dozen times back. Any one of them might be preparing to attack her.

Time travel gave a whole new meaning to the term *incest*.

But none of the men eyed her as if he had designs on

her body. In fact, only Niall looked at her at all, and she saw nothing even vaguely resembling lust in his eyes. He raised his hand and made a motion the other men seemed to understand, for all three headed to the door.

Behind her, she heard the click of the latch that told her she was now alone with the head of this clan. He motioned her to the table behind him.

"I had your dinner sent up here, lass. Have a seat before it grows cold."

Julia didn't move. "Where's Talon . . . the Wizard?"

"He left with his silver. He'll be long gone by now."

She swallowed hard, believing him. "What do you want from me?"

He watched her coolly, lifting a brow. "I assure ye, lass, your virtue is safe with me. I wish only to ask ye a few questions as ye eat."

Julia watched him warily. "Why did they bathe me? I didn't smell any worse than anyone else around here."

"Come, lass," he said, a weary note in his tone. "Eat and I'll explain."

The smell of roast beef reached her nose and her stomach rumbled with answering interest. It occurred to her she'd be a fool to turn away food. She couldn't be certain they wouldn't withhold it from her in the future. She couldn't be sure of anything.

Walking across the wooden floor in her bare feet, she took a seat on the bench and dug into the food. It wasn't nearly as good as what she'd had at Picktillum, or Rayne for that matter, but it wasn't bad. And she *was* hungry.

Niall sat on the throne-like chair, leaning back, his arms casually resting on the arms of the chair as he watched her eat.

"What is your name, lass?"

"Julia," she replied when she'd swallowed the bite she was eating. "Julia Brodie, but you guessed that part."

"Aye. And from whence do ye hail? Ye've not been living in Scotland."

"The accent gives me away every time. I'm from the American colonies. My father was from Scotland, so when he died, I came back here." It almost made sense. Would a woman really just show up in a country in this century with nowhere to go? "I'd hoped to find other Brodies," she added, hoping it didn't sound too lame.

The laird watched her thoughtfully. "The Wizard said you'd lost your memory."

Ugh. "Did he?" She turned back to her food. "I may have told him that."

"And why did ye not tell him the truth?"

She gave a mental groan. The last thing her tangled brain needed right now was to have to follow the logic trails of hers and Talon's contradictory lies. Lying was a pain in the butt.

She shrugged. "Because it seemed like a good idea at the time."

To her relief, Niall nodded as if that response made sense to him. "Who was your father?"

"Duncan. Duncan Brodie."

A small frown marred his angular features. "But he died?"

"Yes. Last year."

"I see. I dinna ken any Duncan Brodie who went to the Colonies." He nodded at her meal. "Eat, lass."

"I'm not hungry. Tell me why the women bathed me."

Niall rested his elbows on the chair arms, steepling his fingers as he watched her. "I suppose ye'll learn the truth soon enough. There's to be a ceremony this eve. Ye are to be a part of it."

"What kind of part?"

He shook his head, a shadow passing through his eyes as he rose. "If ye've eaten all ye wish, we're through. Angus!"

As Angus strode into the room, Julia rose. "What ceremony, Niall?" All her fears came rushing back.

He ignored her, speaking only to Angus. "Lock her up below and prepare the others. The summoning takes place at midnight."

"Aye."

Something primal inside her screamed at her to run and she listened.

As Angus started for her, she lifted her skirts and ran.

But for all his great size, Angus was too quick. He snagged her around the waist and slung her over his shoulder as if she weighed no more than a bag of laundry.

"Is this why Catriona ran from you?" she cried furiously. "Is this why she escaped you?"

Angus froze. The very air in the room went still. And then she found herself dumped on the floor at Angus's feet, Niall towering over her.

"How did you know Catriona?"

Ah, *shit*. How was she supposed to answer that? "What were you going to do to her, Niall? What are you going to do to me?"

He grabbed her face. "Tell me how you knew her."

What the hell. "I met her afterward. After she got away from you."

His face turned into a mask of fury and she cringed, bracing herself for the blow that was sure to come. But instead, he released her and turned away.

"Lock her up."

Angus lifted her over his shoulder, then left the room. Twice her head hit the stone wall of the stairwell as they descended not one but two flights.

Finally, mercifully, the awful turning ceased. Angus carted her through a rough, dirty, dimly lit passage cut out of the rock and into a small, bare room.

A prison cell.

The Brodie hadn't been kidding when he'd told them to lock her up.

Angus dumped her on the ground, slamming her tailbone into the rock floor and banging her head on the wall behind her. Pain shot through her skull. By the time her sight cleared and she managed to struggle to her feet, Angus had already retreated, pulling the heavy wooden door closed with an ominous click. Only a small barred window in the middle of the door allowed her to see out.

"Wait!" she cried, grabbing the bars and trying to see into the hallway. "Angus!" Panic rushed her, sending her pulse careening as she pulled at the bars. "Dammit, let me go!"

A torch on the wall outside her cell let in the only light and it was minimal. He'd left her in near darkness, alone. Why in the hell had they insisted on bathing her if all they'd intended to do was dump her in the dungeon?

Except this wasn't the end of it, was it? Niall had said there was a ceremony she was to be part of tonight. A summoning.

Of *what*?

Images flashed in her mind, the dark images she'd suffered every time she touched the chalice. The blood. *The foot of a woman.*

No, no, no. Her scalp tingled, a cold clamminess rising on her skin. Those images had nothing to do with this. Nothing.

Oh God. What if they did?

What if she'd seen her fate? *Her death.*

Panic tore through her as she leaned back against the door. "Talon," she whispered into the darkness. "I need you."

But even if he knew she was in trouble, even if he tried to save her, he'd never be able to. He might have a bit of magic, but he wasn't Superman. Even with his ring, he couldn't breach a castle. And even if he did, there were dozens of armed men inside. They'd kill him.

There was nothing he could do this time.

She'd followed her heart by coming with him to Loch Laggan instead of staying with Brenna at Picktillum. But though he'd been happy for the company and the sex, he hadn't wanted her heart.

Her legs refused to hold her and she sank to the cold stone floor, pulling her knees tight against her. The last time he saved her, he still thought he needed her to help him find the chalice.

He didn't think he needed her anymore. And she hated him for that. She'd been *fine* on her own. Happy in her independence. In her isolation. Because, dammit, she'd never known anything else.

Until she met Talon. Until he wormed his way into her heart with his charmer's smile, his gentle insistence, and those eyes of his that saw too much.

He *did* need her. She'd seen the pain inside him. He might think he didn't, but he did. Like her, he'd been alone. And like her, he thought he'd been fine with it.

But unlike her, he still thought he was.

She hugged her knees, trying to shield herself from the pain of loving a man who couldn't love her back. And the fear that it wouldn't matter anymore. That whatever the Brodies had planned for her tonight involved blood. And death.

Her death.

As the shaking tore through her body, her tears began to roll.

NINETEEN

The dull clop, clop of a horse and the squeak of a cart sounded nearby. Talon pulled back on the reins of his mount. He needed a way into the castle and he'd long ago learned to ignore nothing when he'd asked for the assistance of the ring.

On the road below, a cart trundled by, filled with barrels strapped to the boards. Likely ale from the nearest alewife. An old man drove the cart over the uneven hill, his tongue clicking to the equally old horse.

"Get ye on, Fia, m'dear. 'Tis gettin' late and the laird will be wantin' his ale."

A small rush of exultation lifted Talon's spirits. This was the boon he'd been looking for. Stifling a groan, he swung out of the saddle and ran over the hill lit only by moonlight to creep behind the cart. Ignoring his aching ribs, he climbed on, hiding between the barrels.

As he'd hoped, the wagon eventually rolled up to the

back gate of the castle. His muscles were sore and cramped, but as the ale man and the guards began to lift the barrels off from the right, Talon dropped to the ground on the left and stole through the massive open door.

Keeping to the shadows, he traversed the passageways, hiding from sight whenever anyone approached. An air of tense excitement enveloped the castle this eve. He heard it in the voices, felt it in the tension of the inhabitants.

This was not simple joy, but something more. Something with a dark edge to it. Which surprised him little, having already seen the dark magic in that chalice.

But what had any of this to do with Julia? *Did* it have aught to do with her or was his concern for her clouding his judgment? Were his feelings blocking his reason?

He couldn't be certain and it no longer mattered. He was here now. He'd not leave without her again.

Voices and footsteps approached and he dove into a dimly lit passage, pressing back into the dark.

"For nigh on a year the laird's had men scouring the land for a by-blow with the Brodie eyes with no success." The speaker was female. "'Tis God's hand that delivered the very lass and the chalice as one. We prayed for a miracle to spare wee Isobel and God has provided."

A second voice, a man's, replied. "Isobel isna spared, ye ken that, lass. Those marked by Veskin will become Veskin's. But the laird's wee daughter will at least get her thirteen years now. The lass delivered to us this day has seen far more than thirteen. 'Tis right for her to die in Isobel's stead."

Die? Talon's pulse began to pound. It was all he could do not to fly from his hiding place and pound the truth out of the pair, but he would do Julia no good were he caught a second time.

Jesu. They meant to kill her. Why? *Because of her eyes?*

"Niall," the man called. "A word, if ye please."

Talon crept as close to the edge of the shadows as he dared, straining to hear.

"The men wish to bleed themselves here, in the castle. They fear the devil's cave."

Niall grunted. "The ritual will be performed in the cave as it has always been done. Just before midnight. Twenty men, myself included. No more, no less."

"Aye, Niall."

The voices moved off. Talon remained with his back pressed to the cool stone of the wall as disbelief swirled about his head. Ritual and blood. Devils and sacrifices.

Julia.

Nay. *Nay.* They'd not have her. They'd as soon rip the heart from his chest. For that was precisely what the lass had become.

"Help me find my heart," he quietly demanded of the ring. "Help me save her. You sent her to me. You'll not let her die!"

The ring had sent her. *Why?* He'd asked . . . what had he finally asked for that had brought her to him? A chill slid down his spine as he remembered. He'd asked the ring to send him that which Niall Brodie sought.

And Niall Brodie had sought, in addition to the chalice, a lass with the Brodie eyes. To sacrifice. To spill her blood in the place of wee Isobel. His daughter.

Why the need for the sacrifice he didn't know, nor did he care.

A sudden thought jolted through him. Was this the reason Hegarty had sent Catriona into the future? *At thirteen.* Had he saved her the night *her* blood was to have been spilled?

Now Julia was here in her place, another Brodie with those same eyes. Doomed to fulfill the destiny Catriona had avoided.

He'd not allow it to happen.

He'd not allow them to destroy the woman he'd come to love.

Huddled on the damp stone floor, Julia heard the soft scurry of a rodent and shivered, a deep pulsing shudder that wouldn't stop, wouldn't ease. She shouldn't even be here! Anger flared inside her. Anger at Catriona for giving her the necklace without any true understanding of the danger of the thing. Why had she given it to her? She should have dropped it into Loch Laggan, where no one would ever find it again.

"Julia."

Her heart gave a leap and she caught her breath, uncertain if that low, urgent sound had been real, or only in her imagination. But her pulse began to skitter and race as she froze, listening.

"Julia."

She heard it again, this time right outside her door, and she leaped to her feet.

"Talon?"

"Shh," he said softly.

Something slid into the lock and the door swung open. Talon stood in the doorway, tall and fierce, like a knight of old.

Julia flew into his arms, burying her face against his chest as he held her against him, his arms like steel bands.

"Are you hurt?"

"No. Just scared. Oh God, Talon, I didn't think you'd come."

His chin rubbed the top of her head. "D'ye still think so little of me?"

She laughed, a small, low sound of disbelief. "I thought you were mortal. I didn't know you'd turned into Superman."

She pressed her cheek to his chest. The truth was, she was never quite sure about him. But it no longer mattered. He was here. *Thank God*, he was here.

"How in the world did you break into a castle filled with armed Highlanders?"

He pulled back, dipped his head, and kissed her hard, then released her to grab her hand. "I'll tell ye once we're away. They'll be here for you soon."

"They mean to kill me, don't they?"

The squeeze of his hand and his silence were all the answers she needed. "They'll not touch you."

But the knowledge that they meant to kill her echoed through her head like the music of some horror flick. The soundtrack to those scenes of the firelit cave and the blood. The severed foot. Whether those visions had been of other deaths, or premonitions of her own, no longer mattered. She was destined for the same if they didn't make good this escape. She knew it. She *felt* it.

Talon led her through a dank and shadowed underground passage. They hadn't gone far when he stilled and pressed back against the wall, telling her silently to do the same. Ahead, she heard a single set of footsteps. A guard? Or Angus on his way to fetch her for whatever they had planned for her?

Perspiration rolled between her breasts.

Beside her, Talon murmured low and she knew him well enough by now to know he was talking to his ring. If they ever needed help, it was now. A diversion.

Holding her breath, she waited, her heart thudding in her ears. And then she heard it. The soft sound of beating wings. Dozens of beating wings.

"Bats," Talon murmured against her ear. "'Tis a favorite of the ring's."

Julia shuddered. But she supposed bats were better than fire. Especially with them trapped in the dungeon.

Talon's grip on her hand tightened. The sound of the bats grew louder, coming from the same direction as the footsteps.

A man's yell of alarm echoed through the tunnels, shout after shout, as if he were being attacked.

"Bollocks," Talon muttered. "Just our luck to get a lad who's afraid of bats. Come." He tugged her hard and fast and they ran down the damp passage, directly toward the commotion.

"Shouldn't we go the other way?" she cried softly.

"'Tis the only way out. And his shouting has likely alerted the entire castle by now."

Talon's words were all too prophetic. They'd barely rushed past the frantic guard when half a dozen armed Brodies barreled into the passage.

"Get back," Talon told her, releasing her hand.

"The ring?" Julia whispered.

"Can only do so much." Talon pulled his sword and launched himself at the guards.

A cloud of bats flew straight through the skirmish, but none of the other guards seemed to notice or care.

Julia felt a hard arm go around her neck, hauling her back from the fray, and knew the bat-phobic guard was back on duty. He shoved her into another prison cell and slammed the door against her.

She lunged for the door and yanked, but she was locked in tight. All she could do was press her face to the high, barred window and watch.

Talon was fighting two Brodies at once, stepping over the prone form of one man who was either dead or injured. The passage was too tight for the others to be able to surround him. But behind him, the guard who'd captured her pulled a wicked-looking knife.

"Talon!" Julia gripped the bars. "Behind you!"

Talon whirled, but not even her Superman could fight

three men at once when they came at him from opposite directions. One blade sliced through his sword arm, leaving a bright ribbon of red blossoming on his sleeve.

As she watched, the guard behind him lunged, blocking her view. But she heard a groan and a hard thud. Then nothing but the heavy breathing of active men.

The fight was over. Talon had lost.

Her skin turned to ice, an ill sweat popping out on her brow.

No. Dear God, no.

She heard the grunts and groans of men lifting a heavy burden, then the sound of footsteps moving away, leaving her in a heartrending silence.

Had they killed him? Would she ever know?

When she died herself in a blood-strewn cave, would he be waiting for her, ready to walk with her into the light?

She slid down onto the floor, buried her face in her hands, and shook.

Julia didn't know how much time had passed when the cell door bumped her in the back and she scrambled to her feet. She'd been so lost in her misery, she hadn't heard the sound of the lock. One of the armed Highlanders grabbed her by the arm and pulled her from the cell, then led her past the blood-soaked stone where she'd seen Talon fall.

Her stomach cramped, a quaking misery shuddering through her as she fought tears. And terror. She would face her death with courage. Because, God knew, it was all she had left.

The man said nothing as he led her up the endless spiral of stairs Angus had taken her down, and back to the room where Niall Brodie had fed her.

He stood, pacing, as the guard led her in.

"Leave her."

Julia watched the Brodie chieftain, her fists clenched at her side, hating him.

He watched her with hard, enigmatic eyes. "Ye'll tell me how you knew Catriona."

"Go to hell." She swiped angrily at the tears trying to cloud her vision. "Why should I tell you anything? You're already going to kill me."

Niall's mouth tightened. "Do ye think I *wish* to kill you?"

Julia stared at him, uncomprehending. "I think you're evil and insane."

She expected him to come after her, to slam her in the face with his fist. She didn't expect him to sink onto his chair and bury his face in his hands.

"Aye. 'Tis evil, true enough." He lowered his hands and looked up at her, a weariness and grief in his eyes that almost, *almost*, made her feel sorry for him. "But I dinna have a choice."

"You have a choice."

He shook his head. "Nay. I thought I did. I tried to end this once. I tried to save my wee sister Catriona. But I failed. And my clan and my kin have paid for my arrogance ever since."

His words throbbed with anguish and she found herself unable to add to his pain.

"Catriona isn't dead, Niall. You did save her."

He stared at her. "I saw the devil take her." He pushed to his feet, his expression desperate. "How do you ken Catriona?"

"I'll tell you. After you tell me what in the hell is going on, why you had to save her, why you have to kill me."

A razor-sharp gleam entered his eyes and for a moment, she feared he would try to shake the truth from her. Instead, he turned away and began to pace.

"'Tis an old tale." The words were laced with gravel. "Centuries ago, during the time of the black plague, the Brodies of Loch Laggan were struck down at a terrible rate. The chieftain's wife was dead, his three sons all buried. Only his wee lassie of a daughter had been left untouched. Seven, she was, and she was his heart. Then she, too, developed the buboes, the swellings, that heralded the black death and he knew he would lose her, too. 'Twas too much for him. He railed at God and the fates, offering his soul in exchange for his wee daughter's life."

Niall turned to her, the look in his eyes not that of a man telling a tale, but of a man recounting a horror he knew all too well. "The devil appeared in the darkest hour of that terrible night, a wee devil with hair as wild as the winds and as black as night. His name was Veskin and he offered to save the lass, but at a price."

His voice dropped, vibrating with a fury and a pain that mirrored her own.

"Veskin had no need for the chieftain's soul. Nay, the debt would be paid in flesh. Once a generation, Veskin would claim his due—a lass. A lass marked for all the world to know she was his and his alone. A lass with eyes of two different colors—the green of the one who'd been saved and the brown of Veskin's own."

Julia scoffed. "That's absurd." She'd been flying along, half-*believing*, right up to the part about her eyes.

"Heterochromia—two different colored eyes—is *not* the mark of the devil."

Niall's jaw clenched. "Always, no. But in the case of the Brodies, aye. They are." He turned away, continuing as if she hadn't interrupted. "Veskin gave the chieftain a golden chalice—the Fire Chalice—and taught him how to use it to summon him. Then the devil made him promise to call him forth on the thirteenth birthday of every marked lass. To tie her and leave her for him in the cave down by the loch."

"Why? What does he want them for?" But the images from the visions she'd had every time she touched that chalice strafed her mind. The blood. *So much blood*. And that severed foot.

She knew.

"He kills them, doesn't he?" And not just killed them. He ripped them limb from limb.

Niall met her gaze, a terrible knowledge in his eyes. A horror that made her recoil even as the words remained unsaid between them. There was no need for the words.

She knew.

Terror hammered at the inner walls of her chest.

"If the clan fails to give the devil his due, the clan will die," Niall continued. "When I was six, my sister Catriona was born with the cursed eyes. My mother wept. I didn't understand the full nature of the curse until the night she was to be sacrificed."

He shook his head, his gaze far away. "She was tied in the devil's cave down by the loch. The ritual was performed to summon Veskin, then all fled, none wishing to risk his own life." His gaze turned to her, defiant and a brother's love flaring in his eyes. "I followed them to the cave that night. And when the others fled, I freed my sister before the devil arrived. Two of my cousins saw us as we escaped the cave. I told Catriona to run while I pulled my sword and held back my cousins. But she failed to get away.

"A second devil appeared, one with hair the color of the setting sun. We all saw him. We all heard her scream. But then he said something to her. He enchanted her with his words and she allowed him to put something around her neck. And then they were gone. Disappeared. Both of them.

"Moments later, the black-haired devil, Veskin, came storming out of the cave, demanding his lassie. I told him another devil stole her, but Veskin wasn't appeased. His eyes turned red and he cursed my clan and disappeared." Niall stopped pacing, a look of anguish aging his face. "Within days, the bairns began to die in their sleep. Within a fortnight, all the weans under thirteen were dead.

"The clan left an unmarked lass in the devil's cave, but the summoning failed. Veskin ignored us. Two lassies were left for him, then three, but Veskin would have naught to do with any of them. And the lasses offered died in their sleep as well.

"From that day to this, no bairn has lived past his or her third year. Not a one. Until six months ago, no lass was born with the cursed eyes to save us. Until six months ago when my wife gave birth to my wee Isobel. For years, I've searched for a lass with the eyes, praying a by-blow was born unnoticed, but to no avail. Until now.

"When Isobel was born, I knew I must sacrifice her too young. Already, there is not a member of the clan under the age of four and thirty. Another thirteen years and too few of our women will still be of childbearing age. The clan will die. A couple of months ago, I went to the wall cupboard where Veskin's golden chalice was locked for safekeeping, knowing what I had to do. Knowing I must sacrifice my daughter for the sake of the clan.

"But the chalice was gone. And the last one who'd seen it, my own father, had been dead for years. I searched the castle for weeks, to no avail. The chalice was gone. Without it—without a means of summoning the devil to break the curse—my clan was doomed. So I hired the Wizard to find the chalice."

His mention of Talon wreaked havoc on her heart.

Niall met her gaze. "Forgive me, lass, but I thank God in heaven, for he answered my prayers when he delivered both you and the chalice to us this day. I have no wish for your death, but I must save my clan. I know ye canna understand, not when you have no love for these people. So I tell you now, I am sorry."

Pity moved through her, an odd pity for the man who would offer her up to be killed. It helped, a little, to know he wasn't doing it out of viciousness. Or evil. She wouldn't forgive him. She wasn't a good enough person for that. But in exchange for his explanation, she could ease his mind on one count.

"The little man who took Catriona saved her. She's fine."

Niall's gaze narrowed, a spark of hope lighting his eyes. "How is that possible?"

"His name is Hegarty and while I haven't met him personally, I know people who have, who call him a friend. He sent Cat to the future, more than three hundred years. To your descendants. They didn't hurt her, Niall. They loved her and raised her and accepted her as their own, though I don't think she ever told them where she'd come from. A couple of years ago, she met a man from the Hebrides and fell in love. They just got married. She's happy. And in that time, alive and well."

He stared at her, his expression a mix of hope and disbelief. "And ye ken this how?"

Julia shrugged. "It's easy enough to figure out, right? I'm from that time. My father was the younger brother of the chieftain, though I wasn't raised in Scotland. I was at Catriona's wedding last Saturday. Afterward, she gave me the stone Hegarty used to send her to the future and told me to take it far away and not put it on. I didn't understand why. I didn't listen."

"Ye put it on."

"And here I am."

His mouth opened, an expression of wonder and joy softening his features. "I saved her."

"Yes."

"And in that time, the curse is no more. She lived. *You* lived."

Julia shrugged. "I guess even devils don't live forever."

Niall's face slowly hardened again, though the regret in his eyes was deep and real. "I thank you for telling me she's happy. Though I ken I deserve no such boon, you've eased my heart. You've given me a gift I've no ability to repay." His mouth tightened. "If you wish, I've a fine whiskey. You must be conscious, but you needn't be sober."

Julia closed her eyes, fear shuddering through her all over again. He might be sorry, but nothing had changed. She was still going to die.

The offer of the whiskey was tempting. So tempting. To dull the pain of Talon's death. To ease the terror of her own.

But no. She wasn't giving up. Hegarty had come when they tried to sacrifice Catriona. Maybe he'd come again. And even if he didn't, maybe she could find a way to fight. She refused to give up until there was no hope left.

And if any chance presented itself, she needed to be sober.

"No, thanks."

Niall nodded, a hint of respect in his eyes. He gave a call in a language she thought might be Gaelic. Angus and another man entered the room. Each took her by one arm.

"It is time," Niall said, his voice flat and hard once more.

As they ushered her out the door, she shied away from the terror clawing at the edges of her mind and reached for thoughts of Talon. Of the way he'd held her as she'd flown into his arms. Of the way he'd risked all to come to her again.

I love you, she told him silently, and felt his presence giving her strength. He'd be there with her, waiting for her as she took her last breath. Easing those last moments before they were reunited again.

He was the only good thing that had ever come into her life. Her memories of him would be the things she clung to as she died.

TWENTY

Talon awoke slowly, the base of his skull throbbing. Swallowing a groan, he pushed himself to a sitting position, feeling damp earth beneath his hands. He blinked over and over, but the darkness refused to abate. Was it still night? Was Julia still alive?

A tight band of fear and fury contracted around his chest. He'd freed her, but the damned ring's diversion hadn't helped them at all. Instead he'd only managed to call down the rest of the castle's guards.

Useless bit of rock.

He rose unsteadily to his feet, his head colliding with solid stone. Jesu. Where was he? The smell of damp earth hung heavy in the air, as did the crawling sensation that he'd been buried alive.

With a growing uneasiness he felt for the ends of his tomb, needing to understand where he was. His hands encountered rock and dirt. And bones.

Human bones.

As his fingers closed around a rack of almost certainly human ribs, the bones shifted. With a crack, the skull landed on his foot.

His pulse pounded. His jaw clenched as he kicked the skull away and moved on. But his explorations uncovered six more skeletons and defined his tomb to be small and circular, little bigger around than the height of two men laid out end to end, and not quite the height of one.

But even as he thought the last, he stepped into the center and felt a faint stirring of air—and no ceiling. He looked up with surprise and saw, high, high above him, the faint flicker of light.

With a slam to his belly that nearly drove him to his knees, he understood.

He'd been tossed into a bottle dungeon—a hole deep in the ground from which there was no escape unless his jailors saw fit to throw a rope down to him.

His six skeletal companions had been given no such reprieve.

Jesu, he had to get out of here! He had to get to Julia before they took her life.

He lifted his ring and pressed the amethyst to his lips.

"If ever I needed ye, old friend, 'tis now. I seek my freedom, ring. And Julia's." Over and over, he demanded and pleaded, begged and cajoled, until a sound above caught his attention.

"Give me my amethyst, laddie, and I'll get ye out of there."

Talon's heart stilled. He peered up through the opening of the pit and caught but a glimpse of a man. But he would know that voice anywhere.

Hegarty's.

His thumb brushed the ring and he muttered at the stone. "Ye answer my wishes, dinna ye? But ne'er in the way I want ye to."

"Hegarty!" he called. "Ye must save Julia. They mean to kill her!"

The wee man grunted. "Sorry, I am, lad, but I cannot. She belongs to Veskin and not even I dare cross that one."

"You saved Catriona from him."

"Nay, her brother saved her. I merely gave her a means of escape."

"Then get me out of here so I can save her!"

"Give me my ring, lad," Hegarty replied evenly. "I'll leave ye there to rot until ye fulfill yer end of our bargain all those years ago."

"I never promised to give it back to you, ye wee liar."

"'Tis of no mind, now, is it? Ye'll not be leaving that hole with the ring, lad, and that be the truth. Whether ye give it to me now while ye still have a chance to save your lassie, or your body relinquishes it when ye die in that place, I'll have my ring."

Talon's breathing grew ragged with his desperation to be free. But not without his ring! How could he save her without the ring's magic?

He paced, thinking. Plotting.

"Get me out of here first, Hegarty. I canna possibly hand ye the ring from here now, can I? If I try to throw it to ye and miss, I'll ne'er find it again in this dark."

And once he was out of the dungeon, he'd find a way to be free of the dwarf without giving away his ring.

But Hegarty was not fooled.

"Take the amethyst off your finger, lad, and hold it in your palm."

Talon's mouth dropped open, a chill stealing over his flesh. The moment he took it from his finger, the dwarf would snatch it away.

No! He'd not give it up. It was all he had. All he was.

As if hearing his thoughts, Hegarty called down softly, "'Tis time ye relied on the gifts God gave ye, laddie. And ye've not much time, if ye catch my meaning. Twenty minutes to midnight. Your lass still lives, but Veskin comes. I feel his foul breath on the back of my neck and I would be out of here when he arrives."

Talon felt the choice like a blade slicing him in two. He would not part with his ring! Yet what good did the amethyst do him when he was trapped in a prison from which there was no escape?

What good was anything if he let Julia die?

Slowly, painfully, his fingers curled around the metal and stone that had been a part of him for so many years. He gripped the ring, his hand beginning to shake, the sweat rolling between his shoulder blades.

It was all he was.

All he would ever be. Though Julia would disagree. What had she said to him? *You don't need the ring. You'd be a better man without it.*

His muscles tensed. She was wrong.

But if giving up the ring gave him even the slightest chance of saving her, he would forsake it all.

With a tug as painful as if he ripped a limb from his body, he wrenched the ring from his finger and set it in his palm.

A heartbeat later, it disappeared.

Talon dug his bare and shaking fingers into his hair. *What have I done? What have I done?*

The rope slapped him in the back of the head.

His means of escape.

Shaking off the deadening pall of his loss, he focused on the only thing that mattered—reaching Julia—and began to pull himself up and out of the bottle pit. When he finally reached the top and hauled himself over the edge, his knees went weak with the relief of being free.

But as he straightened and looked around, his blood turned to ice, then to white-hot fury.

Hegarty was gone. His ring was gone. And he wasn't free at all. The bottle dungeon was locked within a larger cage.

He leaped to his feet and grabbed the metal slats of the cage door, but it didn't give. He might have escaped the pit, but he was still well and truly trapped.

"*Hegarty.*" He retained the presence of mind to keep his voice low, the call no less desperate for that terrible quiet.

His hands hard around the steel bars, his heart began to thud. Rank fear coated his flesh in a cold, acrid sweat.

No. *No.* He wanted to scream to the heavens and rail at God. Julia was about to die and he was helpless to save her. He was helpless to save either of them without his ring, without his magic.

The Wizard was gone.

Talon MacClure alone remained. Powerless.

Useless.

He sank to the floor, his head in his hands, as hopelessness closed over him, sweeping him into a dark pit of despair.

The night was dark but for the torches lighting the way, the air damp with the promise of rain, as the procession followed a well-worn path down the hill from the castle to the shores of the dark loch. Twenty Brodie men.

And their sacrifice, Julia thought bitterly.

Before they'd left the castle gates, they'd tied her wrists firmly in front of her. Niall Brodie kept tight hold of one of her arms while Angus kept a grip on her other, as if they feared she'd escape, which was ridiculous. There wasn't a man among them who didn't tower over her, who couldn't take her down with a single blow.

But Niall was probably thinking of that last summoning, of the way he'd helped Catriona escape, and he was taking no chances of anything going wrong this time.

Though the men said nothing as they escorted her to her death, she sensed their emotions clearly. Excitement. Fear. And a fragile hope.

And in the thumb Niall ran back and forth on her arm, she sensed regret. Yes, he was leading her to her death, but he wasn't happy about it. That was something, she supposed.

But it wouldn't save her.

And it wouldn't save his daughter twelve and a half years from now.

The image of that severed foot rose in her mind and she shied away from the dark terror. Instead, she concentrated on the night, on the feel of the cool, damp breeze along her cheek and the sound of the wind in the boughs above her head. She concentrated on the feel of rocks and dirt beneath her feet, and on holding back the scream that burned and clawed at her throat.

It wasn't fair! This wasn't her time. She shouldn't even be here.

Her swirling thoughts stilled. No, this fate was to have been Catriona's. Catriona, who was, even now, on her honeymoon, her life rich and full with family and love.

While Julia had nothing and no one waiting for her. And the only man she'd ever loved was . . .

A sob caught in her throat. She fought it, shoving her mind away from Talon. If she started crying now, she'd never stop. And she would not meet her death that way.

They led her down the rocky path, her body trembling from head to foot in a deep quaking that had begun when they'd tied her wrists, and refused to stop.

Finally, they reached the cave. One by one, the men placed the half-dozen torches into iron holders attached to the rock walls, illuminating the cave she'd glimpsed too many times in her visions. And her nightmares.

Her captors led her to the far wall, a wall whose rocks had long ago turned black. *From the blood of the girls who had gone before*.

In the middle of the carnage-soaked wall, a large hook protruded, catching her gaze, ripping away the last of her control. Shredding her courage.

Julia fought against the arms propelling her to it, digging her bare feet in the dirt as her heart raced out of her chest and panic flared across her mind.

"No! You can't do this! Don't do this, Niall! Catriona would be horrified. We grew up as cousins. She'd be horrified."

But her pleas fell on deaf ears. Without a word of response, Niall forced her around and pressed her back to the wall. She kicked out, catching him in the shin, but he only grunted and yanked her arms high above her head. Together, he and Angus lifted her, forcing the hook between her wrists, then lowered her to where she could stand on her tiptoes. Yet never escape.

"Niall, no! You bastard. You murderer. Don't leave me here!"

Any empathy she'd felt for him in the castle was gone now. She hated him. She hated them all!

"Are you really going to hang Isobel like this? Do you want to know how she's going to feel when you hang her up to die?" She was beginning to hyperventilate, the air rasping in and out of her lungs.

"She's going to be terrified, Niall. She'll beg you to save her. She's going to hate you, just as I do." Her toes were beginning to cramp, but if she shifted her weight off them, all the weight would be on her arms, the ropes shredding her wrists.

"I hope you see that betrayal in your daughter's eyes

every time you look at her for the next twelve years, Niall. I hope you suffer as she's going to! I hope you suffer a thousand times more."

"The blood of twenty men," Niall murmured, turning his back on her and taking the chalice from one of his kinsmen.

One by one, the men cut their thumbs and squeezed a few drops of blood into the goblet. One by one, the men fled the cave as if terrified of the creature they meant to summon. The creature she alone would be left to face.

Finally, only Niall and Angus remained. Though they'd already added their blood, they did not follow the others. Niall set the chalice on a flat rock to her right that resembled a raised pedestal. Then he took a reed and lit the end from one of the torches. As he murmured in what she suspected was Gaelic, he passed the burning reed over the chalice, back and forth, again and again.

Suddenly, a flame rose up from the chalice, an unearthly greenish glow. As the flame rose, the torches extinguished themselves as if by a witch's wand.

Julia's heart stuttered.

The men exchanged glances, then Niall turned and met her gaze, his face pinched in the horrible green light. "God be with you, Julia Brodie." Then together, the two men fled.

She thought of Catriona in this spot all those years ago, of how she must have felt when her brother stole into the cave, defying everyone to cut her down and help her escape.

She thought of Talon coming for her when she'd been kidnapped.

The memory of that day suddenly snapped into place. How the one man had commented on her Brodie eyes. They hadn't taken her to rape her, she realized, though they might have done that, too. No, they'd been looking for a girl with the Brodie eyes. They'd intended to bring her here. For this.

But Talon had stopped them. He'd saved her. As he never would again.

Talon was gone.

And soon, she would be, too.

Talon tipped his head back against the bars of the cage, hopelessness a seething, rancid poison swirling through his mind.

Julia.

She would die because Hegarty had betrayed him. The dwarf had promised to set him free to save her. Instead the wee bugger had left him caged like a brigand, unable to do anything but wait until the Brodie men found him and tossed him back into that pit.

Damn the dwarf! But Hegarty's words wouldn't quiet from his head. *'Tis time ye relied on the gifts God gave ye.*

Bile rose with the fury. He had no gifts. None. The only thing he'd ever had was the ring. And now it was gone.

Julia.

Her face swam in his mind as she watched him the night she'd told him she loved him. As she'd watched him with sadness in her eyes. Her voice added to Hegarty's. *Deep down, you're a good man, Talon MacClure. A strong, brave, good man. You don't need the ring. You'd be a better man without it.*

If only he could be the man she thought he was. Strong, brave, good.

Bollocks. He leaned forward, his hands pressing at his temple. Bollocks. From the time he was fifteen, he'd held the ring like a talisman against all the ills that had ever befallen him, terrified, deep down, that if he ever lost it, he'd go right back to being what he'd been before.

But he'd grown since then, hadn't he? Losing the ring hadn't turned him back into that scrawny, weak-muscled fifteen-year-old. The boy had grown up. And the ring had had naught to do with it.

Slowly he forced himself to his feet.

The ring had eased his existence. It had provided for him and given him a means to earn coin. But it was not all he was. It had never been all he was.

The thought was a revelation.

And just what was he, then?

He shook his head. He didn't know.

But it was high time he found out just what he had inside him. Or Julia's existence was ended.

With a desperate surge of determination, he turned his mind away from the loss of his ring and focused on the problem at hand. How to get out of the damned cage and escape the castle. Then find the cave and rescue Julia before they killed her. Aye, the problem was simple. It was the solution that was the challenge.

What would the Wizard do?

The knowledge that the Wizard was dead to him twisted like a knife in his belly. He clenched his jaw and pushed the pain aside.

The Wizard would call to the ring for a diversion.

Nay, not a diversion. A feint.

His mind leaped, searching for ideas until one came flying at him. He grabbed the rope and climbed back into the pit, descending only a few feet below the lip where his voice would echo properly, then yelled at the top of his lungs.

"The bottle pit is filling with silver! I'll drown if ye dinna save me! Silver! I am drowning in silver!" Why the guard would believe him he didn't know, but he was willing to wager he'd come to investigate. Which was all Talon needed him to do.

Talon scrambled from the pit, pulled up the rope, and untied the length from the bar that held it. Rope in hand, he pressed back into the corner where none would see him without entering the cage.

He didn't have long to wait. One guard opened the gate, his expression at once wary and excited. But as he edged close enough to the pit to look over, Talon flew out of the corner and hooked the rope around his neck. As the guard's hands flew to the rope, Talon pulled his knife and knocked him unconscious with a quick blow to the back of the head. He relieved the guard of several weapons, then left the cage and ran, praying he wasn't already too late to save the only one who had ever mattered.

Julia.

TWENTY-ONE

The air in the cave changed suddenly. One moment it was damp and normal and the next it blew with a hot, arid breath. As if the gates of Hell had opened.

Julia trembled with a terror beyond anything she'd ever believed possible. Her feet ached, her arms were nearly numb, but the physical pain paled against the sheer terror raking through her, ripping her open with sharp, deadly claws.

She wanted the devil to come, to kill her and get it over with, because the death she was imagining couldn't be any worse than the truth.

The green flame flickered and suddenly she wasn't alone. A small man stood in the middle of the cave, a wizened, black-haired dwarf.

Julia looked at him askance. He looked harmless. "*You're* Veskin?"

He stared at her in horror. "You're old!"

"Excuse me. Thirty is *not* old." Her mind balked as it tried to wrap itself around the fact that this funny little dwarf was the monster that had an entire clan quaking in fear.

"Thirteen." Veskin stomped one foot then the other, his face turning red. "*Thirteen*, I told them. Full grown and enough to fill my belly for weeks, but tender and sweet. You'll be tough as mutton. The only thing worth eating will be your innards and I'll be hungry again in a day."

Julia felt the blood drain from her face. He was going to eat her? *Eat her?*

And suddenly there was nothing funny about her situation at all. All too well, she remembered the vision. The foot.

Oh God, oh God, oh God.

His eyes gleamed with malevolence as he pulled out a small, viciously pointed knife. A knife that would rip open her stomach and literally spill her guts. Which he would *eat*.

Terror pounded in her head until she could barely see, could barely hear. Everyone had to die eventually, she knew that. But not like this. Not like this.

He closed the distance between them until he was standing close enough for her to see the red dots flickering in his eyes and the small, sharp points of his teeth.

Julia's sight clouded with terror, her mind going numb with dread as her body began to quake.

Veskin lunged.

Julia screamed, then clamped her mouth shut as Veskin's knife stopped abruptly three inches in front of her as if he'd plunged it into an invisible wall.

The dwarf snarled. "*Nay.*" He stabbed again and again, but his knife would not penetrate the air around her. In a fit of fury, he threw the knife against the cave wall. As it clattered to the ground, he began to jump from one foot to the other, his hands pulling at his hair, spittle flying from his lips.

As she stared at him, a tentative hope blossomed in her chest. "I don't understand. Why can't you stab me?"

He whirled toward her, his eyes glowing a bright, burning red. "Ye wear a jewel of Kindonan. A talisman."

Julia blinked. "The purple garnet?"

"Aye." His lip curled. "Ye'll pay for this outrage, lassie. I may not be able to eat ye, but I'll kill ye all the same. Mind me well. There are other ways to make ye pay."

"Ye'll not stop this, Wizard!" Niall Brodie cried, his voice low and furious. "My clan will die."

"A pox on your clan!" Talon parried the Brodie chieftain's thrusts, the clang of swords ringing over the loch. At his feet, Angus writhed in pain. He'd come upon the pair standing guard over the cave and they'd stopped him.

From the mouth of the cave flickered an eerie green glow. There was no time to waste. Julia needed him!

Talon fought with desperation, feeling Niall's own desperation nearly as strong. Each fought to save the ones they loved.

And he loved Julia Brodie. With all he was and all he would ever be, he loved her.

With a speed and might he'd long attributed to his ring's power, he carved a bloody gash across the back of Niall Brodie's hand, loosening the other man's sword and sending it flying into the brush. A fast jab through Niall's calf and the chieftain of the Brodies crashed to the ground as Angus had before him.

Talon whirled and ran for the cave, swiping at the blood dripping into his eye. The cut to his brow mattered not. Nothing mattered but reaching Julia before the devil hurt her.

The green light grew as he neared the cave's mouth, flickering wildly. He turned the corner and raced inside, then came to an abrupt halt, his heart lodging in his throat.

Julia hung from a hook on the wall, her hands pulled taut above her, her toes barely touching the ground. She watched the man in front of her—a wee man the size of Hegarty—with an odd expression, a mix of fear and wary surprise. But she didn't appear hurt.

Thank the Virgin, he'd reached her in time.

Veskin's hair was black, not red, but like Hegarty's, that wild mane stuck up from the top of his head in a dozen directions as he shifted his weight from foot to foot.

It was a moment before Talon realized the green glow came from whatever the dwarf held in his hand. The chalice.

"Ye'll pay, lassie," the dwarf snarled in a voice that was not Hegarty-like at all, but dark and sinister. "The flame will burn ye slowly, cookin' ye through. I may not be able to eat ye, but ye'll not be leavin' this cave alive."

Talon had heard enough.

As the creature advanced on her, Talon pulled his knife and threw it hard. Not until the blade had left his fingers did he remember he no longer had his ring to ensure his aim. Fear bolted through him at the thought that the knife might go wild and hurt Julia instead. But even without his ring, his aim was true.

The knife buried itself to the hilt in the dwarf's back, right through his heart. The dwarf didn't fall as any mortal man would have, but whirled, his eyes glowing red, his face a terrible mask of rage.

Talon advanced into the cave, his sword at the ready, wary and uncertain of the nature of the creature before him.

"Talon." Julia's soft cry slid like a balm across his heart, her love strengthening him. But he didn't look at her again, for he dared not take his eyes off his enemy.

The devil tossed the chalice aside. It landed right-side up, the green flame not dimming even a small bit.

"Ye'll pay for this outrage, Brodie," Veskin growled. "I'll eat *your* heart instead."

Talon grinned at him, the Wizard's grin, but why not?

"Come and get me, ye wee bugger. But I'm no Brodie. And 'twill not be my heart leaving my chest this eve, but your own." Yet even as he said the words, he wondered how in the hell he was going to hurt the devil when a blade through his heart had not slowed him at all. "How do you die, fiend?"

"Ye canna kill me, laddie," the creature sneered. "'Tis your death this night." Out of nowhere, twin swords appeared in Veskin's small hands. He rushed forward, moving with a skill and a grace uncanny for one with such short limbs.

Talon pulled his own sword and the clash of metal rang through the cave. Though Talon was by far the bigger and stronger of the two, he felt the slice of steel time after time across his flesh. Blood and fire bloomed on his forearm, along his side, and down his thigh. As the blade tore through leg muscle, Talon nearly went down, staying on his feet by sheer will.

For a few mistaken moments, battling such a small opponent had seemed comical to him. A simple matter. For a few mistaken moments, he'd forgotten the dwarf was not human, but a devil possessed of strong magic. No matter where Talon's blade struck, he drew no blood.

A frisson of true fear melded with the pain burning a hole inside him.

How could he beat a creature he could not injure? And he must win. *He must.*

Or Julia would die.

"Talon!" Julia's voice rose over the sound of battle. "My necklace. You must take it!"

He dodged the flying blades by a hairsbreadth.

"It's the reason he didn't hurt me," Julia called. "The stone acts as a talisman."

"Then it protects you."

"*You* protect me."

For a single, pulsing instant, their gazes met and locked. In the depths of her eyes he saw a trust as deep as the Loch Ness and a belief in him that went all the way to her soul.

A belief in him he'd never shared. Until, perhaps, tonight.

Veskin took advantage of his moment's lapse in attention to stab his forearm.

Talon's mind went white with pain. Indecision ripped him in two. If he took Julia's necklace and failed to stop Veskin, she was dead. But if he didn't take the help she offered, he could very well die.

You protect me. She believed in him wholly.

God in heaven, could he do any less than believe in himself? *He would not fail her*.

Avoiding another lunge by the dwarf, he whirled to Julia. "Aye," he whispered low.

Sweet emotion glittered in her eyes amid an endless well of trust. "It's yours. Take it."

Talon did, pulling it off her head and over his own with a single, swift move, then whirled to protect them both as Veskin attacked.

To Talon's surprise the necklace did nothing to protect him from Veskin's blade, but his own blade was no longer useless. It was enough.

Talon fought like a man possessed, driving the inhuman fiend back, slicing through his arm, his chest. He cut off his hand, relieving him of one of his swords, but the hand grew back in an instant, with the sword still in place.

Jesu, he couldn't win.

He must!

He must end this before it was too late, but how? *How?*

"Take his head, lad. He'll not grow another." Hegarty's voice sounded in his ear, though the red-haired dwarf was nowhere to be seen.

Talon didn't hesitate. He lunged, swinging his blade in a wide arc that left him open to attack. As Veskin's sword sliced a ribbon of blood across Talon's stomach, he cut off Veskin's head.

The green fire went out, blanketing them in total darkness.

Talon fell to his knees, dizzy from the pain and the loss of blood. The only sound that met his ears was the dull thud of the rolling head.

"Talon?" Julia asked softly.

"Aye."

"Is it over?"

"I dinna ken."

"Aye, 'tis over, lass." Hegarty's voice spoke from the cave's mouth. In a sudden flash, light flooded the cave as the torches hanging on the walls lit as one.

"Talon!" Julia's cry of anguish told him he looked every bit as bad as he felt.

Hegarty rushed across the cave, moving without Veskin's grace, his wizened, worried face most welcome.

"He had to die, Hegarty." The words came out breathless. His energy was flagging fast.

Hegarty nodded as he knelt before Talon, shoving his hands against the worst of his wounds. "Aye. And you must live, laddie."

Talon shook his head. "Julia . . ."

"She's fine, if a wee bit uncomfortable. Your injuries come first."

"The ring . . ."

"Is on my finger now, and will increase my healing gifts tenfold. Ye'll be fine in a thrice."

Talon closed his eyes as a warm heaviness flowed through his body as if Hegarty had opened him up and poured warm water into him to cleanse him of all his injuries.

Moment by moment, the pain left him and his strength returned. With shocked surprise, he blinked his eyes open and stared at the man who'd saved him all those years ago.

"You're healing me."

Hegarty nodded once. "Aye." A slow smile crossed the red-haired dwarf's face. "'Tis the least I can do for the man who rid the world of Veskin."

"Truly, ye dinna mind?"

Hegarty chuckled low. "That one has needed dying for a good long while. Nay, I dinna mind." He sat back on his heels. "Ye be healed, laddie."

Talon grinned and shoved to his feet, whirling to find Julia watching him with shining eyes. He lunged for her, grabbing her close as he lifted her up and off the hook and into his arms.

"I thought they'd killed you," she said softly against his neck.

"Nay." When he could bear to loosen his grip on her, he set her on her feet and cut her free of the ropes that bound her wrists.

She moved her arms carefully, easing the stiffness out of her muscles, then slid her arms around his waist and held him tight. He pulled her against his heart.

Together, they turned back to Hegarty, Talon's head full of questions. The dwarf was on his knees beside the body of the fiend, removing Veskin's waistcoat.

"Was it you who took the chalice to Picktillum, Hegarty?"

"Aye. I hid it there myself nigh on ten years ago, where none would find it." He shrugged even as he struggled to pull the dead arm from the garment. "I couldna stop

Veskin from eating the lassies, but I could stop the Brodies from summoning him."

"Where did the chalice go?" Julia asked, staring at the spot where it had landed when Veskin tossed it.

"It was tied to Veskin," Hegarty said. "It ceased to exist when he died."

"So no more Brodie girls will ever be sacrificed," Julia murmured.

"I wonder, Hegarty," Talon said. "When ye saved Catriona, did ye not worry ye'd be sending her to her death in the future? That the Brodies in that time would sacrifice her as surely as the ones here had tried to?"

"Catriona. Was that her name?" Hegarty stroked his whiskerless chin. "I didna ken why they were trying to kill her that night. I hadna realized Veskin was involved until after I sent her away. And after . . . aye, I wondered if I'd only changed the year of her death."

"They didn't hurt her," Julia told him, turning her head to look at him. "They took her in and loved her."

Hegarty grinned, light dancing in his eyes as he clapped his hands gleefully. "Well, there you have it. You were destined to end Veskin's terrorizing all along." He gave Talon a sharp look. "Without my ring."

Wee bugger.

Finally, Hegarty had the garment free and put it on over his own odd assortment of clothes, bloodstains and all.

The red-haired dwarf's gaze swung to Julia. "How did ye get my necklace?"

"Catriona gave it to me. We grew up as cousins. She warned me not to put it on and I didn't listen."

Hegarty nodded. "I must bring her back."

Julia flinched. "No, Hegarty. She just got married. She's happy there. She's in love."

"So she sent you back in her stead?"

"No, she asked me to take the stone to America. Half-way around the world. I think she thought you wouldn't be able to call it from there."

"Nay, I would not have." The little man shrugged. "Well then. I suppose there's no need to bring her back if she doesna wish to come. But 'tis time that I sent you back where you belong."

Talon's arms tightened around her, a wild storm rising in his chest. *Nay.* He'd not let her go. Not now. Not when he'd finally come to understand how much he needed her. How much he loved her.

But, Jesu, she didn't belong here. This had never been her place. He'd known that from the start.

For days he'd wanted her to leave him to his solitary life. Now the prospect made him feel as if he'd been gutted.

All he wanted was to lift her into his arms and to run far, far from Hegarty and his time-traveling magic.

But more than that, far more, he wanted Julia to be safe. And happy.

He had to let her go.

Julia pulled out of Talon's arms, turning to face Hegarty. She was still shaking, but the danger was past. Veskin was dead.

All that was left was the ripping of her heart from her chest. All that was left was saying good-bye to Talon.

Dear God, how was she going to leave him, when she'd just gotten him back?

She reached back and took his hand, not quite able to let him go.

The sound of footsteps sounded outside the cave.

"The demon!"

Hegarty lifted his hand with a flourish and magic tin-gled along the surface of her skin. "That will keep them out for the moment." He held out his hand. "The necklace, lad. 'Tis past time I saw this lassie home."

Talon's grip on her tightened. "Julia," he said softly. As she turned to him, he dipped his head and kissed her, his lips at once soft and fierce.

Slowly, he pulled back and met her gaze, his blue eyes pulsing with a bittersweet ache. His mouth quirked up in that charmer's smile, a smile that didn't reach his eyes.

"Dinna forget me, aye?"

Julia swallowed back the lump that clogged her throat and pressed her palm to his beloved cheek as she fought back tears. "Never."

As Hegarty joined them, Talon pulled his hand from hers and pulled the jewel over his head, dropping it into Hegarty's upturned palm.

Talon met her gaze one last time. "Godspeed, Julia Brodie." His fingers brushed the underside of her chin. "I canna watch ye go, lass." He turned away and picked up Veskin's head by the hair. "I'll give the Brodies what they want, aye?"

Hegarty waved his hand, dropping the barrier that had briefly sealed the cave from outside intrusion.

A pain started deep in her chest as she watched Talon walk away for the last time, radiating out until she could barely breathe. Outside the cave a cheer went up.

"Come, lass." Hegarty reached for her, but she backed away.

"Wait." How could she leave?

How can I stay?

The man she loved was here. In this time. This place.

But it's cold here. And wet. And uncomfortable. I have a life there. I need to get back.

To what? She had nothing there. An empty apartment. An empty life.

She'd spent the past couple of weeks wishing she'd never

put that necklace over her head. She'd spent the past days wishing she'd stayed at Picktillum. But she knew with a certainty born of all the love in her heart that if she went with Hegarty now, if she turned her back on the only person who had ever mattered to her, those regrets would feel like nothing compared to the one she'd live with for the rest of her life.

If Talon wanted her to stay. Because, for all the times he'd risked his life to save her, he'd never said he loved her. And the one time she'd told him she loved him, he'd thrown it back in her face.

Maybe there was no reason for her to stay, but she had to know.

She had to know.

"Give me a minute, Hegarty, please?" Without waiting for his reply, she turned and ran to the entrance of the cave, praying Talon hadn't gone too far.

But when she burst into the night, she found herself alone. He was already gone. High up the hill she heard the cheers and sounds of celebration.

She stood in the light from the cave, uncertain. Doubting. If he'd wanted her to stay, he would have asked her to.

Little by little, the doubts faded away as the truth that had always been at the core of her life washed back in. She swallowed hard against the bitter ache of certainty that she'd always been meant to live her life alone.

Feeling older than her thirty years, she turned back toward the cave, and home.

And that was when she saw him. Talon. Leaning against a tree in the shadows, his head back as if he were in pain. His eyes were closed, his jaw clenched as hard as rock. As she watched, a drop of moisture caught the light on his cheek.

Her heart clenched. "Talon?"

His eyes snapped open and he pushed away from the

tree, staring at her as if not understanding what he was seeing.

"That wee liar! Did he leave ye here?"

As he stormed toward the cave, Julia stepped into his path. "He's waiting for me. I asked him to wait." Her bottom lip began to tremble and she tried to clamp down on it, but it was no use.

He watched her, his eyes narrowed without comprehension. "Why?"

"I just needed to . . ." Her eyes welled with tears and she lost the battle, the sobs overtaking her in a ferocious rush of emotion.

"Easy, lass." She felt his hands on her shoulders, but he didn't pull her close. Did he already guess what this was about? Was this his subtle way of telling her he didn't want her to stay? That he was ready for her to go?

The tears came faster.

Talon's hands caressed her shoulders. "Julia. Ye'll miss me, aye? Is that what this is about?"

The only thing she could do was nod. But she needed to feel his arms. She reached for him, sliding her arms around his waist and locking them tight as she buried her head in his shirt and cried, her heart breaking.

Talon's arms went around her. "I'll miss ye, too, lass. More that ye ken. But ye dinna belong here."

His words only confirmed what she'd feared. She might love him, but his feelings for her weren't that strong. And if she stayed? Sooner or later, she'd be on her own here instead of in the world she knew. And knowing he didn't want her would be unbearable.

With a shuddering breath, she swallowed her tears, pulled herself together, and pulled away.

"Good-bye, Talon."

But as she turned away, she felt his fingers curl around her arm, stopping her.

"I wish ye could stay." His voice pulsed with a sincerity that throbbed within her. "But your life is awaiting ye back there."

"Talon . . . ?"

He pulled her around to face him, his warm palm cupping her cheek. "Julia. Jesu, Julia, I canna let ye go a second time. I tried. Ye dinna belong here, I ken that. But I'll make ye happy, I vow it. Whatever it takes."

Julia stared at him, her heart beginning to thunder in her chest. "What are you saying?"

"I'm saying I love you. I want you to stay. To marry me. To help me be the better man you've seen inside me. I'll be that man for you, Julia." His hands gripped her shoulders, his fingers digging into her flesh with gentle desperation. "But, Jesu, lass, I want you to stay."

Julia began to laugh, even as the tears spilled down her cheeks. "I want to stay. I want to be with you."

Talon gathered her close. "I want ye to be happy, Julia. I want that. Just that."

The tears wouldn't stop, but it no longer mattered. Her heart was full. Her world had tilted on its axis and sent her into the arms of the one man to whom her soul had always belonged.

"The only place I'll ever be happy is with you, Talon MacClure. Only with you."

EPILOGUE

Talon watched his wife with deep and abiding love, and no small amount of amusement, as she showed him the *necessities* Brenna had given her this morn. For the past month, they'd stayed at Picktillum while Brenna taught Julia the things she needed to know to get along in this century of his.

Of theirs now.

Julia looked up at him, her bonny eyes dancing. "You're laughing at me." She grinned that impudent grin of hers he'd come to adore. "You'll be glad for this stuff if you ever get sick. And the rest of it . . ." She waved her hand airily. "Is girl stuff. Brenna's a lifesaver for sharing her stash."

Talon pulled her into his arms. "I'm not laughing at ye." He looked down into her bonny, bonny face, at the love in her eyes as she smiled at him, and thought he might just be the luckiest man on the Earth. "Your happiness lifts my heart, Julia-lass."

She lifted up on tiptoes and kissed him, her lips sweet and sure. "As long as I'm with you, I'm happy, Talon. This is the only place I want to be."

"Aye." And though he still found it hard to believe, he could see the truth of her words shining from her eyes. "Ye'll not mind another sojourn to the Highlands?"

Julia's smile turned wry. "As long as no one tries to sacrifice me." She pressed her small hand to his cheek. "I'm glad you've decided to go home. Even if your parents are gone, your mother's people are your kin."

"Aye, though I canna guess how we'll be welcomed."

Julia shrugged. "I have a feeling they'll welcome you with open arms the moment they get a whiff of your silver. And if they don't, then you won't waste it on them. There are plenty of others who would appreciate it."

He marveled at the ease with which she summed up and discarded the very real possibility he'd not be welcomed at all. And he realized he didn't much care. He went back as a gesture to his mother's memory, nothing more. No longer was his own identity tied to that place. No longer did he blame himself for anything that had happened there.

Before he married her, he'd told Julia everything and she'd helped him see he'd been a victim of circumstances beyond his control.

Circumstances Hegarty had eventually saved him from by giving him the amethyst.

He hooked his hands behind her waist and pulled her close. "And when we've shared my wealth a bit, I vow to ye, lass, a fine home within a day's ride of Picktillum. And a school for the bairns, as ye've asked for, where ye'll teach them all the wonderful things you think they should know. What think you of that?"

"I think . . . I'm in love with you, Wizard."

He stilled. "I am no longer the Wizard, Julia, and ye ken it well."

She cocked her head at him, that impudent grin making him smile despite himself. "I'm not so sure about that, Talon. The night you told me you loved me, you changed my life. You transformed my world. And if that's not magic, I don't know what is."

He kissed her, which was hard to do with them both grinning like lovesick loons. He kissed her soundly, in awe all over again that in giving up his magic, he'd won his heart.

Enter the rich world of
historical romance
with Berkley Books.

Lynn Kurland

Patricia Potter

Betina Krahn

Jodi Thomas

Anne Gracie

Love is timeless.
penguin.com

M9G0907